Zane Presents

WE DIDN'T SEE IT.
Coming

Dear Reader:

Welcome to the upscale, flashy, and prominent world of the Houston Family. From the outside, the Houstons seem like the perfect American dream: successful husband, beautiful wife, and three amazing daughters. Sheltered throughout their entire lives, the Houston sisters are thrown completely off-balance when both of their parents die suddenly on the same day. Without any direction, and having never been allowed to have relationships with men, they are all faced with decisions that they never anticipated having to make until well into the future.

We Didn't See It Coming by Christine Young-Robinson is a true eye-opener on many levels. Skeletons fall out of the mansion closets as the sisters find out that their parents who seemingly could do no wrong had somehow managed to pull the proverbial wool over their eyes over and over again. The sisters find themselves struggling to hold things together, forcing the bond between them to remain strong, and discovering that generational wealth can come with a huge price tag of its own.

As always, thanks for supporting the authors of Strebor Books. We strive to bring you the future in prolific literature today by publishing cutting-edge, inspiring, thought-provoking titles.

Blessings,

Zane

Publisher
Strebor Books
www.simonandschuster.com

ZANE PRESENTS

WE DIDN'T SEE IT.
Coming

CHRISTINE YOUNG-ROBINSON

SBI

STREBOR BOOKS

NEW YORK LONDON TORONTO SYDNEY

Strebor Books
P.O. Box 6505
Largo, MD 20792
http://www.streborbooks.com

ISBN 978-1-59309-566-6
ISBN 978-1-4767-5799-5 (ebook)
LCCN 2014931231

First Strebor Books trade paperback edition September 2014

Cover design: www.mariondesigns.com
Cover photograph: © Keith Saunders/Marion Designs

10 9 8 7 6 5 4 3 2 1

Manufactured in the United States of America

For information regarding special discounts for bulk purchases,
please contact Simon & Schuster Special Sales at 1-866-506-1949
or business@simonandschuster.com

The Simon & Schuster Speakers Bureau can bring authors to your live event.
For more information or to book an event, contact the Simon & Schuster Speakers
Bureau at 1-866-248-3049 or visit our website at www.simonspeakers.com.

Acknowledgments

First and foremost, I would like to thank God for making me a miraclewriter4u.

To my parents, Celess and Ruby Young, thanks for always being there for me and teaching me the true value of love for family and friends.

To my hubby, Joseph, thanks for being such a great husband, father, and grandfather.

To my children, Nishika and Rahim, you're my hearts. Thanks daughter for two wonderful and smart grandchildren.

To my siblings, Tynetta, Maxine and my twin, Christopher, you're my rock. My heavenly siblings, Celess, Jr., Lonnie, and Charlene, I miss you so much but I know you're smiling down on me.

To my mother-in-law, Ola Mae Smith, thanks so much for your love.

To my God-brother, Marc and wife, Laura, Godson, Rahmell, and Goddaughter, Deborah, thanks for your love and support.

To my angel, Mrs. Witherspoon, I thank God for the time that He allowed me to be in your presences. I'll always cherish the fond memories that we'd shared together—Priceless.

To my agent, Dr. Maxine Thompson, you're awesome. Thanks for believing in me as a writer.

To Zane and Charmaine, thanks so much for giving me this opportunity to share my writing with readers. Words can never express how humble and grateful I am. To the Strebor Staff and authors, many of whom I do know and will get to know, I am honored to be in your company.

To the book cover designer, Keith Saunders, awesome job.

To Marvy Moore, Brenda Menoken, Mercy Thomas, Victoria McCornell, Minnie Dix, Tia Wright, Reginald and Rosalind Mitchell, thanks for being supportive in reading my work, listening to me read, and your honest critiques.

To Joan Dash, Pamela Williams, Jo Ann Howard, Robin Duncan, Carol James, Shirley S. Brown, Jean Hopkins, Theresa Thomas, Carmen Hampton-Julious, Gaye O'Neal-Harper, LaShanda Shuler, Sylvia Santiago, Jeanell Brown, Barbara Jones, Vanessa Brown, Sandra Lambright, Faverta Robinson, Sterleita Caldwell, Summiya Dash, and Remmele Young, thanks for your talks, support, and encouragement.

To my sisters-in-law, aunts, uncles, nieces, nephews, cousins, neighbors, and friends, thanks for your love and support. The United Martin Family—Thanks for the love, support and insight to my heritage.

Thanks Tywebbin Creations (Tyora Moody) for your great job on the book trailer.

Thanks Eleuthera Book Club and Cousins Book Club online, for the wonderful book recommendations and discussions.

Thanks to all the book clubs, which I've had the opportunity to meet and will meet in the near future.

To my Cola Wrimo family, I pray that your writing turns into a book. Social media family, thanks for the posts, laughs, and prayers.

Thanks to Eddye Lane, Jacqueline Bouvier Lee, Zina Jenkins,

Kathy Lakin, The crew, (Ron W., Fred P., Stanley P., Grady T., Joe P. and Vincent P.), my words with friends challenger, (Carlos W.), Connie Jenkins, Nicole, Janey, DeBarbara, Sonja, Stephen, Minimah, Nadirah, Maris, Mary T., The Dash Family, Debra Shareef, Tee C. Royal (Rawsistaz) and ACAIC.

To my author-friends, Leigh McKnight, Tracy Price-Thompson, and Mirika Cornelius, thanks for always showing me love.

Thanks to the independent and chain bookstores for giving me the opportunity in the past to book sign with my children's book. I look forward to visiting again, with my first adult novel.

To the adults that purchased my children's books, I thank you for sharing my words with the children, but now, it's your time.

I know I may have missed someone, but it was not intentionally.

I hope all readers have a wonderful journey reading my work. I looked forward to meeting many of you. Please do not hesitate to email me at miraclewriter4u@aol.com and share your thoughts and views.

Chapter 1

Rupert Houston *must pay*, Aniyah, twenty-eight years old, thought as she stared at the number on her cell phone of one of the wealthiest self-made businessmen in South Carolina. She was his mistress—until he decided that she was no longer of use to him.

Without hesitation, Aniyah tapped the touch screen with the tip of her middle finger on her right hand, allowing the call to go through. As she paced the kitchen floor of her apartment, three rings chimed in her ear before his voicemail came on.

"Bastard!" she yelled; she knew he was avoiding her call.

His home phone was next on her list to call. Aniyah did not care who answered. Extremely frustrated with him, she called the number. To her surprise, Rupert picked up.

"Kenley is not home, call back later," Rupert said, assuming that the call most likely was for his youngest daughter.

"Why didn't you answer your damn cell phone?" She startled him.

"How did you get this number? This is a private line. How dare you call my home?" he yelled.

"Obviously, it's not too private. I got it. Again, answer my question: Why didn't you answer your cell phone?"

"What if my wife or one of my girls had picked up? Have you lost it or what?" Rupert was furious.

"I'm one of your girls, too. Don't I count for anything?"

"Aniyah, okay, you made me aware of that. I've left you in my will. I'm willing to give you any money you need right now to take care of yourself, but that's where it ends. My wife has medical problems, and I don't want to do anything to upset her. Her doctor's orders are to keep her calm."

Aniyah listened to him. She had convinced him that she was his illegitimate daughter from his pregnant Mexican servant, Tessa Sanchez, whom he fired years earlier.

"I don't want your pity story. I could bust up your happy home anytime I want to."

"I know that, Aniyah, and that's what I'm over here fighting for you not to do. My girls and my wife think the utmost of me," he said as he pulled a handkerchief out of his pocket. He wiped the sweat that began to moisten his face.

Aniyah giggled. "They won't be thrilled to hear that you slept with me. Your family will flip over the shocking news. I'm the daughter that knows the real truth about you."

Rupert played the situation over and over in his mind, how she was supposed to be his treat for one night on a business trip that ultimately turned into an affair. How was he to know that she was the child of the Mexican servant that he had impregnated and then fired?

"What kind of creature are you? You knew I was your father, yet you still slept with me."

Aniyah laughed out loud. "Get over it. You want a better story than that one? I do have one."

Puzzled, he asked, "What are you talking about?"

"I'm talking about one of your other precious daughters."

"Which one?" Rupert said, wishing he could reach through the phone to grab and shake her for the way she was talking about his daughters. "Just say what you have to say."

"I don't know those damn high-class bitches' names. But one of them is banging your dear lawyer friend." Aniyah laughed wickedly.

Rupert stood up and yelled into the phone, "You're lying."

"Don't call me a liar, you poor excuse for a damn papa. I know what the hell I'm talking about. I may not be one of your high-class daughters, but I can find out shit when I want to!" she shouted back. "If I say one of them is banging the damn lawyer, then she is. Call the bastard and find out."

Rupert slammed the phone down in her ear.

"Oh, no he didn't!" she hissed as the dial tone rang in her ear.

Aniyah tried to call him back but he did not answer. Infuriated, Aniyah began to throw whatever was within her reach across the room. As much as she hated the way that he treated her, there were redeeming factors about Rupert. She admired his natural hair with salt-and-pepper waves. The suits that Rupert wore were tailored for his muscular body. His skin was as flawless as hers. They used to endure facials when they were together, when she was all that he thought about. All she thought about now was that he had to pay. She sat on a plush white loveseat and began polishing her toes in a deep beet-red shade.

Rupert was relieved that he would have some time to himself. After all, his favorite girls were out having a day of their own.

Stepping inside his walk-in closet, which was filled with his collection of designer suits, ties, shirts and shoes, he removed his silk blue tie and tossed it onto an ottoman, followed by his blue pin-striped suit jacket.

Too exhausted from a long day at his construction company, Rupert walked out of the closet and made his way to the double-pane plate glass window. He looked out at Lake Murray to relieve himself of the tension from work and the personal problems that dominated his mind. The water always kept him calm when work became too stressful, but now his personal life was in turmoil, like the choppy waves of the water in the wintertime.

Leaving the vision of the lake, Rupert picked up his cell phone and called his attorney.

"Baron Chavis' office," the secretary answered.

"This is Mr. Houston. Get Baron on the line, Sara." he ordered.

He waited for a moment until his attorney picked up.

"What can I do for you, Mr. Houston?"

Instead of bringing up Aniyah's gossip, even though it baffled him about the accusations she made about one of his daughters, he simply asked, "That new will I had you to draw up...you better still have it on hold. You didn't file it, did you?"

"I have it right here on my desk in front of me. It won't go any further until you give me the okay."

He sighed. "Thanks, Baron; I don't know what I would do without you. I'll get back to you soon enough. I wanted Aniyah to see me give it to you. Talk to you later, buddy."

Rupert hung up and went back to stare out of the window. His cell phone rang, distracting him from a sailboat going by. He looked at the number displayed. No way was he answering another call from Aniyah. The last ring grew silent and he was relieved.

Once again, the gossip that Aniyah shared with him ran across his mind like a marathon runner. *It can't be true.* Everyone who works for him knew the Houston Rule. Plain and simple—nobody dealt with any of his girls. Period! It was his duty to pick the right men for them.

Baron was his longtime attorney for all of his personal and work business. Rupert trusted him like he was his son, but to clear any doubts he called the Chavis Law Firm again.

"Sara, get Baron on the line immediately."

Baron again picked up. "Mr. Houston, you needed something else?"

"Are you or are you not messing with one of my girls?" he asked calmly.

Mr. Chavis hesitated. "Noelle and I only met up one time at a coffee shop. We chatted over a cup of hot coffee," he said, speaking of the second of Houston's three daughters.

"You son of a bitch." Rupert realized that Aniyah's gossip was true. "What happened after that?"

"Absolutely nothing," Baron fibbed to cover himself.

Rupert marched back and forth on the white carpet below his feet; tension etched furrows in his forehead. He didn't believe a word that his attorney was saying.

"I'm warning you, Baron, there better not be anything else."

"I promise you, Mr. Houston, it was a brief encounter."

"Get off my phone." He hung up and called Aniyah back.

"I spoke to Baron and he swore to me that he and my Noelle only met for a cup of hot coffee."

"Your precious girl is your lawyer's whore," Aniyah insisted.

Rupert yelled, "No one bad mouths one of my girls. Aniyah, you're despicable!"

"Your lawyer is lying to protect his ass. He's banging her and I can prove it." The phone beeped.

"Hold on, I'm not finished with you. I have another call," Rupert said as he switched over to another line.

"Yes, Kenley."

"Dad," his youngest daughter said, but was corrected in the background by her oldest sister, Milandra.

"I mean, *Father*, I need to talk to you."

"I'm busy. Make it quick. What is it?" he asked abruptly.

Kenley talked a hundred miles per minute. "My sixteenth birthday is coming up. I realize my sisters had their parties at the yacht club," she explained. She sat across from her mother and two older sisters as they waited on their lunch. "Father, it's a new day. I want to have my party by the pool at home. Can I please break this crazy tradition?"

"Damn it, you called me for that? Speak to your mother!" he yelled and hung up.

Rupert switched back to the other line. "Aniyah, take back what you said about my Noelle."

"Get your ass to a computer."

Rupert went to the far end of the east wing of the house to his study. He logged on to the Internet on his laptop that sat on a desk with a gorgeous cherry finish.

"What's your email address?" she asked curiously.

He was hesitant about giving Aniyah any of his email addresses, but Rupert gave up an email address he barely used.

"You better not be playing around. I have no time for foolishness."

"Shut up! Just get ready to see with your own cutie eyes," she flirted.

The email finally came through to his computer screen. He clicked on it and downloaded the image. There, in vivid color, was his daughter, Noelle, in the arms of Baron. Her breasts were partially exposed.

"Now who's telling the truth, dear Papa? My half-sister looks great in that position." Aniyah laughed. "I'm sure your friends would love to get a copy. Don't play with me; I'm no one to mess with." She threatened and hung up on him.

Rupert called the Chavis Law Firm again. The secretary picked up and turned the call over to her boss.

"Yes, Mr. Houston."

"Baron, you're lucky you're not here right now. I would strangle you to death."

"You can't be serious. You're not still sweating me about Noelle and me having a cup of coffee together, are you?"

"I saw it with my own eyes. I've got the email to prove it. You're sleeping with my Noelle. No one touches my girls, you bastard. You're fired! Send over all the files from my company and my personal files, too. Do it right away and stay the hell away from my Noelle or I'll strangle you with my bare hands."

"Okay, I admit, we had a little kiss. Is that any reason to fire me?"

Houston clearly saw the email image in his mind. "Liar!" he yelled and threw the cell phone across the room, smashing it against the wall.

First Aniyah, now you, Baron, and my precious daughter have betrayed me behind my back. Rupert started to get up and felt lightheaded. He gasped for breath and his chest tightened. He grabbed his chest, attempting to unbutton his shirt, as blood rushed to his head. Trying to make his way out of the bedroom, he tumbled onto the floor.

There Rupert lay with his right hand on his chest. He mumbled, "My life is over."

Chapter 2

On the third Friday of every month, the Houston daughters had lunch with their mother. This was their time to bond.

After they dined on baked chicken parmesan and a Caesar salad, Milandra Houston, the oldest daughter of Rupert and Alana Houston, led the way out of the Italian restaurant. Wearing a two-piece, soft-pink linen pantsuit, she strutted in her open-toe pumps. Her handbag coordinated beautifully with her outfit. Each tap from the heels of her pumps was like a melody being played by a pianist. Her dark-brown hair was combed back off her face into a French roll, enhancing her glowing caramel complexion.

Walking by her side was her youngest sister, Kenley, dressed in a mint-green, sleeveless linen dress. She would have preferred wearing a pair of casual shorts and a tee shirt. Her hair, pulled away from her face, showed off her golden complexion.

Noelle, the middle daughter, took a bite out of a walnut cookie. She fastidiously brushed crumbs from her turquoise linen pantsuit. Her light-brown hair, which bounced against her shoulders, framed her warm milk chocolate complexion perfectly.

"You don't want to mess up that figure you worked so hard to obtain," their mother called as she caught up to them after taking care of the check. Pearl-colored polish gleamed on her perfectly manicured nails as she clenched her black-and-white clutch purse.

She studied Noelle—her lookalike. She admired her daughter for shedding thirty pounds within the past year.

"Noelle, that's about five pounds you've added back onto your waistline or hips," Alana said as she watched Noelle devour the cookie in two bites.

"Unbelievable," Milandra said, noticing her sister, too.

"I'll work it off playing tennis or swimming a few laps around the pool," Noelle said as she and Milandra had taken time out from their tennis games to join their mother for lunch.

They made their way through the door to see that the limo had arrived to pick them up. The driver tilted his black hat as if to say hello. He opened the door.

"What did Father say about your birthday party?" Milandra asked Kenley as she was the first to get into the limo.

"He screamed at me," Kenley whined.

"That's not like Father," Milandra said.

"He's a busy man. He's probably on a construction site," Noelle said in her father's defense.

"You can talk with your father this evening when he comes home," their mother said.

Kenley mumbled, "Discuss it with Mother. That's the last thing he said."

Her sisters giggled.

"It's not funny at all. You two are way older than me. Yacht club parties are not for today's teenagers. A pool party at home is the best. At the yacht club, my friends and I will have to listen to boring piano music. At home, we can listen to current hip-hop and pop music."

"Mother, see what happens when you have an 'oops' baby?" Milandra teased.

"You're plain old mean." Kenley pouted.

Alana Houston was startled when the doctor told her that she was pregnant with Kenley. She knew exactly what day she had conceived. Her husband had not touched her in months. She felt he was going elsewhere to satisfy his sexual hunger. But one night, his so-called meeting must have ended earlier than he expected and he came to bed craving her, as if he was a wild animal starving for food. He awakened her from her sleep. Alana felt as if he was raping her instead of making love to her. He ripped her silk-lace gown from her body. Plunging on top of her, he entered with force. After three humps, he ran out of gas. Kenley was born nine months later. She saw to it that Kenley was home-schooled by a private tutor.

Kenley made new friends with her busy schedule—taking tennis and piano lessons and belonging to social teen clubs. Her sisters coached her in piano and tennis. After all, they were skilled in the same activities. Unlike her family members, who were Harvard University graduates, Kenley's goal was to break the family tradition and attend Spelman College.

Mrs. Houston glimpsed down at her diamond watch. "We have a little time to go pick out Kenley's party dress."

"I'll need a new bathing suit," Kenley hinted.

"Nonsense. You must follow the family tradition. Every daughter of mine celebrates her birthday at the yacht club."

"That's awful! It'll be boring and my friends won't have any fun," Kenley cried.

"It's traditional," her mother reminded her. "Kenley Houston, you will not embarrass me in public the way you talk."

"Mother," Kenley said.

"No back talk." Milandra jumped in as they headed to their next destination.

Kenley looked out of the window as they drove off. She folded her arms and sat back in her seat, pouting.

"Why are you so quiet, Noelle? Is there something you want to talk about?" Alana asked, noticing her daughter was lost in her thoughts.

"No, Mother, I'm just not in a talkative mood. Kenley has a mouthful for all of us."

"Yes, she does," Milandra agreed.

Noelle wanted to spill her thoughts. The secret she held would overshadow her baby sister's argument about a party. It would be a long lecture about what a Houston should do or not do. She wanted no parts of hearing the Houston book of rules, and she dared not share her secret. Her mother would be furious. After having a heart attack a year ago, her delicate heart might not be up to par for such a secret.

"Mother, did you take your medicine this morning?" Noelle asked her.

"Not as of yet. I'm changing my medicine schedule. I'll start taking it in the evening, after supper."

"Mother," Milandra said, "don't go changing things around. You'll take the medicine as soon as you get home."

Alana Houston loved the concern her daughters had for her. Their attentiveness to her health made her admire them even more. "I will. I want to be around to do many lunches with my daughters."

"Mother, this is too much," Kenley told her as she turned around in front of a three-way mirror in the dressing room. She went over to a chair and tried to sit down. The excessive fabric made it difficult for her to sit. "See, I can't sit down," she complained.

"You'll be dancing the night away. No need for sitting," Noelle said as she peeked down into her handbag at her cell phone. She noticed Baron's number displayed on the screen. She was not happy that she was not able to return his call.

"It's lovely, Kenley," Milandra commented.

The final decision was supposed to be her mother's, but as usual, the majority ruled. Therefore, Kenley was outvoted.

The salesperson hung a garment bag over the peach-colored satin dress with a crinoline slip attached underneath, below the bodice. She handed it to Kenley, who carried it out of the boutique. The Houstons loaded up into the limo and headed home.

As they drove up to the front of the estate, Alana surprised Kenley. "I've decided you will be the first to have two parties, one by the poolside and the other at the yacht club."

Kenley scooted over her sisters to give her mother a grateful hug. "I love you, Mother. Thanks so much."

"Mother, I knew you would give in," Milandra said annoyed, looking out at the carpet of grass that covered the grounds. *Any golfer in South Carolina would think the grass was an ideal spot to putt.*

The heat from the sun beamed down on them, but the view of the water fountain in the front yard gave them a vision of coolness. Kenley, the first out of the limo, noticed that the limo her father rode home in every day was parked near the house. She dashed through the front door. "Father, you're home," she called, but got no response.

Her mother followed closely behind her daughter. "Kenley, go hang your garment up in your closet. You have plenty of time to show it off to your father. He's probably handling business in his study."

Kenley made her way up the staircase to the west wing of the house. As she entered her room, a world of bold shades of pink, green and orange showered her with colors. The drapes were drawn, letting in the brilliant sunlight. Before she went and hung up her dress, she glimpsed lots of water from her window—the placid lake and the pool with a cascading waterfall.

Alana made her way up the stairs. Milandra kept talking, holding Noelle up from making her one phone call.

Milandra looked at her mother. "Mother, take your heart pill," she reminded her.

Alana reached the top of the staircase and took a deep breath. She made her way down the long hallway to her bedroom, located in the east wing of the house.

Reaching for the door, she discovered her husband's arms stretched out on the floor into the hallway. Startled by the sight and fearful for her husband, she dropped her black-and-white clutch purse on the floor near his hand. She tried to belt out a loud scream, but her vocal cords seemed numb.

Holding on to the wall, she backed up all the way down the hallway until she reached the top of the staircase. Her daughters noticed the flushed look on their mother's face. They noticed that she tried to speak, but no words came out of her mouth.

"What's wrong, Mother?" they asked.

Alana tried desperately to hold on to the banister. She took one step, and like a falling model, unable to prevent the fall, she tumbled down the stairs. Her head crashed against the hardwood floor with a bang. The girls screamed, running to their mother's aid.

Kenley came out of her room, looked down the staircase to see her mother spread out on the floor below. "Mother, Mother!" she screamed.

"Call an ambulance," Milandra suggested.

Noelle reached into her handbag and pulled out her cell phone. She keyed 9-1-1 into the dial pad.

Maintaining her composure, Milandra looked up at Kenley and ordered: "Find Father quick. Go find Father!"

Noelle, busy on the phone, tried to speak to the operator between shedding tears. "They want to know if Mother has a pulse," she cried.

Milandra placed her fingers on her mother's wrist; she felt no pulse. She screamed, "I don't feel a thing. Tell them to stop asking so many questions." She was losing her cool. "Just hurry and send an ambulance. We need help."

Kenley ran to the east wing of the house. "Father! Father!" she bellowed. "It's Mother! She's fallen and she's unconscious."

One shock was too many. When Kenley reached her parents' bedroom and saw her father laid out on the floor, her scream became like a siren. "Aw…!" Kenley now realized what had made her mother fall down the stairs. "Mother discovered Father on the floor." Full of tears, she ran to get help. She looked down the stairs at her sisters and pointed toward the east wing. "It's Father! He's unconscious, too, just like Mother."

"Stay with Mother, Noelle. I'll see about Father," Milandra said, taking control back, making her way up the stairs.

Kenley sat down on the hall floor against the wall. She placed the cell phone on the floor. She buried her head between her knees and became a human waterfall. Tears dampened her dress.

Chapter 3

Reared back in his seat, Baron wondered how Rupert had found out about his brief encounter with Noelle. He had told him the truth, but Houston insisted that he still was a liar.

Rupert was protective of his daughters, but to have one of them followed was a bit too much to believe. He concluded that Rupert had had a private investigator follow and photograph their brief kiss.

Now Baron was losing his biggest client because he had challenged the Houston Rule for a second time.

The first time was because of Tessa Sanchez. He remembered walking up to the front door of the Houstons' home years ago. Tessa appeared at the door—as beautiful as ever—with gorgeous, long dark hair. She wore a black maid's uniform with a white apron that hugged her slender waistline. She gave him the biggest smile ever.

"Hello, welcome to the Houston Estate," she had said in her Spanish accent.

Her large eyes mesmerized him.

"Thank you. I'm here to see Rupert Houston."

Tessa moved aside and led him down the art gallery hallway. Lots of art in gold and bronze frames hung against the lemon-colored walls. She escorted him into a room that Mr. Houston had named The Gentleman's Lounge. It was furnished with two brown leather loveseats with creamed-colored cushions, and it was accented with multicolored striped pillows that sat between round Chippendale sofa tables. A reddish, burgundy-colored ottoman sat on top of a rug that highlighted all the colors in the room. He noticed a pool table in the room a few feet away from where he stood.

"Have a seat. Mr. Houston will be with you in a minute. May I get you anything while you wait?"

He wanted to say to Tessa, "It's you I want." But instead he answered, "I'm fine. Thank you for your warm hospitality."

She left the room as Rupert came in. "Hello, Baron. How are you?"

"I'm fine; just admiring the beauty of your housekeeper."

"Yes, Tessa is a pretty girl and a very hard worker."

"She deserves more," Baron said with a sparkle in his eye.

"I see you're having an instant crush on my help," Rupert said as he gave him a stare.

Baron explained: "I recognize beauty when I see it."

The men went on with their business deals. After that day, Baron made it his obligation to come over as often as he could. Any invitations from Rupert were always accepted.

Rupert's jealous ways manifested one particular day when Baron came to his home.

Tessa was busy polishing silver in the kitchen. "Hello, Mr. Chavis." She smiled.

"To you, it's Baron."

"I'm sorry, but Mr. Houston gave me strict orders to only call you Mr. Chavis."

"Never mind him; it'll be our secret. Is he in?"

"Mr. Houston said to tell you he'll be in shortly."

Baron came close up behind her. He laid his hands over hers as she tried to continue to polish the silver. She trembled as he touched her.

"You're so pretty. I've wanted to touch you for a long time."

Blowing kisses on her neck, Baron traveled his hands through her hair. Her hair felt like silk to him.

"Please, I don't want to lose my work."

"Tessa, I can take you away from this job. You can become the lady of my house."

"Mr. and Mrs. Houston have been good to me since I came here from Mexico. I could never leave them. I'm forever loyal to them."

He turned her around and pulled her closer to him as he tasted the sweetness of her lips. She tried to pull away, but the force of his lips on hers made her submit to the hunger she also had for him.

Rupert made his way into the kitchen where he witnessed them kissing. "What's going on in here?" he shouted.

Tessa pushed Baron away. "Sir, please don't fire me," she cried.

"Run along, Tessa. I'll deal with you later."

She left the room. The two men came face to face. Baron could see the wrinkles of frustration and anger forming on Rupert's forehead.

"I knew you had a crush on her. But that's as far as it goes from here on out. I don't allow my help to deal with any of my colleagues."

"I have feelings for her and she obviously feels the same."

"Baron, we have formed a great business and personal relationship. Let's not destroy it over poor-class help."

"I see more to her than someone under me or you. I see a beautiful woman that has a lot to offer a man."

Rupert went over and grabbed a glass from the cupboard. He filled it with water and handed it to him. "Cool off. Remember, I made you what you are, and I can destroy you at the blink of an eye."

Baron did not utter a single word.

He had the power to ruin Baron's career.

Baron took a swallow of the water. "There, I'm cooled off. Let's get down to business."

Nothing else was said of Tessa. Baron admired her from afar. She stayed out of his sight as much as she could when he visited the Houstons' home. The young attorney thought of many ways he could make her his own. He had to find a way to get to her without Rupert finding out.

At the time, the Houstons had planned to take a trip with their only daughter, Milandra. The other girls weren't born yet. This was the ideal time for him to see her. He made his way over to the Houston Estate. The servants' quarters were a separate residence on the property. Each servant who lived-in had his or her own private room. Each one had an outside entrance into their room.

Baron made his way to Tessa's room. The sky was dark, but a light pole glowed in front of each quarter. He walked up to her room. The door was ajar. As he eased the door open, he saw the soft glow of low, dimmed lights coming from inside.

In the room, he saw a mahogany bed made up with a dark-brown blanket. A colorful Mexican blanket was folded at the foot of the bed. Two lamps sat on the mahogany nightstands. The polished hardwood floors reflected the shine from the light.

Baron looked over at the window seat. He locked eyes with Tessa. She looked over the shoulder of a man. He saw that the man wore a suit jacket, but his slacks were dropped down to his calves, exposing his legs.

Tessa cried in agony as the man continued to penetrate her. A tear ran down her face as she screamed, "Mr. Houston, it's Mr. Chavis."

Rupert let go of her. He turned around, pulled up his pants, and zipped them. Tessa was fully exposed in all of her glorious nudity.

Baron stared at what he had wanted so much to touch—her body. She covered her breasts with her hands as she ran to the bed, got the Mexican blanket from the foot of it, and covered up.

Out of anger, Baron ran over to Rupert. He tried to grab him by the collar, but Houston got to him first, pushing him away from getting any closer to him.

"Don't you dare ever attempt to come at me. You walk out of this room and forget what you ever saw—or ever wanted. Tessa is mine now. Get out of here," Rupert ordered.

"I thought you had feelings for me," Baron said as he looked at her.

"You don't have the money to give her or to take care of her the way I do," Rupert called.

"I thought you were out of town," Baron blurted as he walked toward the door.

"Alana took Milandra away. As you can see, I have business to take care of here. You have no need to question my personal life. Get out!" he yelled.

Dejected, Baron left the room. He swore that one day he would get even with Rupert. And this was the reason he met with Noelle. She had a crush on him.

Noelle could barely look at him without blushing. He thought she would be the perfect way to get revenge on her father. He had just begun to put his vengeful plan in motion, but Rupert was one step ahead of him.

He had to give Rupert time to calm down. Hopefully, he could salvage the mess. He had gotten in trouble with women that he had never gotten to first base with before.

Frustrated, Baron picked up the manila folder that held the latest lawsuit against Houston Commercial Construction Company: a young man who had fallen off a ladder and broken his leg was claiming expenses for damages. As always, Baron tried to help the company pay little or no money on claims against the company. The more he tried to drown himself in the case, the more he wondered what reaction his client would have with Noelle.

He went to pick up the phone to contact her, but his secretary tapped on the door. "You may come in, Sara."

Holding his appointment schedule in her hand, Sara entered the room, dressed in a beige skirt outfit. Her once brownish hair was beginning to streak with gray strands. She looked over at her boss, a man she longed to have in her personal life. Despite all the years she had worked for Baron, she still grew nervous in his presence. She would have given anything to tell him her true feelings, but loyalty to her job kept her quiet. "I thought maybe we could go over your next few appointments."

"Let's take care of that first thing in the morning. Do me a favor: cancel any appointments I have for the rest of the day. I need to run out."

"Yes, Mr. Chavis."

"Thanks, Sara; you're a lifesaver." He smiled.

Sara blushed because she felt comforted knowing that he relied on her. She closed the door behind her.

Baron leaned back in his seat. His thoughts went to the day that he first met Rupert.

He had exceeded his ultimate dream, passing the Bar exam, which led him to a job at a local law office called Newman Law Firm. The first case assigned to him was from Houston Commercial Construction Company. Rupert was one of Newman's biggest clients.

Baron met with Mr. Houston and shared a pot of coffee in one of Newman's meeting rooms. They discussed—detail by detail—what Rupert expected from the case. Simply put, he was to pay no money to a man who pretended to have damaged his knee while working for him. He was to prove the man's injury was pre-existing. Through investigation and long hard work, Baron did exactly that. He saved Houston Commercial Construction Company over fifty thousand dollars.

Rupert was impressed with the eagerness that Baron showed in his job. He began to give all of his business, and personal cases, directly to him. Then one day he asked the hardworking attorney to leave Newman Law Firm to come work as a personal attorney for his company.

Baron could not resist. This meant more money for him. He worked diligently until he opened his own private practice, Chavis Law Firm, inside one of Houston's office buildings. He handled all of Houston's business and personal legal issues.

Now, Baron felt that he had to make amends with Rupert. He was thankful for all of the help he had given him professionally, but the pain of losing Tessa left him heartbroken on a personal level, and he directed his anger toward Rupert.

Baron leaped out of his seat. This wasn't the right time to get totally even with him. What was he thinking? Rupert had handed him a few more cases in the last month, keeping him swamped with work. He smoothed out his suit jacket and made his way out of the door.

Inside his black Lexus, he called Noelle. He wondered whether she was aware that her father knew of their brief encounter. Her phone rang, but she did not answer.

"Come on...pick up, Elle," he said as he called her the nickname he had given her.

He drove in the direction of the Houston Estate. He hoped Rupert had cooled off some. He had to undo the damage that might cause the cases he had on his desk to be revoked.

Cases equaled dollars, and those, Baron did not want to lose.

Chapter 4

Noelle pulled out her cell phone and called Baron.

He answered, "Hello, Elle. I've been trying to reach you."

She cried, "Tragedy has struck our family. It's Mother and Father! I think they're dead!"

"Dead?" he questioned, as he couldn't believe what he had heard. "I'm already here. I was coming to see your father. I'm getting out of the car as we speak. Hang up."

Noelle shut her cell phone off. Baron made his way into the house. Noelle rushed into his arms. He patted her on the head. "Stay calm."

He looked to see Alana lying on the floor. He took her pulse and realized that she was gone. He ran up the stairs and found Kenley still curled up against the wall. "Stay calm," he said to her as well.

He went down to the east wing. Milandra sobbed as she held on to her father. Baron lifted her off of him. "Come on, Milandra. Stay calm." He led her to where Kenley sat. "You Houstons need to comfort each other."

Baron went back down to the east wing, but this time he went to Rupert's study. He hurried over to his laptop computer. Rupert was still logged on. Baron strolled down through all of the emails in his mailbox files until he saw the email that he was looking for. He saw that the email came from juicyascanbe. He deleted it.

He ran back down the east wing and stepped over Rupert to enter the master suite. He looked around until he discovered the destroyed cell phone on the floor. He dared not put any of his fingerprints on the phone. This was a crime scene until the cause of death was pronounced.

Baron stepped back over Rupert to leave the suite when he noticed his eyes were still open and as sharp as a blade. He knelt down and closed Rupert's eyes.

"Damn! I wanted to pay you back, but not to this extent." Baron became sentimental over the death of the man who had helped build his career. He wiped his watery eyes as he stood up and noticed the paramedics approaching the room. "Hello, I'm Baron Chavis, the Houstons' attorney and friend."

"Do you know exactly what happened here?" one of them asked.

"No, I'll have to get one of his daughters to tell you. I arrived shortly before you," he explained.

Baron made his way to get Milandra, since she was the oldest. She was huddled down on the floor with her sisters, in tears.

"The paramedics need to speak to you. They need to know what might have happened," he said.

Milandra wept as he helped her to stand up. He placed his arms around her and led her down the hall. She trembled as she explained to the paramedics what happened. "My sisters and I had just come home from a day out with our mother. Mother was on her way into her room to take her daily heart medicine when she discovered Father on the floor. I guess the shock of seeing him lying there was more than she could bear. She tried to warn us but was unable to speak. She gasped for breath, and the next thing we knew she had tumbled down the stairs. My father, I have no clue as to what happened to him. Is he okay?" Milandra hoped he might have just fainted.

"I'm afraid not; your father is also dead. From the look of things he had a massive heart attack, and so did your mother."

"No, not Father and Mother. They're our life. We breathe for our parents. My God, what will we do without them?" Milandra ran back to her sisters. She cried. "Father is dead, too."

Her sisters heard her loud and clear. Kenley stomped her feet rapidly on the floor. Noelle banged her fist against the wall until a colorful painting of a floral arrangement fell and crumbled into tiny pieces of glass. Milandra leaned against the wall and sobbed.

Baron came to their rescue. "Girls, try to get control of yourselves. Think of what your father and mother would say if they were here."

The sisters thought of what their parents would say. They knew that their words would be empowering: that no matter what troubles happen in their family, they must stand tall and gain strength from each other. And when joy comes their way, they should rejoice in unity, for they are forever Houstons.

Just like robots, the girls wiped away their sobbing eyes. They brushed off their linen clothes. They went downstairs into the open-spaced kitchen adjacent to a family room where a plasma television showed the news. In a matter of time, their family's sadness would be plastered over the television screen, as well as the front pages of every local newspaper.

"Kenley, get something cold out of the refrigerator for us to drink. Noelle, you get the glasses," Milandra instructed.

Kenley opened the refrigerator door that was hidden behind a wooden cabinet. She spotted a bottle of sparkling cider.

Noelle took out three crystal glasses. She filled one with extra ice, for which Kenley could not do without. She filled the glasses with cider. Each sister held up her glass.

"We're Houstons. We'll get through this," Milandra toasted.

"It's going to be so hard," Noelle admitted.

"Why did this have to happen? I wish I hadn't given Mother such a hard time about where I wanted my party. I hate becoming sixteen. How can I have a birthday party without Mother and Father?" Kenley wept.

"Just stop it, Kenley," Milandra scolded her. "Your sixteenth birthday celebration will go on. It's tradition."

"Cheers," Noelle said as she tapped her glass against her sisters'.

They took a sip from the glasses.

Kenley sat down at the table. She put her glass down and bowed her head. "Milandra, I'm not as strong as you and Noelle." Tears flowed down her cheeks.

Noelle placed her glass on the table. She put her arm around her sister. "Go ahead, Kenley, cry all you want. We all should cry ourselves to sleep tonight."

"How can you both forget that fast what Mother and Father have taught us?" Milandra asked.

Kenley jumped up. "It hurts, Milandra. It truly hurts."

Noelle wiped the tears from her baby sister's face. Milandra came over and they both comforted her for a few seconds. She spoke, "I can't sit here and do nothing."

Milandra exited the kitchen to help finish handling their family saga.

After a while, Baron entered into the kitchen. Kenley and Noelle were busy watching the television screen for any breaking news of their sorrow.

"I'm so sorry about all this tragedy that has come down on your family," he said.

"You're family, too," Noelle said as she found the strength to give him a smile. She got up, went over to him, and gave him a hug. She pressed close to him.

"I appreciate the love," he said as he moved on and gave her sister a hug.

Kenley wondered, "Where's Milandra?"

"She's seeing everyone out. She's giving the housekeepers the night off."

"The bodies…sorry, I didn't mean to say bodies. Your parents have been taken away. I told Milandra I'd handle all of the funeral arrangements," he said.

"We do thank you, Mr. Chavis," Noelle said; she wanted to call him by his first name.

Milandra made her way back into the kitchen. "The coast is clear. Maybe we should go and take a swim."

"That'd be a good way for you all to relax. Or better yet, go out and sit by the lake."

"I don't want to see any water. I want my parents," Kenley cried.

"Don't be difficult. That is what mother would say to you. Now go put on your bathing suit," Milandra demanded.

Kenley got up and ran from the kitchen.

"Mr. Chavis, I'll speak to you later. I'm going up to get ready for a swim and to make sure Kenley is doing the same."

"Since you relieved the help, I'll tidy up the kitchen. I'll be up in a minute," Noelle said.

Milandra exited the kitchen. Noelle waited until she didn't hear any sound of heels tapping against the floor. She rushed into his arms. She kissed Baron passionately.

"Baby, I've been wanting you to comfort me. Let's tell Milandra and Kenley about us. We no longer have any reason to keep our relationship a secret," Noelle whispered in his ear.

He delicately pulled her away. "We need to wait. I don't think Milandra will take it lightly hearing about any contact we may have had. Right now is not the best time. She'll think you defied your parents. This will bring friction between you and your sisters. You need each other more now than ever."

Noelle knew that what he said was true. Kenley would think nothing of it, but Milandra would be furious.

"I agree," she said. "But as soon as things calm down, we'll find a way to share the news about the love we feel for each other. I love you, Baron, with all my heart."

He barely got the words out of his mouth. "I love you, too."

Noelle reached again and smothered his lips. He eased away from her.

"I better go," he said. "Go take that swim with your sisters. Be strong."

Tearfully, Noelle said, "I wish you didn't have to leave."

"I'll see you soon," he said and hurried out.

Chapter 5

Baron got into his car. As he loosened his tie, he could still smell the scent of Noelle's perfume. He could not believe that she actually thought a cup of coffee and a peck on the lips would imply that they were a romantic couple. Right now, however, he couldn't concentrate on her, but in due time he had to find a way to let her down gently because there was no future for them.

His concern was whether or not Rupert Houston's discovery about them had led to Rupert's and his wife's deaths. He felt deeply guilty for Alana's death, but he felt only a slight bit of guilt for her husband.

Rupert always wanted to be in control of everything, from his family down to his business. Everything was a possession to him. He did not want to share anything with anyone unless it was on his terms.

Baron made his way down the road, thinking of Rupert's illegitimate daughter. He had to call Aniyah and give her the sad news. He called his office and got the number from his secretary, then called her.

"Hello!" she answered in a high pitch.

"This is Mr. Chavis. I got your number from Mr. Houston's files. Do you remember me? I'm the attorney for your father."

"How can I forget a hottie lawyer like you? You're the one that holds my future. You know I was added to Papa's will."

"I have some disturbing news. Are you sitting down?"

"I know he didn't kick me to the curb?"

"No, it's something more serious. Mr. Houston died not long ago; so did his wife."

Aniyah almost lost her balance. Dollar signs flashed across her eyes. She became a sobbing actress. "Papa is gone?" she bellowed.

"Yes."

"Oh, I didn't even get to spend that much time getting to know him. Oh, Papa," she cried.

"Are you okay?" he asked as he listened to how hysterical she was.

"No, I'm not okay! I have no one here! Please come over. I need to be with someone. I can't take this," she sobbed.

He heard the phone drop onto the floor. He called, "Aniyah!"

She didn't answer. He heard her crying in the background. "I'm on my way over to you," he said as he hung up the phone. He was quite aware of the location where Rupert had set up house for her. It was the same apartment he had used in the past for many of his female encounters.

Baron made a sharp U-turn and headed to her aid.

Aniyah clicked off the phone. She became hysterical with laughter. "Jackass, I knew you would fall for it."

She didn't want anything going wrong. She wanted to make sure that what she estimated was due to her would be no problem getting to her, and Baron was the one to do it.

Aniyah stepped out of the short, sleeveless dress that she wore. She found her way to her suitcase and pulled out a black bikini, slipping it on. Her breasts bulged from the top and her hips stretched the bottom to its limit. She went into the shower and soaked her bathing suit, not letting the water touch her long black hair. Her hard nipples were exposed through the top.

In her galley kitchen, Aniyah took out an onion and held the onion up to her face until it brought tears to her eyes. She stuffed the onion back into the bottom of the refrigerator.

Baron buzzed the bell repeatedly. "Open up, Aniyah," he called.

She made her way to the door and unlocked it. He heard the click of the lock. Aniyah left the door and sat on the bed. He turned the knob and came into the apartment.

"Are you all right?" he asked.

"My papa is gone," she cried, tears flowing from the effect of the onion.

She got up and turned her back to him. Baron tried not to look at her, but the wetness of the bathing suit clenched to her body turned him on. His eyes traveled up her legs to see her cheeks peeking out from under the bottom of her bikini.

Aniyah turned around and ran over to him. She lay in his arms. Her wet bikini dampened his suit.

Baron looked down at her breasts pressed against his chest. He stared at her as he did the first time he met her in his office. She reminded him so much of Tessa with her flowing black hair.

"You look so much like your mother."

"I don't look like my papa?"

Baron tried to find some resemblance to Rupert or one of her half-sisters, but there was no resemblance. He felt that with her resting on him, he had been given a second chance with the woman that he loved. Temptation weakened him. He pushed Aniyah away. He saw a chair nearby and sat down.

"Yes, you look so much like him," he lied.

"I was at the pool before you called. That's why I'm so wet," she said as she eased her hand down her body. "Would you like a drink? I sure could use a stiff one," she said, sniffling.

"I could use one myself." He tasted the dryness in his mouth.

Aniyah went into the kitchen and returned with two plastic cups in her hands. Under her arm she held a half-filled bottle of rum. She poured nearly a cupful of rum for Baron but only poured herself a little.

Aniyah handed him the cup.

"You have a heavy hand, I see," he said as he noticed the amount that she had given him.

"Drink what you want. Tell me what happened," she said as she sat on the bed. She leaned back on her arms to give him a good view of her body.

Baron began to speak but tried to keep his eyes on an empty wall. He took a sip of the drink as he spoke. One sip too many and he became relaxed. He no longer cared to look at the empty wall. Instead, he feasted his eyes on her. She watched him gulp the drink down and went back to pour him more.

He touched her on the hand. "Tessa," he called her.

"I'm Aniyah," she reminded him.

He smiled. "No, you're really Tessa."

"Is that who you want me to be?" Aniyah asked as she took his hand and placed it on her cleavage.

"Yes," he said, as he caressed her breasts.

Aniyah was curious about what connection he had to Tessa. "So why are you so fascinated with my mother?"

"I was in love with her, before your father stole her from me. The bastard knew I loved her. I wanted to take her away from being a maid, but Rupert forbade me from having any physical contact with her. He took her for himself."

"You're saying my papa was a bastard?"

"Yes."

"A bastard he could be at times," Aniyah whispered in his ears as she pulled him up out of his seat.

Baron fumbled a little but kept his balance. He took a strand of her hair and rubbed it on his cheek.

Aniyah helped him out of his suit jacket. She unbuttoned his shirt and pulled it out of his pants.

Baron leaned over and kissed her. "Soft lips."

Aniyah unzipped his pants. He kicked off his shoes. She helped him out of his pants and striped boxers.

Aniyah slipped out of her bikini bottom. She untied her bikini top to fully expose her breasts to him. They were two naked souls.

Pulling him by the hand, Aniyah pushed him down onto the bed. She dove on top of him, working her magic all over his body.

"Tessa!" he screamed as he exploded.

He fell asleep. Aniyah sat up and looked at his limp body.

"Men—so weak," she said as she lay near him. "I guess I have to put up with your ass for the rest of the night."

Before she went to bed she took a snapshot of the two of them in a compromising position.

Chapter 6

The sun beamed through the sheer panel curtains in Milandra's bedroom. She awakened to the aroma of turkey sausages and bacon, cooked by the servants.

She sat up, stretched her arms, and yawned before she got out of bed. Sliding her feet into her slippers, she went to wake up her sisters. She called. "Kenley and Noelle; it's morning time."

Noelle awakened right away, but Kenley took her time getting up. The ladies went to their own bathrooms to wash their faces and brush their whitened teeth.

Making their way to the lower level of the house, dressed in white linen bathrobes, they entered the kitchen to see that Elsa, the head servant, had garnished the table with a bowl of assorted fruits, buttered biscuits, and a blend of juices in crystal pitchers.

Elsa ran over and gave each one of them a tight squeeze. She wiped her eyes with the bottom of her apron. "Lord, I barely made it through last night. I'm sure going to miss your daddy and mama," she wept.

Kenley started to tear up. Elsa patted her on the back. "I don't mean to get you upset, baby girl. Go on and have a seat. Put some food in your belly."

The sisters sat at the table. Elsa stood over them and blessed the food. Another servant came behind her and scooped grits onto their plates. They helped themselves to the rest of the food, pampering their tongues with the taste of Elsa's morning breakfast.

"Everything is delicious, Elsa," Kenley said.

"Take your time," Milandra said as she watched her sister gulp down her food.

Of course, Kenley finished her meal first. She was about to get up out of her seat when Milandra announced: "We have an appointment right after breakfast."

"I'm going to stay in my room and return my friends' calls," Kenley informed.

"No, you're not. They're calling to be nosy for their parents," Milandra replied.

"Kenley, I do understand you want to talk with your friends, but I believe Milandra is right. For now, stay away from talking with your friends. We sisters can do things together today," Noelle said as she got up. "What do you have planned for us?" she said, directing her attention to Milandra, who had already finished her food and stood up.

"I have three massage therapists waiting for us in the Spa Suite. This will help us to deal with the loss of Mother and Father," Milandra said, tossing her French roll up in a ponytail.

"Fine, let's make our way there," Noelle said. Her hair was, as Kenley's was, pulled back from her face.

Kenley said nothing. She followed her sisters to the lower level of the house, but lagged behind.

Three masseurs were in the massage salon of the Spa Suite to relieve the tension built up in the sisters. There were three tables in a row in the room, where Alana and her oldest two girls had enjoyed getting massages together several times before. Kenley, however, always found her way to the meditation salon of the Spa Suite. She would drown herself in the softness of the pillow-top mattress and plush covering on the king-sized bed. Or at times, she found her way into the spa tub with aromatherapy-scented bath oils.

Today was no exception. Kenley tiptoed into the meditation salon, removed her bathrobe, and jumped onto the bed, covering herself with organic linens.

Noelle and Milandra made their way to the massage tables. They removed the white linen bathrobes that they wore and settled under a white sheet.

Milandra was the first to notice that her baby sister was not on her table. "Kenley, come in here," she called.

"I'm sleepy; I didn't get much sleep last night," Kenley said as she rested on the bed. She listened to the soft music that played on a radio. The curtains were drawn shut to block out the sunlight. The trickle of water from the tabletop aromatherapy fountain relaxed her. A few candles glowed and gave the room a fragranced vanilla scent.

"Kenley, the massage therapist is waiting on you," Noelle called.

The last masseur stood like a body builder near the empty table. Kenley came into the room to see her sisters lying face down on the tables. She looked over at the masseur as he stood there and the other masseurs who worked on her sisters. "I'm not taking my robe off until they leave the room."

"Please leave until my sister gets undressed," Milandra said.

Kenley held on to the belt of her linen bathrobe until the masseurs exited. Once they were gone she removed her bathrobe and got on top of her table, face down.

The men returned and began to massage each of them around the neck.

"Relieve yourself," one of the masseurs said to Milandra.

"This feels so good," Noelle admitted, wishing the hands that were on her body belonged to Baron. She thought of him as the masseur continued. A tingling sensation spread between her legs.

Kenley jumped. "Ouch! That hurts!"

"Sorry, Miss Houston," the masseur said as he slowed the rotation of his hands on her shoulders.

Kenley laid her head back down on the white cushion pillow. She tried to shut out the discomfort she felt from his hands. "This isn't relaxing at all. Spa tubs, now they are relaxing."

Kenley wrapped herself in the sheet and got up. She snatched her bathrobe and dashed out of the room.

"Tell me we weren't as bad as Kenley is as a teenager," Noelle said, wondering.

"Mother always said Kenley was her most challenging child. She never wants to follow the family rules that have already been set for her."

They calmed down into a mellow mood, their bodies absorbing the lotion from the firm hands of the masseurs.

In the farthest part of the Spa Suite, Kenley sat in bubbling heated water. Her head rested on a spa pillow. She thought of how in the next few months she would be the only sister in her family without her parents to share her sweet sixteenth birthday. Earlier yesterday she debated with her mother about where to have her party, the Lake Murray Yacht Club or at the poolside? By the middle of the day she had persuaded her mother to let her have two parties. By the end of the day, she was left without either parent. She would return the dress. What would a celebration be without her parents being there to shower her with love and gifts?

Kenley held back the tears. She reached over on the spa tub and hit a button. A television screen slowly popped up from the foot of the spa tub. She changed the channel to see her parents' faces plastered on the news and news reporters camped out on the grounds outside the gates of the estate, hungry to share her family's tragedy with the world.

Kenley was familiar with the media reporting good and bad things about her family, but the one thing that startled her was the last statement that one of the reporters had said. "The question is, where is the fourth daughter?"

"The nerve of them!" she shouted.

Kenley turned the television off. She pressed the button and the television disappeared back into the caddy on the spa tub. As she got out of the tub, she splashed water on her hair.

Dripping water onto the hardwood floors, in her two-piece bikini, Kenley ran to the massage salon. "Milandra! Noelle!" she yelled. "Guess what I heard on the news."

Milandra looked up at her, recalling how thin her body used to be, like Kenley's. She noticed her sister dripping water onto the ceramic tile floor. "Kenley, get a towel."

Noelle wondered what was reported about their family. She prayed it wasn't anything about Baron and her. "What's on the news?"

The eldest sister watched the masseurs diligently focusing on Kenley. "You're dismissed," she ordered. The masseurs marched out immediately.

Milandra sat up and put on her robe. Noelle followed.

"Kenley, you must be careful how you speak around the help and others. We're the Houstons. People feed off of gossip about us."

"What did you hear?" Noelle demanded to know.

"On the news it said, and I quote, 'The question is, where is the fourth daughter?'"

Milandra's eyes lit up. "Fourth daughter? They'll go to any length to make up such gossip about our family."

Noelle agreed. "Yes, that's going too far."

Kenley busily dried off with a towel. "Well, we know they're not talking about Mother. So they must be speaking of Father. Could it be true?"

"Kenley, I wonder about you sometimes. Are you loyal to this family?"

"How dare you, Milandra, think I'm not loyal to my family? But Father was a handsome and powerful man. He could have had any woman he wanted."

Milandra went up to Kenley. She snatched her by the arms and shook her. "Stop it! Stop talking that way about Father and he's not even buried yet."

Noelle pulled Milandra away from their baby sister. "She has a right to her opinion," she commented.

"Are you turning against the family, too?" Milandra asked as she turned to face Noelle.

"Never," Noelle said. She knew that if her sister found out about Baron she would think she did.

Kenley stormed out of the room and cried, "I want Mother and Father."

"See what you've done. It's only been one day since Mother and Father's death. Please, I beg you, Milandra, let's not grow apart."

The sisters hugged. "The media is cruel," Milandra said.

"Yes, we won't read nor watch any television to hear the vicious lies."

"We need to call Mr. Chavis," Milandra suggested. "He'll handle such gossip."

Milandra called him but got no answer.

Every chance Noelle got she tried to contact him and she, too, received no answer.

Chapter 7

Baron woke up, covered with a sheet, but realized that he wasn't in his house. His head throbbed from the after-effects of the rum. He felt as if he had a couple of paperweights on his forehead. Peeking under the cover, he discovered that he was stripped of his clothes.

The Latin music playing didn't help his aches and pains. He looked up to see Aniyah dancing. She twirled her nude body to the music. "You like?" she asked.

"Oh, no, Aniyah, tell me I didn't."

She threw herself on top of him. He tried to push her away, but she swung her arms around his neck.

"This is a serious mistake. Whatever part I've played in this, I'm deeply sorry."

"You were drunk. You thought I was my mother."

He recalled his old love, Tessa Sanchez. "Oh God, forgive me."

Baron grabbed Aniyah and tossed her off him. He got up and looked at his cell phone to see that he had numerous missed calls, one or two from Milandra, but most of them from Noelle. "I have to get out of here. I should be planning your father's funeral. Shit!" Baron recalled who she really was. He slipped on his clothes.

Aniyah laughed. "You called my papa a bastard last night."

Astonished, Baron wondered what else he had said while under the influence.

"It must have been the rum talking." He looked over at her nude body. "You've got a bathrobe. Put it on."

She walked up behind him and put her arms around his waist. She licked his neck. "I want you to be my lover." She pushed her hands down in his pants.

Baron pushed her hands off of him. "You're tempting, but I can't."

Aniyah came around him and stood in front of him. She pierced her eyes on him. "You will be whatever I choose you to be."

Throwing her arms around his neck, she kissed him, rubbing her breasts against him. Taking her left knee, she pushed it up into his crotch.

For a moment, Baron kissed her back; but again, he fought her off. "I can't do this. Aniyah, you're beautiful. You're so much like your mother in looks, but you could never replace her."

Aniyah became annoyed. "You're the bastard. I know exactly what you told me last night."

"What did I tell you?"

"You told me that Papa found out about you and my half-ass sister."

Baron kept a straight face. He could not believe that, as an attorney, he had been that dumb to share the information with her.

"I never said any such thing."

Aniyah laughed. "I know all about you and her. What would my other sisters think of you if they knew you caused our parents' deaths?"

"From my understanding, your father had a heart attack," he informed her.

"Because of you, asshole. He saw the picture of you making out with her."

Baron couldn't believe what he had heard. He had deleted the email.

"How in the hell do you know about the picture?"

"Because I sent it to him." She laughed.

"How did you do it?" he yelled. "I never slept with Noelle. We only had a quick kiss. Whose body did you attach to her face?"

"This body, the one you really made out with." Aniyah pranced around the room. "I have a copy of the picture."

"Why are you doing this?"

"I want all that's coming to me, and that includes you."

The music continued to play. Aniyah began to dance, shaking her body. She came closer to him. Grabbing him by the hands, she placed his arms around her back.

Aniyah reached up and hugged him around the neck. Baron was hypnotized by her dark eyes. She kissed him, forcing her tongue into his mouth. He submitted, as she knew he eventually would.

Baron spread her legs apart and entered her. Aniyah moaned from the force of his manhood. He smothered his lips on her neck, sniffing her natural body scent. Together they cried in ecstasy. As much as he enjoyed her, he had to find a way out of this one. His cell phone rang.

It must be Noelle, he thought. Noelle lusted for him too, but his heart would forever belong to Tessa. No woman could ever satisfy his hunger for her, not even her daughter. In his mind he whispered: "Forgive me, Tessa."

Aniyah finally felt secure that she had Baron where she wanted him. She stepped back and let him take a shower.

Baron freshened up and came out of the bathroom tying a knot in his tie.

Aniyah held up her digital camera and snapped a photo of him. He furiously grabbed the camera from her.

"Give that back to me," she said as she wrestled to take the camera from him but did not succeed.

Baron walked away and reviewed the photos in hopes that he would find the image of him and Noelle. Instead, he discovered the photo Aniyah took of the two of them in a sexual position. He pulled the SD memory card out of the camera and broke it in half.

"Go ahead and tear the damn thing up. I still have the picture of you and my half-ass sister safely put away. And it damn sure isn't in this apartment."

Baron put the broken pieces of the SD memory card into his pocket. "Goodbye, Aniyah."

"See you at the reading of the will. We can have it all."

"You're not coming to the funeral?" he asked as he walked to the door.

"Right, the funeral. I'll be around." She smirked.

"Well, if you come, just stay far away from me."

Baron left.

Aniyah turned the music up loud. She celebrated. "These people with money are dumber than I thought. Next fight to win is with them bitches; oops, my half-ass sisters." She giggled.

Chapter 8

The speed limit wasn't an option for Baron as he drove on the highway to his office. Keeping his eyes on the traffic, he reached for his cell phone and clicked on the voice activation to make calls.

Milandra would be his first call. Baron knew that she was basically a female version of her father when it came to business. Everything had to be in order.

Milandra picked up and scolded him: "Mr. Chavis, why haven't you answered my calls?"

"I took a sleeping pill to get some rest last night. It must have been pretty strong or I was just plain tired. Overslept, what can I say?" he lied.

"I want my parents' funeral to be carried out with dignity," she demanded.

"Arrangements will be finalized today. Your father kept everything in writing."

"Yes, I assumed you have his will. He always said you kept good files of all his legal matters."

"Yes, everything is in order. We'll have the reading of his will as soon as you say so."

Baron, distracted by a driver in a red car who tried to cut in front of him, blew his horn.

Milandra heard the loud noise through the cell phone.

"Mr. Chavis, call me when you get to your office. You'll have a wreck trying to drive and speak on the phone at the same time."

In the room with Milandra was Kenley. She hollered, "Before you hang up, ask him about what I heard on the news."

"I will not. I won't entertain garbage," Milandra said as she put her hand over the mouthpiece of the phone, moving away from her sister.

Baron had heard Kenley clearly. "What's on the news, Milandra, that I should know about?"

"You know how the media can get. They're asking, where the fourth daughter is?"

For a moment Baron lost control, almost swerving into another car. He pressed down on his brakes and regained control, wondering how the media had gotten wind of Aniyah. He prayed that she had not turned the photo that she was blackmailing him with over to the media.

"Stay away from the television and newspapers. I'll investigate any gossip."

"That's what I told my sisters. It's trash talk to destroy our family's good name."

"Exactly," he agreed, relieved Milandra didn't buy into the gossip.

"Call me as soon as you get things in order."

Milandra hung up.

Baron pulled into his parking spot at his office. Several reporters awaited him.

"Damn!" He panicked.

They shouted, "Mr. Chavis, do you have any idea what happened at the Houston Estate? Is there a fourth daughter born out of wedlock? If it is, who is she? Who's the mother? Will his oldest daughters take over running the company?"

Cameras flashed at him. "I'm not answering any questions at this time. Please, do not bother Mr. Houston's daughters. They're in mourning for their parents." He said no more and entered the office building.

Sara greeted him. "Hello, Mr. Chavis, you've had lots of calls concerning the Houston family.

"Hold all my calls. I need to focus on making final arrangements for the Houstons."

One thing Rupert loved about Baron was that he knew how to run his law firm.

Baron settled at his desk and went straight into work mode. He was searching among the stack of files on his desk labeled "Rupert Houston" when the ring of his cell phone alarmed him.

Looking at the number, he saw Noelle was trying to reach him. Baron decided to answer her to avoid having to delete another message from the numerous messages she had left on his voicemail.

"Hello, Elle."

"Baron, where have you been? I've been ringing and ringing you. Why are you ignoring me?" she asked frantically.

"I don't mean to ignore you, but work must be done."

She wept, "I need you so much now. I don't know if I can handle all this."

"Elle, lean on your sisters for strength," he said abruptly.

Noelle was startled. "It's like all of a sudden you don't want to be bothered."

"I do. But right now it's best we stay away from each other. With the media and all, we don't want to be in the spotlight. You know Milandra would be furious with us."

Noelle couldn't help but agree. Her sister would attack her. She would say she wasn't loyal to the family. Also, Noelle knew her sister would be hurt on a personal level.

Milandra never dated. She waited for Rupert to match her up with a perfect gentleman. After all, she honored her father.

Noelle was in the same position as her sister. She also had waited on her father to match her up with a perfect gentleman. She remembered asking him once, "Father, have you found a suitable gentleman for me? I would love to have a companion."

Rupert had sternly replied, "There's no one in the United States I see fit for you. I'm searching out of the country for a suitable gentleman. It's a matter of time. Be patient, my dear." He smiled. "Run along. Tomorrow I'll bring you home a special gift."

As always, he lavished her with jewelry, but that did not fill the void she felt for a man. Seeing Baron over and over at the estate made her heart begin to ponder over him. She flirted with him when her father wasn't around. She figured that her flirtation had paid off when Baron secretly asked her out for coffee.

"Talk to you later" Baron said, but there was no response from Noelle. "Did you hear what I said?"

"I apologize; I was lost in my thoughts. What did you say?"

"I must go now."

"Okay, but call me as soon as you can," she humbly submitted.

The attorney banged his fists on the desk. His involvement with Noelle was supposed to be to get back at her father. Now Rupert was dead and he was stuck with Noelle clinging to him from mere kisses that she had planted on his face. He giggled for a moment. "Damn, if I gave her sex she would turn into a stalker."

Aniyah added to the flames burning in his life. He labeled her psychotic—nothing like her sweet mother. He should have seen it coming—the wet bikini she was wearing when she had greeted him at the door, and the full glass of rum with no Coca-Cola in it. Just like a mouse, he went for the cheese. She looked good but tasting her had become damaging to his life. He blocked out his thoughts of his personal life and went on to find the Houstons' file.

On his desk, below other cases, he pulled out a file labeled: "Rupert Houston Estate." He pulled out Rupert's wishes in the event of his death.

After several calls, it was not long before the Houstons' funeral arrangements were finalized.

The last two pages in the file were the will. He looked over it, studying the name Aniyah, as one of Rupert's daughter.

Rupert demanded him not to file the will, but that was a request that Baron had disobeyed.

Baron recalled the day that Rupert had come to him.

"Baron, this is my new will. Don't file it, you hear me?" Rupert insisted as he handed him a sealed envelope.

"Why would you hand me a will that you don't want to be filed?"

Rupert stared at him. "Follow orders, don't question me."

"You're mighty cranky. What's got you so uptight?"

Rupert decided to let him in on his secret. "I told you years ago that Tessa up and left her job with us, but that wasn't true. She was pregnant."

"Pregnant!"

The child should have been mine, Baron thought.

"Yes, the baby she had is no baby anymore. She's a beautiful, grown girl, but on the wild side. She thinks I'm going to leave her something in my will. That's a joke." He chuckled.

"She's your daughter, too. Why wouldn't you leave her something? You owe that much to her and Tessa."

"Baron, be quiet and stay in your place. She's right outside in your lobby. I'm warning you, don't say a word about what I'm doing," he ordered him.

Rupert went out the door and asked Aniyah to come into the

office. She strutted in and posed in front of the desk. Her dress fit every curve of her body.

"This here is my daughter, Aniyah," Rupert introduced.

"Nice meeting you. You're your mother all over. Beautiful," Baron said as he took her hand and kissed the back of it.

Rupert, annoyed by the behavior of his attorney, grabbed Aniyah by the hand. "Come on, let's go. You—" He pointed at Baron. "—take care of that envelope for me."

The attorney watched as they left out. Aniyah looked back and winked her eye at him. She switched her hips, giving him no choice but to feast his eyes on her. He furiously held up the envelope. Rupert reminded him that he was the one that had won Tessa over.

"To hell with him," Baron said with no hesitation and filed the papers.

Closing the file, Baron made up his mind that the reading of the will would be the day that he would introduce Rupert's daughters to their new sister.

Chapter 9

B ad news is like a contagious virus—it travels fast. Word had already made its way from Lake Murray, South Carolina, to Cancun, Mexico.

Julia, Tessa's sister, was busy cleaning a home where she and Tessa worked.

She dusted a night table in one of the bedrooms. Going over to the other side of the bed to dust the other night table, she picked up a morning newspaper and the story on the front page caught her attention.

"Look, Tessa, there's sad news in the paper about the family you worked for," she spoke in Spanish as she ran to the kitchen.

Tessa, dressed in a floral dress, busily removed the mop from the pail of water. She had just finished mopping the floor. Drying her hands, she took hold of the newspaper.

She stared into the eyes of an older photo of Rupert. Alana's photo lay on the page next to his.

Too weak, Tessa went and sat on a bench in the hallway. Her sister followed and stood over her.

Reading the article word for word, Tessa clutched at the rosary beads that hung around her neck.

"Oh, my God," she said in Spanish. Her eyes watered as she

recalled how wonderfully Alana Houston had treated her. The pretty clothes Alana no longer wanted, she handed to her to share with her family in Mexico.

Alana thought of her as being a fragile-built girl. She passed on the leftovers from meals for her to take back to her room at the servants' quarters for snacks.

"She's so beautiful. She deserved a better man than Mr. Houston," Tessa said to her sister.

"Was he a bad man?"

"Yes, very cruel man," she tearfully said. "It's because of him I had to leave."

"What do you mean, Tessa?"

She touched her stomach. "It was his child I carried within me."

"You messed with a married man? How could you do that to his wife? You said she was nice to you."

"You don't understand."

"Tessa," her sister said as she sat next to her on the bench, "you came back home, pregnant and quiet, never wanting to talk about your problems. Please, tell me the truth about what happened."

Tessa's memory was clear as if it had happened yesterday. She wiped the tears from her eyes and spoke.

"My heart was with another man, but Mr. Houston didn't like it. He threatened me. I needed the money for our family. I did what I had to do. I slept with him." Tessa lowered her head. "I'm so ashamed."

"I never met the man and I hate him, too, for what he did to you."

Tessa cried, "God punished me." She kissed her rosary beads. "That's why I lost my baby girl."

"Oh, Tessa, that's not true. It must have been from all the sadness you had on your heart."

"I should have been stronger. I put money before my belief in God," she cried as she ran off and left work.

Julia wanted to run after her sister, but in order for them to be paid, she had to finish the day's work for both of them.

Tessa made her way into the house that she shared with her sister. She put a teakettle on the stove before she went into a bedroom, which was barely big enough for a twin bed and a small wooden dresser.

Opening a dresser drawer, she removed a black dress and a white apron from underneath her undergarments. She stared at the maid's outfit she had once worn when she worked for the Houstons, and then she held it close to her and cried.

She thought of what she read in the article. The Houstons' longtime attorney and friend, Baron Chavis, made the funeral arrangements. Just the thought of Baron's name made her smile. She would love to have seen a photo of him in the newspaper. *I can speak to Baron now.* A relief came over her. Rupert was no longer a threat.

Tessa got up and pulled a box from under the bed. She opened it and counted the money that she saved, in hope of using the funds to help her sister hire a private detective to find her runaway daughter. But, as with anything else, things always came up that she needed to use the money for.

The Houstons' deaths were another situation that she would have to use the money for. Tessa got up and looked inside the closet for her black suitcase. She packed it with a few clothes.

The whistle of the teakettle called her back to the kitchen. She made a cup of tea and sipped on it. Setting the cup down on the table, Tessa picked up the phone and made her reservation to go back to Lake Murray.

Tessa held on tight to her purse as she took her seat on the airplane. The memory of her last time in Lake Murray was devastating.

Nothing stayed on her stomach. Every morning she felt so nauseous. Alana demanded for her to go to bed. "I think you're having a baby," Alana said, "just like me."

Tessa panicked. "Oh no, not me! It's something I must have eaten."

"Nonsense." Alana smiled. "I'll have Doc come over and give you a checkup."

"No, Mrs. Houston, that won't be necessary."

Doc, the physician who aided all of the help, made his way to the servants' quarters. He examined her.

"You're pregnant!" he announced. "I've already shared the news with Mrs. Houston."

Doc left. Tessa trembled, knowing that she carried Rupert's baby, the same time as his wife was with child. If Alana had ever found out, she would have hated her.

Rupert got word of her pregnancy and made his way to the servants' quarters.

He came up to her, as she lay balled up on the bed. He snatched her from the bed.

"You crazy bitch. Don't you know anything about birth control?"

"Sorry, Mr. Houston, please help me get rid of it. I have no money."

Rupert slapped her across the face, shoving her back onto the bed. He got on top of her and ripped off her clothes, forcing himself inside of her, pumping as hard as he could, as if he was trying to destroy the baby.

"Pack all your things. Tonight, you're on the next plane out of here."

Rupert zipped up his pants. Tessa cried as she held the covers over her naked body. He turned around to see that she hadn't moved.

"Hurry up. I'll be waiting right outside." Rupert left, leaving the door ajar.

She grabbed all of her clothing, including her work outfit and shoved them into the same black suitcase she carried now.

Rupert waited for her outside in a limo.

Tessa went to the door and looked back at the bed that was in disarray, leaving the lights to burn and the door wide open. She jumped in the back seat of the limo with her suitcase resting on her lap, staying close to the window, and leaving plenty of space between her and Rupert.

The driver looked up into the rearview mirror to see her face was full of tears.

"Keep your eyes on the road!" Rupert shouted.

They reached the airport. Rupert instructed the driver to take a walk. The driver got out and got lost.

Houston leaned over and grabbed her by the hair. "My wife is pregnant. That's the only baby I'm looking forward to. I'll destroy you if word gets back to her that you're carrying my baby, too, Forget you ever knew me, much less my family. You hear me?" he shouted as he yanked her hair.

"Yes." Tessa trembled, praying that she would make it to the airplane.

Rupert kissed her on the lips one last time. "It was good while it lasted." He opened the door and pushed her out of the limo. She almost fell over her own suitcase.

The driver witnessed her getting out. He saw to it that she got on the airplane and stayed put until the flight took off.

She made it safely to Cancun, Mexico, finding her way to her sister, Julia, and her newborn baby. Tessa lay in bed for days depressed and sad. She hated that Rupert's selfish ways denied her the chance to have true love with Baron.

Depression took a toll on Tessa until the day that she went into the bathroom and her water broke at seven months. She cried for Julia, who had experienced delivering a baby. After so many pushes, Tessa delivered a baby girl. Her sister cut the umbilical cord. The baby had problems breathing. Mother and baby were rushed to a hospital. Due to renal complications, her baby died.

As time passed, Tessa recovered. She found work cleaning in Mexico. It did not pay much like the Houston Estate. The income was insufficient so she got up enough nerve to send Rupert a photo of her sister's little girl, who resembled her. She wrote on the back of the photo: "Mr. Houston, this is your daughter."

Rupert received the photo at his office. He panicked. To keep Tessa away, he mailed her three hundred dollars a month, for what he called support.

The flight attendant's announcement for passengers to fasten their seat belts brought Tessa back to reality. She fastened the belt and reached into her purse to find a stick of gum to help with the signs of nausea that might come on due to the high altitude.

Inside her purse was the stub from the last of the three hundred-dollar money orders she had received monthly from Rupert. She started to ball it up and throw it away; but instead, she left it in her purse. She found the stick of gum and chewed on it.

The roaring sound of the airplane's engine taking off made her brace herself. The plane began to move slowly until it picked up speed, faster and faster. Her hands clenched the arms of the seat. Up in the air she went, looking out the window to see the land of her heritage disappear before her eyes.

A flashing light appeared ahead, giving the passengers clearance to remove their seat belts. Tessa unlatched her seat belt. She took out the article on the Houstons and read it again. Her eyes stayed glued to Rupert's photo. A male passenger who sat next to her noticed the photo as well.

"Such a loss. He was a great man."

"So you say."

Tessa folded the paper, shoving it back in her purse.

"I think I'll take a nap. I see this might be a longer trip than I expected." The male passenger closed his eyes.

Tessa wondered how Rupert was so nice in front of high-society people, but behind the scenes, he treated the common folks so cruel. She witnessed his cruelty against female servants.

Every female servant was under thirty years old, except for Elsa, the head servant. The male servants were older men. She assumed that he didn't want any younger men around to seduce his wife or daughters.

As with her, and many of the women servants, he would pat them on the backside. Many cried when he would fondle their breasts. Then it was those he thought were sexier—the women servants whose legs he spread apart and took them for his liking in the servants' quarters.

The women took the abuse because it was all about the pay. She remembered the day she was hired. Rupert interviewed her for the job. Alana was nowhere to be found. His pleasant smile was of such charm.

"You'd like a job at the Houston Estate, I see?"

"Yes, I'm a hard worker," Tessa had said excitedly. "I clean, cook, and wash very, very good."

"Stand up," he ordered.

She eased out of her seat. A long trench coat covered her from the chill of the winter air.

"Remove your coat."

Rupert leaned back in a chair.

Tessa jumped to his command. She removed the coat, to show off a solid beige dress she wore to her knees.

"Take your hair down." He grinned and constantly kept his eyes on Tessa.

She untwisted her hair that was up in a ball. Her hair fell down to flow down her back.

A lady that she met while washing clothes at a Laundromat had told her about work at the Houston Estate. The lady warned her about the interview process. But she shouldn't fret, because it would lead her to making lots of money.

"Turn around," he ordered as he drooled over her.

Tessa shyly turned around, feeling degraded, even with her clothes on. She prayed that the interview would go no further.

"You have the job," Rupert said as he got out of his seat. He passed by her and tapped her on the shoulder. "Report tomorrow to the head help. Her name is Elsa."

Tessa was familiar with where she was to go. The next morning she reported to Elsa, who handed her a black dress, a white apron, and a white bonnet. She remembered her conversation with Elsa.

"Mr. Houston is a nice man."

Elsa pointed a finger at her. "You want to keep this job a long time?"

"Yes," Tessa answered, frightened by her tone.

"Stay away from Mr. Houston. Don't give him any reason to have a conversation with you."

"How come?"

"How old are you?"

"I'm almost nineteen."

"Whatever girl helped you to get this job only told you about it to get him to stay away from her. He must be having his way with her. You do understand what I'm talking about?"

Tessa was upset that maybe she had made a mistake by taking the job, but she needed the money. Bravely, she said, "I'll work long enough to make lots of money and then find other work." With that said, she put on the uniform.

Elsa laughed as she placed her hands on her hips. "That's what I said fifteen years ago. Look at me, I'm still here." Her grin changed to a frown. "I've had plenty of talks with Mr. Houston, mostly in bed. I've had one abortion and one miscarriage Mr. Houston never knew about. I'm fat and worn out to him. I don't know what it is about me, but he kept me around and made me head maid. I guess I was one of his first maids."

Tessa was frantic. "None of that will ever happen to me. No more talk. Where do I start?"

Elsa smirked. "Welcome to the money hell house."

Tessa followed her out to her first job of cleaning the kitchen.

"Something to drink?" the flight attendant asked as Tessa jumped.

"Yes," Tessa said, but smelled the roasted peanuts on the rolling cart. "Peanuts, please, if that's okay."

The flight attendant handed her the drink and peanuts. Tessa enjoyed the snacks, until she fell asleep. She woke up to the flight attendant making an announcement, "Ladies and gentlemen, we have just been clear to land at Columbia Metropolitan Airport. Please make sure your seat belts are securely fastened."

Chapter 10

The Houstons and Baron received the official news from the autopsy that both Rupert and Alana died from massive heart attacks. This allowed them to proceed with the combined funeral as planned.

Many came to Lake Murray Church to the services of Rupert and Alana. Rows of flowers lined the front of the church. The funeral consisted of masses of men dressed in black suits. The women were dressed in sleeveless black dresses. Some wore black hats on their heads to avoid the burn of the hundred-degree weather.

The Houstons stepped out of the limousine from oldest to youngest. Each sister was dressed in a white linen sleeveless dress. Milandra made sure of that. Kenley insisted on not wearing a white hat like her sisters. Her hair bounced on her shoulders.

Inside the church, with their heads up high, they walked down the aisle holding each other's hands. Milandra gave strict instructions—especially to her baby sister—that there would be no tears shed in the public eyesight. No photographer would dare print photos of the Houstons' daughters crying in a newspaper. No mockery would be made of them.

Kenley held tight to her tears. At times, she felt the pressure of trying to stay true to being a Houston. Too many rules came with it. She looked over at her sisters and followed the stern look on their faces. The only thing that dripped down their faces was perspiration from the humid heat. They went up to the caskets and took one last look at their parents.

"I can't do this," Kenley said as she tried to pull away from her sisters.

Milandra gripped her hands tight. "Kenley Houston, if you really loved Mother and Father, you'll not embarrass them in this way. They wouldn't care for you behaving improperly in front of the public."

Milandra jerked her hand discreetly and Kenley stood along with her sisters, saying good-bye to her parents for the last time. She closed her eyes tight when she felt the need to cry. Noelle took deep breaths to keep from falling apart.

Baron made his way down the aisle and leaned over to speak to them: "Hello there, ladies, do you need any tissues?" He held up a box of Kleenex.

"Mr. Chavis, we're our parents' daughters. Don't dare bring tissues to us in front of the public," Milandra said, embarrassed.

"Calm down. I was only checking," he said as he sat in the front row on the right side.

Noelle wanted to defend him, but it wasn't the right time.

Aniyah, dressed in a hot pink suit, entered the back of the church. Her top clung to her body and her skirt stopped nowhere near her knees. Dark shades covered her eyes. A wide-brimmed, pink straw hat was pulled down over her face.

Aniyah stood up on high-heeled sandals to match the rest of her outfit. She sat in the first row that she came to in the back of the church. She slid all the way over to the far right of the pew.

People continued to flow into the church. Aniyah looked up, and to her surprise, Tessa walked in. She slid down in the seat, turning her head away from the aisle, to avoid being noticed by Tessa.

Tessa was dressed in a black dress. A small black hat accented her dress. She wiped her tearful eyes. She strolled to the front until she approached the Houstons. "It's been a long time," she said as she looked down at Milandra, now all grown up.

"I'm sorry, but I don't know who you are?" Milandra said.

"I used to work for your parents when you were younger. The prettiest girl I ever did see. You had such a beautiful mother."

"What's your name?" Milandra asked, curious.

"Tessa Sanchez."

"Hello, Tessa. I do remember you. You're the help who used to let me lick the spoon from your chocolate cake."

"You remember that?" Tessa smiled.

"This is my sister, Noelle, and our youngest sister, Kenley."

Tessa looked over at Noelle. She realized that if she had not lost her baby, Rupert Houston would have two daughters the same age.

Across the aisle, Baron studied the back of Tessa, but when she turned around he could not believe his eyes.

"Tessa," he whispered. She was just as beautiful to him as when he had met her decades ago. Her long, black hair flowed down her back. Her body had gained a few pounds—in all the right places—which made him hunger for her more.

Baron wanted to go up to her, but the guilt of his encounter with Aniyah kept him in his seat. He held his head down, hoping that she would not notice him.

Tessa went up and viewed the bodies. She glanced over at Rupert's body while standing at Alana's casket. She cried, wiping tears from her eyes. "Forgive me," she said as she made the sign of the cross with her right hand. She held on to the rosaries around her neck and moved away to let others take their last view.

The services were short, and so was the last resting place ceremony. Aniyah didn't stay for the services. She exited the church while Tessa viewed the bodies.

Baron looked for signs of Tessa at the Houston Estate. Hopefully, she had come back to the servants' quarters to visit old friends, like Elsa, who didn't make it to the funeral. Milandra ordered that she stay at the estate and prepare the food for their guests.

Once the house was cleared of family and friends, he sat down with the Houstons.

Elsa took charge and poured them hot tea. She kept her ears open to hear what their conversation would be. She wondered if her job would still be secure now that Rupert and Alana Houston were gone.

Milandra waited until she finished pouring them a cup of tea.

"Excuse yourself, Elsa."

"Yes, Miss Houston."

Elsa made her way out of the room. Milandra brought her attention to Baron.

"Let's get down to business, the reading of the will. My sisters and I want to see what Father has put into place for us now that Mother is gone, too."

"Do I have to stay and listen to all this?" Kenley asked, not caring for any talk on business. She wanted to run along, get rid of the clothes she had on, and change into a pair of jeans. She was ready to contact her friends to drown out her pain.

"Of course you do," Noelle said. "This is your future we're speaking of also."

"Kenley, grow up. You have no idea who you really are," Milandra said.

"I'm a teenager!" she shouted. "I'm not old enough to be handling paperwork and all that stuff. May I be excused?"

"How dare you raise your tone of voice to me? I forbid you to speak to me in front of company in such a way. Apologize to Mr. Chavis," Milandra scolded her.

Kenley pouted. "I apologize. I wish Father and Mother were here," she cried out, falling back onto the sofa, no longer sitting in an upright position like her sisters.

The attorney took over the conversation. "Well, tomorrow in my office we can have the reading of the will. If there is anyone else to notify, I'll do it this evening."

"What do you mean?" Noelle asked.

He hesitated. "I was speaking in general as a lawyer. But I must go over the paperwork one last time to make sure everything is in order. I should be going."

"That means I can go, too," Kenley said, beating him out of the seat.

"See you in the morning at eleven o'clock. Is that sufficient?"

"Mr. Chavis, we'll get an early start. Make it nine," Milandra said.

The sisters saw him out. Noelle wanted her sister to escape right along with Kenley, but Milandra was her twin for that second.

Chapter 11

Aniyah tossed her hat onto the bed. She raced to a newly purchased bottle of rum and poured a drink. She spoke out loud, "What the hell is wrong with you, Tessa? How could you come back here to see a dead man who took your innocence? He threw you away like garbage. Are you crazy or what?" she asked, as if her aunt was there in the room with her.

Aniyah took another gulp of the rum. She continued to speak out loud: "How weak can you be? What is it that made you return here to spoil my chance of living the rich life? I may not be your daughter, but I'm your blood. Everyone says I look just like you, but in no way do I act like you. No man stomps on my heart and gets away with it. No man stomps on my family's heart and gets away with it. The man—dead or not—must pay. Tessa, go back to Mexico!" she yelled. "You won't mess up my good fortune."

Aniyah threw the glass across the room, shattering it against the wall. She kicked off her shoes and put the bottle of rum up to her mouth, swallowing a mouthful.

After a few swallows she passed out on the bed, spilling the bottle of rum and soaking her ruined hat.

She awakened at the time that most people would be leaving work. She realized that the funeral services were over and Rupert was covered with the soil of the earth.

Her head throbbed and she drank a glass of tomato juice.

Baron ran across her mind and she picked up the phone and called him.

"Hello," Baron said, praying that she had vanished.

"When are you going to read the damn will? I can't wait any longer. I want what is rightfully mine."

"I've spoken with the Houstons. The will will be read in the morning at my office."

"Did you tell them bitches about me? I hope you did."

He paused. "I'm afraid not. They're emotionally drained. Today wasn't the time for me to tell them the news about you."

"You're saying they're more important than me because I'm his bastard child?" Aniyah replied.

"Calm down," he said, but at the same time he thought, Women! "I'm not saying that. I know you're grieving, too." He remembered the service. "Your mother, Tessa, came to the funeral, but you weren't there with her. How come?"

"I was there. You didn't notice me because you were too busy taking care of my freakin' sisters. Did you speak to my mama?" Aniyah wondered, hoping her secret was still intact.

"Things moved so fast. I didn't get a chance."

"We aren't speaking," Aniyah said, thinking quickly. "She didn't want me to find my papa."

"Your mother knew what kind of reaction your father would have. She probably didn't want you to be rejected."

"Where are you?" Aniyah wondered.

"I'm on my way home. Another long day."

"Come over, please. I need company." Aniyah saddened.

Baron drove in the direction of his home. Tessa Sanchez was back in Lake Murray. Whatever chance he had to rekindle his relationship with her might be squashed. His closeness to Aniyah had put up a blockade between them.

"It's late. The reading of the will is at nine o'clock in the morning. Get a good night's rest. See you in the morning." He hung up.

Aniyah ran and got the brand new telephone book she had seen on the ground outside of her apartment door. She searched for his home address and she called a cab.

Fifteen minutes later, the cab was parked outside her apartment complex waiting on her. She jumped in.

"This is where I want to go." She passed the driver a slip of paper with the address on it.

The driver blew a kiss at her. "Hot! And I don't mean the heat from my cab."

The cab driver pulled off, but peeped at her every so often. He tried to figure out what nationality she was. "So, what are you?"

Aniyah had heard those words so many times. "Black-Mexican."

"Girl, if I can make a baby girl as pretty as you, I'm going to find me a Mexican girl to have sex with."

She laughed. "Go for it, but make sure you can take care of it."

"Done deal," the driver said.

The cab driver drove about twenty minutes. He pulled up to a large house in a subdivision, not secluded and gated like the Houston Estate. A wide porch accentuated the front of the house. The only light Aniyah saw lit in the house was in one room on the second floor.

"Boyfriend got a little cash, I see," the driver teased.

"Shut up and take this money." Aniyah paid the driver ten dollars; the amount shown on the meter.

"Do you need a pickup or you and your boyfriend plan to handle things all night long?"

"I'll tell you what, if he doesn't work out, who knows, I might call on you," Aniyah teased.

"I'll be the best baby daddy." He grinned, hoping things didn't work out for her.

Aniyah got out and slammed the door. She stepped onto the porch. A few chairs lined the porch. She rang the doorbell.

Baron, about to step into the shower, stepped back at the sound of the bell. Leaving the shower water running, he grabbed a royal blue bathrobe and tied it around his waist.

As Baron made his way downstairs, he wondered if his receptionist was at the door with some important documents to sign that he may have overlooked at the office. He flicked two switches and the inside foyer and outside lights came on.

Aniyah stood in bright lights, as if the sun was rising instead of setting.

Baron opened the door. The screened door separated them. Startled, he asked, "What are you doing here? How did you find out where I lived?"

"Thanks to the telephone book." She laughed.

He looked past her. He saw no parked car. "How did you get here?"

"Unfortunately, I'm not like my sisters. I don't have free limousine services. I took a cab."

"No you didn't," he said, looking out the door to see if any neighbors had noticed the goings-on at his house. "Where's the cab, Aniyah? Get back in it and go home. Be ready for tomorrow."

"Cab is gone. No way to get home." She smiled. "Let me in." She pulled on the doorknob.

"What's the number? I'll call you another one?"

"Hell no! Let me in, or would you rather I scream rape?"

He unlocked the door reluctantly. He could see that she was ready to give her lungs some exercise.

"Thank you," she said as she entered the house. "Wow! Beautiful!"

Aniyah loved the daintiness of his home. Everything looked like the background on a soap opera.

"Girl, what do you want?"

"Tonight, I want you." She moved closer to him.

Baron backed away. He remembered the shower was still running. "Stay right here." He ran up the stairs.

Everything is happening right on time. She kicked off her shoes and rushed up the stairs, following his lead through the master bedroom to the master bath.

Baron leaned over and turned the water off. He turned around and came face to face with her. He jumped. "Aniyah. Girl, you're adding difficulty to my life."

"I'm bringing spice to your life," she said as she shook her body.

He went to walk around her but she blocked his way. She slipped off her skirt to let it fall. Baron was faced with the natural tan of her body. Moving fast, she pulled the tie of his bathrobe. It flung open.

"I love coffee," she said as she stroked his chest.

He flung his head back as he tried to come up with an excuse as to why it was okay for him to have another sexual encounter with her. The rum from the other night was no longer an excuse he could get by with.

Too weakened by her touch, he grabbed the back of her hair and brought her closer to him to feel her heartbeat. He kissed her and his lips traveled her body. Aniyah moaned. She gradually reached over into the shower and turned the water back on.

Pulling him by the hand, Aniyah led him in. She took a bottle of body wash and lathered her hands with it. In return, he did the same. Together they massaged each other's bodies with the lather. They let the sprinkling water wash the suds away.

Baron took her into his arms, kissing her. He pushed her against the wall and there he made passionate love to her. As always, in his mind he thought, forgive me, Tessa.

Aniyah turned the water off as Baron reached for a towel. He handed it to her.

"So, when are you going to give me that made-up picture of Noelle and me?"

Instead of drying herself off, she towel dried his back. "When I become Mrs. Chavis."

"Mrs. Chavis! No marriage for me."

Aniyah took the towel and patted him in the front.

"You will." She laughed. "But first thing's first: I must find out about my fortune. I'll even share some of it with you. How do you like that?"

"I'm not worried about any fortune. I want the picture you took. Anyway, whatever Rupert left for you, the Houstons will fight you on it; especially Milandra."

Aniyah confronted him: "That is where you come in. You'll make sure they don't or everyone will find out about you and your women. They'll think we planned all this together."

"So that's what this is all about."

Baron snatched the towel from her. He left out the bathroom and put on a pair of pajama shorts. "There's the phone, call a cab." He pointed and jumped in the bed.

Aniyah found her way in the bed and under the covers. She tickled his manhood. Baron pushed her away. She jumped on top of him. Her breasts dangled in his face.

Aniyah would be hard to get out of his house without putting up a big fuss. He had already milked the cow so why not go for more milk? Reaching up at her, he found himself locked in her arms.

The next morning, Baron woke up while Aniyah still slept. He checked the clock, eight o'clock.

"Aniyah, wake up. We're going to be late. Hell, I'm going to be late."

"Good morning," she said as if she were his wife.

"I have to be at the office at nine o'clock. The Houstons are prompt."

"What about me? I have to be there, too. You'll drive me."

"I can't drive you. Me, drive Rupert Houston's illegitimate daughter to the reading of his will? Are you out of your mind?"

"How else will I get there?"

Baron knew about the time it took for a cab to arrive, and to take her home to get a change of clothing, she would be late for the reading. "Here's the deal: I'll drive you there under one circumstance. You have to kneel down so no one sees you. When we get to the office, you'll get out and go in first. It will appear that you were waiting on me to come in."

Aniyah grinned, for she had gotten her way again. She put back on the outfit that she had worn to the funeral. Baron got dressed.

He led her to the garage. She lay down in the backseat and off they went to his office.

Arriving, he parked in his usual parking spot. He looked around to see the limo hadn't yet brought the Houstons.

Out of the car, he opened the back passenger door on the driver's side and stood in front of the door while Aniyah crawled out. She squatted down and walked around the car, passing two cars before she stood up again and went inside.

The attorney entered the office building a few minutes after her. "Good morning, Sara. The Houstons haven't arrived yet?"

"No, but there's an Aniyah Sanchez here," Sara said, pointing toward her. "Miss Sanchez says she's here for the reading of the will."

"Good morning, Miss Sanchez," he said as he shook her hand.

"Nice meeting you again." Aniyah smiled.

"Sara, please escort Miss Sanchez to the meeting room."

Aniyah stood up, pulling down on her skirt that had risen up to almost expose her private parts. She followed Sara down the hall.

Baron went to the left to his office. He pulled out the Houstons' file, and then Sara buzzed him.

"They are here. Do you wish for me to direct them to the meeting room?"

"No. Send them into my office," he replied.

Chapter 12

The sisters strolled into Baron's office from the oldest to the youngest. Kenley purposely dragged far behind them. Inside her bag, she carried an iPod that she wanted to listen to and tune out all of the family's business.

Baron smelled the different fragrances that the two older sisters wore. "Come in and have a seat."

Milandra sat in the closest seat to his desk. He pulled two more chairs up for Noelle and Kenley. Not too far away was another chair for their surprise guest.

Noelle tried to be discreet in making eye contact with him, but Baron now played his business role of Attorney Chavis. He showed no signs of looking into her eyes.

This is why Noelle was falling in love with him. Baron reminded her so much of her father, so professional. He was also a man who showed so much attention to her family. He would make a great family man to his own family.

He sat behind his desk and opened the file. He clenched his hands together, leaning back in his leather executive chair.

"Something has come up," he said softly.

"Excuse me," Milandra said, leaning forward to clearly hear what he had said. "Speak up, Mr. Chavis." She saw the flushed look in his face. He kept his eyes on the file. There was trouble in the will. "Speak up," Milandra repeated.

"Please, Mr. Chavis, hurry up so I can get out of here," Kenley pleaded.

"Mr. Chavis, whatever it is, just tell us," Noelle said.

He spoke up loud and clear. "Something has come up," he repeated.

"Just tell us," Noelle said.

"It's that fourth daughter the news was talking about. It's true," he said.

"Who is she?" Kenley was excited as she rambled on at the mouth. "How old is she?" She forgot all about leaving. This was the kind of gossip she heard about from some of her friends about their fathers.

"Be quiet, Kenley. And you, Mr. Chavis, control your mouth on tabloid lies," Milandra said.

"It wasn't in the tabloids; it was on the news," Kenley corrected her.

"It's the same thing," Milandra insisted.

"I'm sorry, Milandra, it's the truth. You have a sister you knew nothing of," he said.

"I knew in my heart it was true. Maybe lots of bad things written in the paper about Father were the truth and we knew nothing about it," Kenley said.

Milandra went over and slapped her across the face. "Don't ever disrespect Father. He has given us his heart and soul!" she yelled.

Noelle pulled Milandra by the elbow, urging her to go back to her seat. Kenley sat crying.

"We must not fall apart on this news. Maybe it's a mistake. Someone is looking to cash in on Father's fortune," Noelle said.

They settled back into their seats. Baron didn't know whether or not to get Aniyah out of the building and deal with the will later. After all, following two intimate moments with her, the tabloids would report him as her lover or bed partner. He decided that since the can of beans was half open, he might as well open the can all the way.

"She's here for the reading of the will," he said.

The sisters looked back toward the door. They shouted in unison, "Where?"

"She's sitting in the meeting room," he said.

The sisters had many questions. But one question Milandra blurted: "Why is she here for the reading of the will?"

"Your father indicated her in his will," the attorney stated.

"Father acknowledged her? It must be true." Noelle cried.

"She wasn't raised in our home under the family name. She'll never be family to me." Milandra said as she sat back in her seat with her head up high. Milandra pulled out a handkerchief and wiped the sweat from her neck.

"Father probably left her a few dollars in his will, no big thing. Let her get her few dollars and be gone," Kenley said, annoyed.

Milandra smiled. "You can speak like a Houston when you want to," she said to her sister.

Baron paged his secretary. "Sara, send Miss Aniyah Sanchez in."

The door opened and the Houstons turned to see Aniyah walk in. Aniyah's smile was brighter than the sunlight shining in the room. They could see she had to be a child of one of the Mexican servants.

"Unbelievable," Milandra said.

"As they say in the hood, a hoochie," Kenley said.

Noelle didn't express her thoughts. *Whore* flashed across her mind, though.

"Hello, half-ass sisters; that's not a way to welcome me." Aniyah smiled.

From under her skirt, the sisters could see that Aniyah's legs were exposed up to her thighs. Her breasts bulged out of her outfit. The hot pink color that she wore turned the business mood into a room for partying. Bangles jingled on her arms. The platform heels raised her high off of the floor. She flung her hair.

"Have a seat, Miss Sanchez," Baron said.

"Yes, sugar," she said as she winked at him.

Aniyah sat down and crossed one leg over the other. She gave him a good view of her whole right side up to her thigh.

Noelle wanted to rip her eyes out. This was something she was supposed to be doing to arouse him.

"Mr. Chavis, please get on with the reading of the will so we can get out of the presence of such company," Milandra said.

"Bitch, you got a problem with me? Don't hate. Now I know why Papa always said I was his favorite and fun daughter," Aniyah teased, continuing to play in her hair.

Kenley was annoyed for she had always considered herself as her father's favorite daughter. If he were still alive, she would run to ask him if he loved Aniyah more than her.

Milandra was appalled. "How dare you?" She stood up.

Aniyah stood up, too. "Bring it on," she said as she waved for Milandra to come near her.

Baron rushed out of his seat to attend to them. "Please, let's handle this with intelligence."

"Whores don't know anything about being intelligent—just spreading their legs," Noelle spoke.

Aniyah was quite aware that it was the photo of Noelle she had copied and pasted on the computer with Baron. This was the sister she was blackmailing him with.

Aniyah laughed. "So, it's you?"

Puddles of sweat gathered on Baron's forehead. "Please, have a seat, Miss Sanchez, and be quiet," he begged.

Noelle didn't forget Aniyah's words. "What do you mean, it's you?" she asked.

Chavis answered in response for Aniyah, "You and Aniyah are the same age," he explained.

"Oh, Father, how could you do this to us, even to Mother?" Milandra sobbed.

"Father had two women pregnant at the same time," Kenley said.

Aniyah laughed. "Yes, Papa had a bed in the big house with his black wife and a bed in the maid's room with his Mexican honey."

"Who's your mother?" Milandra demanded to know.

"Tessa Sanchez."

The girls recalled the woman coming up to them at the funeral and how she remembered Milandra as a little girl.

"Your mother was at the funeral. But for you to be Father's daughter, how can you be here for the reading of his will, but not attend his funeral?" Milandra was appalled.

Aniyah pointed at Milandra. "Girl, get your facts straight. I was there. In and out—just like he did with my mama."

"Despicable," Milandra said. "I have no other words for you. Mr. Chavis, read the will."

"Ladies," he said, "no matter what is read, please don't interrupt."

Baron read the will from beginning to end. Tears flowed down the Houstons' eyes, except for Aniyah, who sat with a big smile on her face.

"Fabulous," Aniyah said, excited.

The words he read spun over and over again in their heads.

Rupert had left in his written will that Baron would be executor over the construction business and estate. He left huge sums of money to his daughters. He explained that they had lived at the Estate all their lives and now it was Aniyah's turn.

Their father stipulated that Kenley could stay in the house until she finished college, after which she could move on. And in any event, upon Aniyah's death, the estate would go back to the rest of his children to sell and divide equally. His daughters should move immediately into his other property, the Houston Villa in Lake Murray. A smaller home, but cozy enough for them. All the servants who wished to stay, their jobs were secure. Elsa would remain head servant until she either retired or passed away.

Baron showed no emotions of joy about being executor of the Houston Estate, as the will also stated, until Milandra turned fifty. He could build his own empire by then.

Kenley looked over at Aniyah. She could see the glow in her eyes. "Father expects me to live with a total stranger," she said, even though she knew all of the Houstons' rules would be doomed.

"Girl, I'm not a babysitter. You need to get to stepping with your two sisters sitting over there," Aniyah said, snapping her finger at Kenley.

Milandra screamed, "This has to be some mistake! This matter must be investigated. Mr. Chavis, do what you have to do to cover this matter and report back to me."

"The only thing that has to be done, bitch, is for you to pack your stuff and get out my house," Aniyah retorted.

"We will not!" Milandra yelled.

"No fighting anymore. If this is Father's wish, so be it. We have each other." Noelle wept.

Milandra looked over at Aniyah. "Never!" she screamed. "I won't accept her moving into what's rightfully ours."

"Listen, if you don't move out of my house, I'll call every newspaper in America and tell my story," Aniyah bluffed.

Milandra knew a scandal in the media would destroy what good was left of their family name. She stood up and looked back at Baron. "Handle it. Come on, Noelle and Kenley, let's leave. We have work to do."

The sisters left the office. Once they disappeared, Aniyah burst out laughing. She slammed the door behind them.

Baron came from around his desk and shook her. "This isn't funny. I've never seen them so lost and hurt."

Aniyah snatched him by the tie. "Don't worry about their pain. Your only concern should be my pleasure." She reached up and kissed him, leaving her lipstick on his lips. "I'll take a limo back to the apartment and pack. Call me one. Put it on my bill. No, you pay for it, Executor." She laughed.

He got on the phone and called her a limo. Somehow or some way, he had to get her out of his life.

Chapter 13

Tessa made her way, in a private cab, to the Houston Estate. She looked out of the window as she crossed the bridge into Lake Murray. The rising sun beamed on the smooth waves of the lake.

Reaching the Houston Estate, the cab stopped at the security station. A security guard, or as Tessa remembered Rupert called his security "security help," came up to the cab.

"Yes, may I help you?" the security guard asked, dressed in black with gold patches on his shirt.

Tessa rolled down the window. She pulled out an old work badge and held it up to the man. "I worked for the Houstons many years ago. I've come to see an old friend, if she's still here working. Elsa is her name."

The security guard smiled, speaking in his deep-toned voice, "Elsa is an old shoe around here."

The guard called her on the radio dispatcher. "Elsa, you have a guest. Her name is Tessa Sanchez."

Elsa's voice came through loud and clear. "Oh my God, let Tessa in the gates. Tell her I'm in her old room."

The man turned back to Tessa. "Do you remember how to get there?"

"Yes, I could never forget."

The guard pushed a button inside his small security booth office. The gates opened.

The driver was amazed as he proceeded into the estate. "Wow! I've always wanted to see what this place look likes. It reminds me of the Biltmore Estate."

As far as the driver could see there was nothing but manicured green lawn. Nowhere in sight was any visibility of unwanted weeds.

"Follow the road to the left," Tessa said, as the right would lead them to the house.

The driver drove up to a row of small, attached houses. To him it was like the apartment complex he lived in.

"I won't be long. Please wait for me," she begged.

"I'm enjoying every bit of this." The driver cut the engine off. He got out, taking his own private tour around on the grounds of the servants' quarters, hoping he could strike a job. "The Houstons have their own tenants, I see."

"Not at all, this is where the live-in workers stay."

"This is the kind of job I need. Hook a brotha up."

Tessa looked at him to see unshaved gray whiskers under his chin. Rupert would have hired him on the spot. The driver wouldn't have been any threat to stealing his wife.

She knocked on the door. Elsa opened the door dressed in a burgundy uniform.

She recognized her plum cheeks.

Elsa reached out her hands to her. "Give me a hug. Lord, I prayed for you every day."

Tessa embraced her. Elsa stepped back from her, extending her arms to rest her hands on Tessa's shoulders.

"Let me take a good look at you. You're still pretty as the day I first met you. Got a little meat on your bones." Elsa chuckled.

"I hope it's in the right places."

"Come on in your old room. I'm here getting things ready for a new girl."

Tessa walked into the room. No brown spread covered the bed. A burgundy spread covered it. Pictures of floral arrangements accented the wall. The room gave her a sense of home, instead of a servant's quarters.

"Everything has changed."

"Oh yeah, Tessa, that's because of Mrs. Houston. She came to me one day and said she's going to ask her husband to let her have fun decorating our rooms. You know, to keep her happy, he gave her the okay."

Tessa thought of how he could treat his wife with such dignity but degrade any other woman, or maybe it was just the ones who he felt were beneath him.

"Child, she asked me to help her. I felt like we were sisters, not by race, but by blood."

"I'm happy for you and the others."

"Sit down on the bed and rest yourself."

"I don't want to mess it up. It's so neat."

Elsa sat down on the bed. "It's not neat anymore." Tessa sat next to her.

Elsa put a hand under her chin. "You got to tell me what made you leave here. There's been rumors, like one of them was you were buried somewhere on this property. And you know I didn't believe that one."

"No, I'm here and alive."

"Then what was it?" Elsa wondered.

Tessa became tearful as she looked at the windowsill. The window seat looked inviting, a few magazines sat in the corner next to a throw pillow. She eased her hand across the bed covers.

"I kept my mouth shut, Elsa. I had no contact with Mr. Houston. I did my work very good. But that didn't help me. Mr. Houston still came to my bed."

"That's strange. He usually doesn't take girls to his bed unless they start making talk with him."

"Mr. Houston was jealous because I talked to Mr. Chavis. He got mad and told Mr. Chavis to stay away from me. That's when he started to come after me." Tessa cried.

Elsa took a tissue out of the pocket of her uniform. She patted Tessa's eyes to absorb the tears.

"So to keep him from touching you, you left," Elsa concluded.

Tessa placed her hand on her stomach and patted it. "Like you, I became pregnant with Mr. Houston's baby."

"You had a child by him?"

"Yes."

Tessa couldn't tell her all the truth. After all, Rupert had sent her money every month for a baby that did not exist.

"I'll bet that man went to his grave and didn't know he had a baby."

"He knew, Elsa. Remember I was sick that day? Mrs. Houston sent a doctor to check on me. The doctor told her I was with baby. She told Mr. Houston. He came to my room and had sex with me one last time. He made me throw my things in my bag and put me on a plane back to Mexico. I wish I could have kept my pregnancy a secret like you did."

"Yeah, I did what I had to do to keep my job. It was heartbreaking. I even let Mr. Houston take me after one of my abortions. Blood was everywhere. He thought I was on my period. Nasty bastard!" Elsa yelled.

"Why'd you stay here with so much hurt?"

Elsa nodded. "A plain fool, I guess…a fool for a good dollar."

Tessa smiled. "Maybe you really stayed here to warn and protect other girls. You did that for me."

"It didn't help."

Tessa patted Elsa on the hand. "Your warning prepared me for the worst, and I'm also sure you've saved some other girls around here from him."

"Can you believe he's gone?"

"It feels weird. That's why I had to come and see for myself."

Elsa tapped her knees. "I'm somewhat nervous. Don't know what's going to happen now. All our jobs may be gone."

"I'm certain his daughters will keep you on. You've been good to them."

"I don't know. You remember their little girl, Milandra? She's all grown up."

Tessa nodded. "I saw her at the funeral."

"She sure enough got ways like her daddy—not gracious like her mother. Noelle has her mother's ways. And that Kenley, the baby girl, she's in a world of her own."

They smiled.

"Tessa, did you know that Mrs. Houston was pregnant the same time as you were?"

"We both had girls."

"You have a girl?"

"Yes," Tessa said with a nervous voice.

"She didn't come with you?"

Before Tessa could answer, a knock turned their attention to the door.

"Come in," Elsa called.

A young girl, barely out of high school, entered. "Hello, I'm here for job," she said, speaking her best English.

"Hola," Tessa said.

Elsa flagged the girl to come over to a closet. The girl carried her small suitcase.

"Bags in here." Elsa pointed into the closet. "Fresh uniform on the hanger. The bathroom is right over there," Elsa said as she pointed in the direction of the bathroom. The girl hurried to change.

"I'll leave now," Tessa said. "My ride is waiting."

Elsa wondered about Tessa. "Got yourself a husband?"

"No, never married."

"Mr. Chavis never married either." Elsa saw how her eyes lit up. "You really liked him, didn't you?"

"Yes, but that's the past."

"Have you seen him since you been in town?"

"Not at all."

"I say you're prettier now than before. You're free now. You'll never know what could have been if you don't go and see him while you're here. The man may still have you in his heart. Run along and find your king."

"I don't know about that."

"I thought you listened to my words," Elsa replied.

"Goodbye, Elsa." Tessa giggled as she stood up to leave.

"I think you'll see more of me than you bet on. Call me. My number is still the same."

"I still have that number, but I was too embarrassed to call you."

"You have nothing to be ashamed of. Pick up the phone."

Tessa left knowing that Elsa was right. The only way to bring peace to her heart was to visit Baron.

Chapter 14

The Houstons stepped out into the lobby. Kenley was almost in tears. "I can't wait to get home."

"Maybe it's still *your* home, but it's not ours unless one of us strangles her," Milandra said.

"I'm not living with any stranger," Kenley wept. She wiped her eyes with the back of her hands.

"Forget that, first things first. We must get to Father's office and pack all his personal belongings," Milandra said.

"We can leave that to Mr. Chavis," Noelle said, confident that her so-called man would handle things.

Arriving at the elevator, Milandra tapped repeatedly on the down button until the elevator doors opened. "After what just happened, we'll look into Father's personal things."

They stepped into the elevator, taking it to the top floor, or as their father called it, the Penthouse.

As they got off the elevator, they were greeted, one after another, by the employees of Houston Commercial Construction Company, who offered them their condolences.

Milandra nodded her head while her sisters thanked them for their kindness. They reached their father's office, noticing his bronze nameplate had been removed.

Milandra turned around. "Who took my father's nameplate off his door?"

The employees became silent, not uttering a word. They kept their eyes glued to their computer screens; others acted as if they were on business calls.

"Don't say a word and every one of you will be fired," Milandra sternly said.

A woman in her mid-forties got up from her desk and spoke up: "I believe it was taken down by one of the cleaning crew. No one here would dare stoop that low."

"Then what's up with the silence?" Milandra asked.

The woman turned around and looked out amongst her co-workers. She mumbled, "Scared, I guess."

"Have it put back ASAP," Milandra ordered.

"I will, Miss Houston," the woman said as she tried to walk away fast in the straight ankle-length skirt she wore.

Milandra joined her sisters. They went inside their father's office. "One of you close the blinds," Milandra said as she shut the door.

Noelle closed the blinds on a glass window that gave a good view of the employees at their desks.

Kenley sat in the leather chair where her father handled his business. She giggled as she looked on the desk to see a photo of her as a kid posing at a piano recital.

"Get up," Milandra said as she nudged Kenley.

"You're so bossy," Kenley argued.

"Watch your mouth," Milandra said as she took a set of keys out of her pocketbook. She searched each key until it opened the desk drawers.

"Run and ask for some boxes, Kenley," Milandra instructed her.

"Why me?"

"Just go," Milandra insisted.

With her arms folded and her lips poked out, Kenley stormed out the office.

Noelle stood over Milandra to see if she found any other information about their father that they were not aware of.

Milandra felt her breathing over her. "Don't stand over me. Go check one of the files to see what you can find."

Noelle went over to a cherry file cabinet. She tried to pull a drawer open but it was locked. "I can't open it. I need a key."

"Try one of these keys."

The keys dangled as Milandra handed them to her sister.

"Father had too many keys."

Noelle fumbled through several keys before she finally opened the file cabinet.

"I bet Father's employees are gossiping."

"Let me hear them. I'll fire them."

Noelle giggled. "You sound like Father."

Kenley came back in the office. Her sisters noticed she had one small box.

"All these personal items that Father has, and you bring back a tiny box," Milandra said.

"The woman who spoke to you, Milandra, is getting the custodians to bring us big boxes," Kenley said. "I think she's kissing up to us."

"The woman could happen to be nice," Noelle defended her.

"She wants to be nosey," Milandra said. "No one comes in here. Kenley, you guard the door."

"You're treating me like help. I'm a Houston; have you forgotten?" Kenley asked, making her way to the door.

The woman came to the door. Kenley stepped out of the office.

"Please leave the boxes here. We'll come out and get what we need."

The woman helped one of the custodians place the boxes outside the door. She tried every angle to peek into the office, but Kenley kept a close watch on the door opening.

Once the woman left, Kenley carried in the few mid-sized boxes.

"Let's dump everything we think is personally important in the boxes. We can sort things later," Milandra supervised.

Kenley stacked the photos from the desk and around the room in one of the boxes. Noelle went through the file cabinet and gathered up personal financial files. Kenley cleared out her father's desk.

They left one portrait of their father on the wall.

Once they had searched the entire office, the boxes were ready to be carried out by the custodians.

"What are we going to do with the boxes now?" Noelle wanted to know.

"Take them to the Houston Villa," Milandra said.

"I know we're not going there right now. I'm hungry," Kenley said.

"No food. We have to get this done," Milandra shouted.

"Can you and Noelle do it without me?" Kenley asked.

Milandra gave her a "don't mess with me look." She picked up the phone on the desk and called in the movers to move the boxes.

The movers followed their limo to the Houston Villa.

The sisters pulled up to see a home approximately four thousand square feet. They got out of the limo and stood looking at the brick house surrounded by trees. Pine straw scattered on the grass.

"This is unacceptable. Father knew I have allergies." Milandra sniffled.

"He always told you not to run away from any problems. Deal with it," Noelle said. "I guess this is one of the things he meant."

"Be quiet," Milandra said.

They walked up to the house. Milandra pulled the screen door open. She unlocked the steel white door. Inside, the home was heated with the outside warmth.

They fanned as they walked throughout the house. The kitchen was half the size of the one in the Houston Estate.

Rupert had furnished the house with cherrywood furniture. There were photos of his daughters in the family room. They went upstairs to the bedrooms. There was no east or west wing; only a small hallway to the three bedrooms. Each bedroom had a small-scaled bathroom. The queen-sized beds were covered with quilted spreads, not like the lavish comforter sets at the Houston Estate.

Noelle came to tears. "This is nothing compared to our real home."

"I changed my mind. I'm staying with the crazy half-sister," Kenley said.

Milandra rolled her eyes at Kenley. "Father is testing us. He wants to see if we can be strong."

"This isn't a test, Milandra. Father is gone. It's for real," Noelle argued.

Back downstairs, Kenley and Noelle got lost checking out the backyard. They left Milandra to inspect the rest of the interior and oversee the movers.

One of the movers came in carrying two boxes stacked on top of each other. His muscular arms were exposed from his sleeveless shirt. "Where would you like these boxes placed?" he asked in a deep voice.

It was something about the way he looked at Milandra that caused her to blush. It was unusual for her to smile. "You can take them to the family room." She pointed in the direction of the room.

The mover placed the boxes down on the floor in a corner. "It's warm in here." He wiped sweat from his forehead as he looked at Milandra, thinking of how efficient she was. It turned him on.

Milandra fanned. "It is hot in here."

She wanted to turn on the air conditioner but had no idea where to begin looking for the thermostat controls. The mover knew by her manicured nails, flawless skin, and her upright posture that she was raised letting others do for her. He found her to be sexy in her straight black skirt and tailored white blouse.

He volunteered, "I'll get some cool air stirring in here."

Relieved, Milandra said, "Thank you."

The mover went down the hall to find the thermostat on the wall. Milandra followed him for future reference. Her first task for the place would be to hire help.

The mover adjusted the temperature. She studied him, noticing how clean-shaven he was. His arms shined as if they had been polished with Vaseline. The cologne he wore overpowered the staleness of a closed house.

"By any chance, would you be interested in changing jobs?"

The mover smiled. "I'll have to shut down my business. I'm the owner of Rice Moving Company."

Milandra felt embarrassed. "Oh, I'm sorry, Mr. ..."

"Call me Nolan." He grinned. "Everyone calls you and your sisters the Houstons, but what's your first name?"

"I'm Milandra." She reached out her hand.

Nolan extended his hand to shake hers. "Nice meeting you, Milandra. Pretty name."

"My baby sister is Kenley and my middle sister is Noelle. I truly apologize for being out of place. I assumed the wrong thing."

"I'm not a big time moving company, but I hold my own. Listen, you and your sisters have suffered a great loss. It takes time to get things in order."

Nolan handed her a business card. "Call me. I'll help you out in whatever way I can."

"That's kind of you, but I don't want to take you from your work."

"I wouldn't miss the moment to catch your pretty smile," he flirted.

Kenley and Noelle came back into the family room. They witnessed their sister blushing.

"These are my sisters. Kenley and Noelle, this is Nolan."

"Hi." Kenley stared. "Man, you're cute."

"Kenley," Milandra said. "You have to excuse my baby sister."

"She thinks you're cute, too. But she'll never admit it." Kenley giggled.

Noelle placed her hand over Kenley's mouth. "Enough."

"I'll go and get the rest of the boxes." He smiled.

"We have some things we're going to need moved from our other house to here. My sister would love to have you move it for us," Kenley instigated. "Wouldn't you, Milandra?"

Milandra rolled her eyes at Kenley. "Yes, I completely forgot. You have the job if you'd like, Nolan. I'll give you a call when we're ready."

"Thanks," Nolan said and left the room.

Kenley and Noelle teased their sister.

"I can't believe you, Milandra, smiling up in a man's face. I've never seen your eyes pop open so wide," Kenley said.

"They were not," Milandra said. "You are silly."

"He's hot. And it's about time you have a man. You have to pick your own; Father isn't here to do the picking for you," Noelle said, wanting to spill her guts about her feelings for Baron.

"I don't understand how come you two never had boyfriends," Kenley said.

"Father said he would find the right men for us," Noelle said.

"I plan to have one as soon as I find one," Kenley said.

"Oh no you won't, young lady," Milandra said. "You'll wait until you're as old as us."

"Never!" Kenley yelled.

Nolan made his way back in the room with more boxes. The sisters waited until he finished. They locked up the house. Their next stop was the Houston Estate.

"We will have lunch by the lake and then pack up our things," Milandra said.

The girls sat out on the patio overlooking the lake. Dining on tuna sandwiches, potato chips, and a melody of fruits, they watched the neighbors out and about on their sailboats. The sailors reminded them of their father, as he too used to love to take his boat out on the lake.

"I can't sit here and pretend like everything is fabulous when it's not." Milandra sounded annoyed as she finished crunching on a chip. She took a sip out of a glass of cold iced tea. "This can't be happening to us. This kind of thing only happens in the theater. Leave this house to that thing of a whore. Father, give us some kind of sign that she's a liar."

"Milandra, calm down. The help might hear you," Noelle warned.

Milandra took another sip of the cold iced tea to cool her anger. She broke down in a cascade of tears. For the first time, her sisters witnessed her emotional outpouring.

"We'll get through this, Milandra. We have each other," Noelle consoled her sister.

"If it makes you happy, I'll live at the Houston Villa. But no bossing me around or I'm out," Kenley said.

"You don't have to live with us if you don't want to. At least one of us gets to stay here," Noelle said.

Milandra blew her nose. "Oh, yes, she has to come right along with us. We've lost Mother and Father. I'm not about to lose my baby sister, too."

"How sweet of you, Milandra. I didn't know I meant that much to you," Kenley said as she got up out of her seat and ran over to give her sister a hug. "I'll tell you what I'll do," she said and took her seat to continue eating. "I'll visit the estate often to make sure Miss Half doesn't turn it into a whorehouse."

"Miss Half?" Noelle giggled. "Kenley, that's not nice."

"I happen to think the name complements her," Milandra said. "Hurry up, let's finish. We have work to do."

The girls left their mess for the servants to clean. They went to their rooms and packed loads and loads of clothes with care. Their next stop was their parents' master suite.

Noelle led the way. "What will we do with Father's and Mother's belongings?"

"We'll give it to one of Mother's favorite charities," Milandra said.

"How about we give it to the help?" Kenley said.

"No!" Milandra yelled, as she went into their mother's walk-in closet. She began removing clothes from the rack.

"I think that's great," Noelle said. "They've been good to our parents. They've worked hard, especially Elsa. Come on, Milandra, it's the right thing to do."

Milandra stirred in the closet. She pulled out three white linen summer dress suits. "Okay, but I want some to go to her favorite charities."

"That's fair," Noelle said. "I'll call Elsa."

Noelle went over to the intercom. She called Elsa, who was busy in the kitchen.

Elsa came into the room a few minutes later. "Yes, Miss Houston," she said, not knowing which sister would answer, but noticed the clothes on the bed.

"Elsa, I rang you because we want to share some of our parents' clothes," Noelle said.

"Oh my, I sure do appreciate it. Your mother wore the prettiest things."

"Yes, she did," Noelle said. "Now everything that's left on this bed will be for you and the other help to browse through. Take all you want."

Elsa admired the suits, blouses, and dresses on the bed. "Thank you, Miss Houston. Y'all are so kind. I hope I get to keep working for you."

Milandra came out of the closet when she heard her say those words. Elsa looked at her.

Milandra didn't crack a smile. "You don't have to worry about your job. Father has left in his will that as long as you are alive your job is secure."

Elsa couldn't believe Rupert had done that for her. She wondered if this was his way of asking her for forgiveness of the things he had done to her. "Thank you, I feel so blessed. Thank you again."

Milandra knew she was appreciative by the rapid clap of her hands. Kenley sat on the bed admiring her mother's clothes. Milandra saw her sister was being of no help.

"Kenley, go into Father's study and clean off the top of his desk. I'll handle what's inside the drawers," Milandra said.

Kenley hopped off the bed, leaving her sisters to tackle the clothes.

"Elsa, let the help know that at this time we won't be firing any-one. But there are going to be some major changes around here. My father has another daughter," Noelle said, spilling her father's secret.

"Noelle!" Milandra was annoyed. "Why are you telling Elsa about that girl?"

"Milandra, she's going to be moving in here. She has to know."

Elsa listened as the sisters argued. She wondered why Tessa didn't tell her this, nor did she know of her daughter coming to stay at the Houston Estate. She remembered asking Tessa about her daughter but the doorbell had rung, interrupting their conversation.

Noelle paid her sister no attention. Telling the truth would alleviate twisted lies and stop the servants from gossiping about her family.

"My father, in his final wishes, has allowed our half-sister, Aniyah Sanchez, to live in the house. You'll be basically working for her, but under the trust of Mr. Chavis. We're moving."

Elsa stood with her mouth opened. "Tessa's daughter?" She re-called Tessa telling her about her pregnancy.

"You knew my father had a daughter?" Milandra screamed at her.

"No, Miss Houston. I just found out about her. Tessa came to visit me. She told me she had a daughter. She says her daughter was Mr. Houston's child."

"Where is this Tessa now? I want to speak to her. I bet she plans to live in this house, too—evil and vicious woman," Milandra said angrily.

"Miss Houston, Tessa said nothing about moving in here or her daughter moving in here. Really, she talked as if she was going back to Mexico."

"Are you telling me the truth?" Milandra screamed.

"All this yelling is not necessary, Milandra," Noelle said. "Elsa has done nothing wrong."

"Miss Houston, I don't have any way of contacting Tessa. I did ask her to keep in touch. Mr. Chavis may hear from her," Elsa blurted, not realizing what she said.

"Why would she call Mr. Chavis?" Noelle asked curiously.

Elsa didn't know what to say. "I guess to say hello. He was one of the people she remembered when she worked here."

Noelle was relieved, hoping there were no secrets between her and Baron. She had to get to see him. It had been a while since they had snuck around and been together. In her mind, he kissed her goodbye and left her hungry to taste more of his lips.

"Mr. Chavis will inform me if he hears from her," Milandra said.

"May I be excused?" Elsa asked. "I will miss you girls around here." In reality, she would only miss the two younger sisters. Elsa couldn't wait for Aniyah to move into the estate. The sweet personality of Tessa had to have rubbed off on her daughter.

"Leave," Milandra ordered.

In the next room, Kenley cleaned off her father's desk, basically throwing everything in one box, except his laptop. She turned it on to have some goof-off time.

Kenley started to click on a game of solitaire, but instead her eyes were drawn to the file labeled *Documents*. Inquisitively, she moved the mouse to click on the files. There she scanned different files. All of them pertained to his work, except for the last file. Kenley clicked the file. The image slowly came up. Her eyes opened wider and wider right along with the image. "Talk about Sex." She could see two people flesh to flesh.

The image became clearer to her. It was her sister, Noelle, with her head back and Baron leaned forward, kissing her. Noelle's breasts were partially exposed.

"No way," Kenley mumbled. "Noelle making out with Mr. Chavis. And she acts like she so innocent."

Kenley wondered what the image was doing on her father's computer. How did he get it? Why didn't he say anything about it? Why did Noelle and Baron Chavis pretend like they had no connection? But the big question to Kenley was when did her father learn about them? His cause of death was a heart attack. He had a look on his face as if he had gotten disturbing news. Was this what drove her father to his death?

She closed the file and wanted to run to Noelle and show her that she knew the truth about her. *Milandra would be mad.*

Kenley decided to keep it a secret, for she would watch Noelle and Baron. See if they had the guts to come clean about their relationship. One thing she knew, Milandra would fight her for the laptop. But this was one fight her older sister would not win. This was hers to keep.

Kenley logged off the computer. She closed it down, unplugged it, and carried the laptop out of the office and back into the master suite where her sisters continued to pack their parents' belongings.

Milandra noticed her carrying the laptop. "Hand over Father's computer."

"I'm keeping it for myself. Father always let me have fun on it," Kenley said as she held it tight.

"No, you're not. There may be important files on there," Milandra said.

"I'm computer smart. There's nothing on it. Father only used this one to surf the Internet, not for work. He would never let me play games on a computer he handled his business on."

"Kenley, leave the computer in his office," Milandra ordered.

"Can things ever go my way? Everything has to be what you say?" Kenley yelled.

"Don't bargain with me. Just listen," Milandra said, going through her mother's jewelry.

"Look at you picking out jewelry you want to keep from Mother. Neither Noelle nor I get to have any say so on what you get to keep or take from Mother or Father."

Milandra knew this was true, as always, because she was the oldest, and as the oldest she carried the role of being a mother figure to them.

Noelle, the peacemaker, jumped into the conversation. "Milandra, let her keep it. She's grieving Mother and Father, too. Come, Kenley, share some of Mother's jewelry," Noelle offered.

Kenley recalled her mother wearing diamond studs. "Just save me a pair of her diamond earrings," she said as she left the room. Noelle was saved from her revealing what she found on the computer. If Noelle had taken sides with Milandra regarding the laptop, her secret would have been known.

Kenley placed the laptop near her belongings. She wished she knew her father's password for his email. She would check for that, too, in search of more hidden secrets.

After a day of exhaustion, they were packed and ready to move out. Milandra called Nolan, the mover, to come move their things.

"I didn't know I would be hearing from you this fast," he said as he held his cell phone to his ear.

"Yes, my sisters and I decided to get things over with. The sooner we get settled in our new lives, the sooner we can begin to heal and move on."

Nolan made it over in less than an hour.

"You didn't bring help." Milandra noticed he was alone.

"I can handle it on my own."

"If you need assistance, I can get some of the help."

"I'm used to it," he replied.

Nolan carried the boxes out and loaded them into the truck. Milandra was impressed by how he took charge and had pride in what he did. He carried the boxes with caution to avoid any damages to their belongings.

Nolan placed the last box in the truck. He waited in the truck to follow them to the Houston Villa.

The sisters stood outside of the house. They held hands as they tearfully said goodbye to the Estate.

Many of the servants, including Elsa, watched as they stood tall in unison. Milandra was still suited down, as her mother would have been dressed. Her French roll was still neatly intact.

Noelle was casually dressed in a pair of slacks and a tank top. Curls fell to her shoulder. Kenley sported a pair of jeans and a tee shirt. Her hair was pulled back high into a ponytail.

A limo driver awaited the Houstons as Nolan watched from his truck.

Elsa went over and gave them each a hug. Other servants followed, crying for them. No matter what they thought of Mr. Houston, they knew the feeling of losing a loved one. They left the Houstons to say their final goodbyes.

"Maybe this is for the best," Noelle said. "The house died the day Father and Mother did." She cried.

"I don't believe that. In my heart, I feel this is a temporary move. God is giving us a chance to heal. There are too many wonderful family memories in this house for any pain to flow through it right now. God is letting us relieve our pain somewhere else. When we come back, we'll restore the house with nothing but joy," Milandra said.

"I'll be back and forth. Since Miss Half is half, then she'll be sharing half of the house with me. Don't worry, I'll be watching her. She won't turn my parents' house into a whorehouse," Kenley said.

"Kenley, be careful. People can be real vicious at times," Noelle warned her.

"Please. Let Miss Half bring it on," Kenley said.

The driver opened the door and they got into the limo.

Reaching their new home, the Houstons noticed the pine straw was raked and used as skirts for the trees.

"You had a gardener to clean the yard?" Noelle asked.

"No. I don't know who tidied this," Milandra said, surprised.

They got out of the limo. Nolan stepped down from the truck. He called. "I hope I did a good job on your yard," he queried.

Noelle and Kenley left Milandra to talk to him. They could see Nolan was focused on their sister.

"Please, whatever the cost is, add it to the bill," Milandra said.

"That won't be necessary."

Kenley ran outside with a cold soda in her hand. "Milandra! Thanks for having supper on the stove. Fried chicken, potato salad, and string beans. The refrigerator is filled with cold drinks. I was wondering what we were going to do about food," Kenley said.

"You didn't do that, too? Did you?" Milandra asked.

"My pleasure." He smiled.

Milandra pulled out her checkbook. "Please, let me pay you."

Nolan pointed to his truck. "I'm going to empty your boxes out of my truck to work up an appetite. All I ask is to let me have a bite to eat when I finish."

"Of course you may share a meal with us, but that's not payment. You're eating the food *you* purchased."

"Yeah, but I'm eating for free at your home. And, I get to look at beauty for free while I eat." He smiled.

"All right, I see you can be as stubborn as me," Milandra admitted.

Nolan went on to unload the truck. Kenley giggled. "Milandra has a boyfriend," she teased.

"Hush, he might hear you," Milandra said as she pulled her sister to walk toward the house.

The aroma of fried chicken filled the house. Noelle sat at a wooden oak table as she bit into a chicken leg.

"This is delicious," she said. "Nice and crispy."

"You know we can sit down at the table and have supper together," Milandra said.

"This is a snack," Noelle said.

"I'll have a snack with you," Kenley said as she took a chicken wing out of a KFC box.

"Come, Milandra, have a chicken wing," Noelle said.

Kenley sat down at the table next to her sister. "She's not hungry for chicken; she's hungry for the mover," Kenley instigated.

Milandra tried not to blush. "Nonsense!" She left the room and went on the patio deck. She called Baron.

"Hello," he answered.

"Hello, Mr. Chavis, this is Milandra. Any new update on how we can fight my father's will?"

"Sorry, Milandra, but there are no loopholes, yet. Realize that even if I find one, we could be in court for a very long time."

"Whatever it is, I want the estate back. Father should have left this house to her; it's enough space for one person."

Milandra jumped when Nolan came up behind her and tapped her on the shoulder.

She turned around to come face to face with him. She immediately said to Baron, "I have to go." She clicked the phone off.

"Talking to your man?" Nolan asked.

"No, my lawyer."

"Didn't mean to interrupt you. I'm finished bringing in the boxes."

"Hungry?" Milandra asked.

Nolan patted his six-pack. "Oh yeah!"

Milandra insisted that he go in first, but Nolan, being a gentleman, said, "Ladies first."

He watched her from behind. He feasted his eyes on her curves. He would have to do overtime to get with her.

Milandra felt his eyes on her. Never had she felt so uneasy in front of a man. She had been around many of her father's workers, but none brought her this much tension.

Back in the kitchen, her sisters' plates were left with chicken bones on them.

"Thanks for the food. The chicken is good," Kenley said.

Noelle got up and disposed of her plate.

Kenley left hers on the table. "We should have brought some help with us."

Milandra agreed. "I'll make a call and start interviewing help tomorrow."

Nolan listened to them. He went on and made himself a plate of food.

"Are you going to eat?" Nolan focused his attention on Milandra.

"Yes. Kenley, prepare me a plate of supper."

"Me? I'm not one of the help."

Nolan placed his plate on the table. Next to his seat he pulled a chair out. "Have a seat, Miss Houston," he said as he flagged Milandra.

Kenley playfully went to sit down.

"I forgot there're three Miss Houstons in this kitchen. I meant you, Milandra."

"Excuse me." Kenley giggled.

Noelle pulled her by the arm. "Come on, baby sister, I think you need to go with me. Let's start unpacking."

Milandra sat in the seat. Nolan's mannerism was the class act she loved. As fast as she took a seat, she went to get back up. "I haven't cleansed my hands."

"Don't move," he said.

Nolan ran over to the sink and wet a paper towel. He brought it back to her. Milandra wiped her hands while he made a plate of food for her.

"What part of the chicken would you like, Miss Houston?"

"I'll take a leg. That'll be fine."

Nolan placed the plate in front of her. He folded a napkin in front of her with a fork on top of it. "Enjoy your meal," he whispered in her ear.

Nolan sat down and took charge, blessing the food.

Milandra sat erect eating her food. Taking small bites of the chicken, she constantly wiped any food particles from around her mouth. She had never felt so nervous eating in front of a man. Her father would have forbidden it. She was defying him at this very moment, but her inner being led her to stay put in the seat.

Nolan noticed the trembling in her hands, that she wasn't relaxed. He broke the ice by making small talk. "My belly has been waiting for a meal all day."

"You haven't eaten today?" Milandra asked but kept her eyes on her plate.

"I drink water all day in this heat. It keeps me hydrated."

"Speaking of drinks, I have to hire help right away. A Southern table must always have a pitcher of cold homemade iced tea."

"No problem, I'll be your temporary help." Nolan got up and went to the refrigerator. "You can have iced tea, but it's not homemade." He held up a gallon of store bought lemon tea.

"I never had iced tea from a container. I'll try it." She smiled.

Nolan filled two glasses for them. He placed one in front of her.

She took a sip of it. "It's nice and lemony." She smiled. "I'll buy several containers for the house."

Nolan grinned. "You should only buy a couple at a time. You want it nice and freshly brewed."

"Will do."

Nolan saw that Milandra became somewhat more relaxed around him. But more work had to be done to get her to want him as much as he wanted her.

"Is there anything else you need done around here?"

"Well, starting tomorrow, I'll have help around here. I won't bother you, unless I need something moved."

"Oh, that's no good." Nolan wondered what he could do to keep coming to see her.

"I offered you a job that you don't need."

Nolan laughed. "Yes, you did."

"I promise, if I need your help, I'll call you."

"That's it; you wouldn't call a friend just to say hello?"

Milandra looked up at him. "We're friends now?"

"I thought you knew that," Nolan teased. "I'm not the type of guy you would have for a friend?"

"Nolan, I have no male friends."

"You have one now. Me."

He got up out of his seat and cleaned his spot. "Finished?" he asked, looking over at her empty plate.

Milandra handed her plate to him. She got out of her seat. "I guess I'll go help my sisters unpack. I'll walk you out."

Nolan made his way to the front door. "Milandra, you made my day."

"With all that my sisters and I have been through, you have alleviated some of our problems. So I graciously thank you." Milandra bowed her head.

"Speaking of problems, your Jacuzzi in the backyard is malfunctioning. Also, out near the ramped walkway to the lake, there's a slope in the ground. Come, I'll show you."

"How do you know all of this?"

"Let's just say I made sure everything was safe for you ladies to move in."

Nolan led the way out back. The walk to the lake gave them a peaceful view of the sun starting to disappear among the clouds. He came to the slope in the ground. "Right here," he said as he tapped his shoe on the spot. "It needs some filling in with dirt." Nolan looked down at her ankle to see a diamond anklet. "I wouldn't want you to twist your ankle."

"I'll have it fixed. Kenley would be the main one to trip in the hole."

"We wouldn't want that," he said. "I'll take the job, if you don't mind. It won't take long to get it filled, and I'll fix the minor problem with your Jacuzzi."

"You're a mover," Milandra reminded him, but happy that he volunteered.

"That's my day job. This will be my evening project."

"My sisters say I'm stubborn. But I see I have a twin," she joked.

Nolan took his ultimate chance and extended his hand out to her. "Friends."

Milandra's hand got lost in his. Nolan caressed her hand as he shook it. He stared into her brown eyes. Milandra felt guilty and let go of his hand. Her eyes began to water.

Nolan could see the tears forming. "I feel so bad. I'm making you cry."

"It's not you. Don't flatter yourself. I'm overwhelmed—just a worn-out day," she said, but the tears started flowing.

Milandra hurried inside the house. It was like she had come

down with the flu and her body ached for him, or better yet, the comfort of any man.

Nolan ran after her. He wanted to console her and break the hard shell that Milandra hid behind.

Inside the house, Milandra ran right into Kenley watching television on a leather sofa. Nolan came in behind her. Kenley could feel there was more heat between them than outdoors.

"Humph! It looks like the cat is chasing the mouse. But the mouse doesn't want to be caught," Kenley observed.

"Hush such talk. What are you doing in here?" Milandra asked.

Kenley smirked. "What were you doing out at the lake?"

Nolan could tell Milandra was embarrassed by how outspoken her sister was. He interjected, "Good night," and found his way out the house.

"Talk about being humiliated—what's wrong with you?"

"Did he try to kiss you? That's why you came running into the house?"

"I wasn't running." Milandra wiped her face to show no signs of her tears.

"He kissed you, and you ran from him. Is he a good kisser?" Kenley asked as she puckered her lips.

"Aren't you supposed to be unpacking boxes?"

"You did kiss him. Please tell me, is he a mushy or juicy kisser?" Kenley asked as she got up from the sofa and pulled on her sister's arm.

"Let go of me. I didn't kiss any stranger." Milandra pushed away from her sister.

"Gosh, Milandra! You're an adult. You met him, you like him, and then you smack him on the lips," Kenley said as she puckered up her lips.

"Father would slap you if he heard you talking and acting in such a way."

"I wish I was older. I would have such passion with him—like what I see in romance movies."

"Kenley Houston, stop such talk."

"I bet if Miss Half sees him, she'll scoop him up as if he was ice cream."

"Good night, Kenley," Milandra said and left the room.

Milandra went into her new bedroom and fell across the bed. After meeting Nolan, she yearned for him to come back and visit.

Chapter 15

Aniyah called Baron constantly until he agreed to escort her to the Houston Estate. She dropped her bag in the back-seat of his car, then made her way to the front passenger seat. Without warning, she reached over and landed a kiss on his lips.

Baron pushed her away. "Please, we're in the public eye."

"That's okay, sugar," Aniyah said as she pulled down on the spandex dress she wore.

Baron kept looking straight ahead. He didn't want to get distracted from the spillover coming out of the top of her dress.

"After today, we won't be seeing each other. I'll help you get settled at the Houston Estate and that's where it ends."

Aniyah reached over and touched his crotch. He took one hand off the wheel and pushed her hand away.

Aniyah tickled. "I know you're just playing games."

"After today, we'll keep our distance. I feel guilty after seeing your mother," Baron said sternly.

"Get over it. You and I can have a love nest at my new house. I can't wait to get there."

Aniyah took out a nail file and began to file her nails. She couldn't believe her eyes when they drove up to the Houston Estate. The security buzzed Baron in through the gates.

"Dang, this is like being in jail, behind bars."

"You've been to jail?" Baron asked.

"One damn time. I stayed overnight for drunk driving. Rum had me mad and speeding."

"What happened to your car?"

"It wasn't mine. It belonged to the dude I was messing with. My license is still on lockdown."

Baron looked over at her. He couldn't comprehend how he had allowed her to manipulate him.

They drove to the right of the estate. "The workers' residences are that way," he said as he pointed to the left.

"Look at the flowers. I could pick roses to put in my hair."

"Yes, you can do that."

He pulled around until the house began to show.

"This is not a house. It's an apartment complex," she said. "I think I'll rent rooms."

"Oh no, you can't do that," he said. "I see you have a lot to learn."

"I got you, baby, to teach me," she said as she touched him on the neck.

He pushed her hand away. "Keep your hands off me. Please, behave when you get in front of the staff."

Baron drove up to the front and got out. Aniyah jumped out of the car. She pulled her dress down. She held a big red pocketbook on her arm. He opened up the front door and Aniyah strutted into the house. She began to dance around. "This is beautiful. Look how clean it is. I won't be able to find my way around here."

"You will in due time," he said.

Elsa appeared at the sound of their voices. "Hello, Mr. Chavis." She smiled.

"Hello, Elsa. This is Aniyah Sanchez, Mr. Houston's daughter. She'll be living here from now on."

Baron knew that word had already gotten back to the help about Rupert having a daughter with one his servants.

"Give me a hug," Elsa said. She embraced Aniyah.

"Be careful, don't wrinkle my dress," Aniyah said.

"Oh, I'm good at ironing." Elsa chuckled as she got a good look at Aniyah's dress code. "I see you look just like Tessa, but you don't dress like her."

"My mother dresses pitiful. She's not hot like me." Aniyah grinned as she spun around. She shook her body briefly. "Where's the music around here? It's so quiet."

"The Houstons only play music in the family room in the evening, except that baby girl listening to music with her ear plugs."

"Those heifers better not be here, are they?"

Elsa was mesmerized by the way Aniyah spoke of the Houstons. "No, they moved out."

"They're too uppity for me, conceited, rich broads."

"I see you do speak your mind," Elsa said, surprised.

"I'm thirsty. Where's the fridge?" Aniyah wondered.

"It's not too far down the hall." Elsa pointed in the direction of the kitchen.

Baron, ready to leave, interrupted their conversation. "Elsa, I'll leave Miss Sanchez in your hands. I'll be going. Show her to the bedrooms."

"Hold up. I don't want a woman showing me where the bedrooms are. That's a man's job." Aniyah said as she put her arm under Baron's arms.

He gave in, not wanting Aniyah to expose any information about them to Elsa. "I'll go ahead and escort her to the bedrooms."

Right away Elsa noticed that Aniyah had a crush on the attorney. "Sassy gal," she mumbled as she left the room. Elsa couldn't wait for Tessa to call her. She understood why she didn't brag about her daughter. The girl was wild.

Baron led Aniyah up to the second floor. He first showed her the west wing and then the east wing. He showed her the master suite where Rupert and Alana had slept.

"I'm not sleeping on any dead folks' bed. I'm dumping all this mess."

"Mr. Houston has a storage place on the property. Ask Elsa to get someone to move the furniture for you."

"Come on, for now you can sleep in the guestroom," he said as he took her to a huge room with a king-sized bed covered in a white eyelet bedspread. A bouquet of roses in a crystal vase accented a table near the window. Aniyah went into the bathroom. It was bigger than the apartment she had once shared with a boyfriend before they were evicted for nonpayment of rent.

"Put your bag in the closet."

Aniyah went into the huge walk-in closet. Two long bar rails awaited lots of clothes.

She only had the spandex dress she wore and two other garments to put in the closet.

"Everything is so dang big."

"Maybe you don't want to live here in such a big house. You can trade with the Houstons. They would be very happy to move back here."

Aniyah went up to him and yanked on his tie. "No way in hell!" She released his tie. "Take me, baby," she begged as she reached up and swung her arms around his neck.

Baron pulled her arms off of him. "There are too many people around here. We could get caught." *This was his excuse and he was sticking to it.*

"Who cares? We're both single."

"Anyone finds out about us and they'll think you and I had something to do with Mr. Houston's death. Milandra Houston would see that I'm disbarred."

Aniyah went over and closed the door. "Now, no one will see us," she said as she pushed him, catching him off-guard. He fell back onto the bed.

She jumped on top of the white eyelet spread. Her spandex dress rose to where she could feel the conditioned air on her rear. Her breasts popped out. Baron came eye to eye with her nipples. He was back in the trap he didn't want to be in. It was Tessa he wanted, not her daughter. But his hunger for motherly milk led his mouth to her right nipple.

Elsa came to the top of the stairs. She had brought up two glasses of cold iced tea. She saw the door closed. Putting her ear to the door, she heard Aniyah giggling, but no sound from Baron until he let out a loud moan.

"Well, Father help me," Elsa whispered. "Tessa has lost her man to her daughter." She hurried back down the hallway, spilling iced tea on the hardwood floors.

Baron got up from the bed. He put his pants back on. "I must leave," he said as he headed to the door. *This can't happen again.*

Aniyah stood up and pulled down on her dress. She made sure her breasts were covered.

She followed Baron into the hallway. They noticed a male servant had begun to mop up a spilled substance on the floor.

"What happened here?" Baron asked as he straightened his tie.

"Elsa said one of the help wasted tea," the servant said.

Baron knew there were no spills on the floor when he and Aniyah came down the hall. He wondered if Elsa or one of the servants who brought up the drinks had heard them.

Aniyah gave her attention to the young man. She admired the darkness of his hair and the muscles in his arms from days of hard work. "You're Mexican?" She smiled.

"Yes," the young man said as he tried to keep his eyes off the dress that was drawn up her legs.

"I'm Black-Mexican," she announced.

"So am I," the young man said.

"What's your name?"

"Pete," he said.

"How old are you?" she asked.

"Eighteen, almost nineteen."

"I have another job for you," Aniyah flirted. She took the mop out of Pete's hand and passed it to Baron. "On your way out, Mr. Chavis, drop the mop off wherever it goes? I have a real man's job for Pete to do," she said as she winked her eye at him.

Baron stood holding the mop in his hand as he watched Aniyah pull Pete by the hand down the hallway. Pete nervously went with her.

Baron called, "Isn't he a bit too young for you?"

Aniyah turned around. "I'll teach him what you old farts lack." She laughed and kept walking away with Pete to her new bedroom.

Baron listened to them as they spoke, but didn't understand their dialogue at times because they spoke in Spanish. They vanished into the bedroom, with Aniyah shutting the door behind them.

He placed the mop against the wall. He went back to the bedroom and eased the door open. He looked in and saw that Pete was his replacement in a snap.

Inside the room, Aniyah unbuttoned the white, short-sleeved shirt Pete wore. He stood tall with his arms by his side. She removed his shirt.

"Strong arms for a young man." She admired him.

"Thank you," Pete shyly responded in Spanish.

Aniyah assumed this was going to be his first time having sex. She could sense that he was nervous by the way sweat accumulated on his forehead. His hands trembled as she placed one of them on her left breast. Right then his hand froze; it lay numb on her breast.

She laughed. "Sugar, relax."

"I've never been with a girl before," he admitted.

"See, you have graduated to the head of the class. You get to be with a woman who can teach you how to handle them young thangs."

Aniyah placed her arms around his neck. She smothered his lips and kissed him with force. She then ordered Pete to remove the rest of his clothes.

Pete followed her instructions. Rupert had recently hired him. He was the first young male that Rupert had ever employed. Due to Alana's heart trouble, a young man stealing his wife didn't threaten Rupert.

Pete was happy that he had a job that gave him room and board. As sexy as he thought Aniyah was, he realized that it was wrong for what he was doing. But to stay working at the Houston Estate, he submitted to her demands just as the women servants had done with Rupert.

Aniyah pulled him over to the bed. "Lay down," she insisted.

Pete did as he was told.

She studied his manhood as she removed her dress.

His eyes popped open. The fullness of her breasts turned him on. His manhood responded. It stood erect.

Aniyah crawled on top of him. She gave him the ride of his life.

Afterward they lay under the covers. She held him close. She looked over Pete's shoulder to see Baron peeking inside the room.

"You're better than any other man I've ever had. I loved it." She smiled.

Baron mumbled, "Crazy bitch." He left the door ajar. He hurried out of the house, leaving the mop where it was. Being a man… his ego got to him. He was jealous, but happy that she might let up on him.

Elsa glimpsed Baron leaving as she headed upstairs. She saw the mop against the wall. *Where was Pete?*

Elsa heard voices and walked to the room Aniyah occupied. "Lord, have mercy," she mumbled as she peeked inside. She listened to them.

"Sugar, this is your new job around here," Aniyah said as she played in his black hair. "You're my human vibrator." She giggled.

"More pay," Pete wondered aloud.

"Big pay," Aniyah said as she kissed him. Again they absorbed in their ecstasy.

Tessa Sanchez's daughter is hot in the pants, Elsa thought as she watched them. Lord, she's going to bring more gossip around here than her daddy did.

Elsa made her way back down the stairs to resume her daily activity. She couldn't wait to hear from Tessa.

Aniyah dismissed Pete once they were finished. The discovery of sex was how she had started her life at the age of sixteen, when she met a guy who went by the name of Danny.

It was during the time of year when tourists vacationed in

Cancun, Mexico. Aniyah loved to go and watch the tourists shop for souvenirs.

Danny, as he called himself, saw her from afar. She wore a midriff top and a long, flared skirt. Her hair was covered with a sombrero to avoid the hot sun.

Danny came up to her. "Excuse me. Can you tell me where tourists go at night for a good fiesta?"

Aniyah's eyes lit up. She loved to dance. She hadn't been to any of the nightclubs, but she knew the locations. She began to name a few of the places.

Danny saw that she was full of life. She was the bait he was looking for. "I may need you as a tour guide. I'll pay you."

Aniyah grew excited. This was a way to bring money into her home. After all, her mother and her aunt worked long hours cleaning for barely anything. "Yes, I would love to. How much you pay?"

"Believe me, top dollar." Danny grinned.

Aniyah could see the man was in his early twenties. His chest was exposed from the opened floral shirt he wore.

"So what's your name?" he asked.

She paused. "Aniyah Sanchez," she blurted.

"Pretty name. You can just call me Danny," he said, not giving her his true name.

Danny asked that she meet him in the same spot after dark. Aniyah went home. She didn't tell her mother or her aunt about the man. It was her secret. They would never approve of her going anywhere with him. Although that's how she came into this world. Her mother had had a one-night stand with a tourist of African American descent. Her mother thought there was something special between them. The man went back to his home, never knowing he had a baby. Aniyah was disgusted with her mother because she didn't even get the man's name. All she got was a twenty-dollar bill on the nightstand.

"Aunt Tessa," Aniyah said, "it's so hot tonight. My friends are all at the hotel pool. May I go and swim?" she asked because her mother was sound asleep.

Local teens that had parents working at the hotel usually swam there during tourism time.

"Don't stay too long," Tessa said.

Aniyah got ready to leave the house. She still wore the same clothes from earlier that day. She carried her bathing suit in her hands. Once out of the house she dropped the bathing suit behind a trashcan. She would pick it up on the way back home.

She met Danny, who stood dressed in a pair of navy pants and a print shirt. His shoes had been shined. He held a plastic bag from the hotel in his hand.

"I thought you stood me up," he said as he looked at his watch.

"I had a hard time getting out of the house," she admitted.

"You mean to tell me your parents don't know you're out. How old are you?"

"Almost eighteen," she lied because she didn't want him to stop her from making money.

Danny saw that she was dressed in her same clothes. "Girl, you still have on your shopping clothes. You need a little more spicy rags to wear on that hot body of yours and a little makeup to perk up that pretty face."

"My face is ugly, and this is not good enough?" Aniyah asked as she looked down at her skirt.

"A little lipstick never hurts, and I've got the perfect dress for you," he said.

Danny pulled out a spandex black dress and a makeup kit. Aniyah thought of the dresses she had seen in teen magazines. She thought this was one of those dresses.

"You can get dressed in the bathroom in the lobby of the hotel where I'm staying," he said, starting to walk in that direction.

Aniyah followed him. She was going to be the prettiest tourist guide in Cancun tonight.

They went through the lobby in the hotel. They heard Latin music playing.

"Looks like a party is going on in here that I didn't know anything about." Danny was excited.

Aniyah shook her body to the music. "I love to dance," she said as she danced her way to the bathroom.

She pulled the dress over her head. It clung to her body and showed off all of her curves. She turned sideways to the mirror and saw that her butt filled the dress. Her full breasts protruded slightly from the top. "I'm chili pepper hot." She smiled.

She smeared the red lipstick on her lips. She lined her eyes with eyeliner as she had seen her mother and auntie do many of times.

"Very pretty," she said as she admired her look in the mirror.

Aniyah found her way out of the bathroom to reveal her new look to Danny.

His eyes lit up. "Sweet mercy," he said. "I knew that dress was you. And your lips are as juicy and red as a cherry."

"You like?" Aniyah asked as she spun around. "Such a pretty dress. I wish I could go dancing in this dress."

"Girl, you forgot you're my escort. Let's go," Danny said.

"Come on, I'll show you where the night life is."

"Why waste the good music? We'll hang out here."

Aniyah followed him to the entrance of the hotel nightclub. The man at the door stopped them.

"How old is the senorita?" he said.

"You mean my wife?" Danny said, not a smile on his face.

Aniyah looked at him in shock. Danny placed his arm around her shoulder. He kissed her on the forehead. "Come on, baby, let's party."

The man stepped aside and they went in. The music played. They found their way to a small table in the corner of the club. A waitress came over to them. "What are you drinking?"

"Two rum and Cokes," he said.

Aniyah had never drunk before. But she was getting paid to entertain him. So she went with the flow of things. This was one of the happiest nights of her life. Danny took her on the dance floor. She showed him how to Latin dance. He gave her a few tips on how the Decatur, Georgia, people got down. The few drinks led her to be open to anything. She wobbled her way off the floor to the table.

"I'll have another."

"No more, baby," he whispered.

"I'm having the best night of my life."

"It gets better the later it gets," he said. "Let's get out of here."

Danny got up and pulled her close to him. She held on to him, as she tried not to fall down from intoxication. They reached the outside of the club. Danny pulled his room key from his pocket.

"I need you to do one more thing for me tonight," he said, "and I'll pay you big."

"I love this work. I get to have fun while I show you a good time." She giggled.

They went up to his hotel room. Inside he tossed his shirt off. Aniyah made her way to the bed. She lay back on it. Her dress rode up her thighs.

Danny pulled her up off the bed. "Come here, baby," he said and kissed her.

Aniyah felt like a woman. She had heard of other girls talking about their encounters with men. Now, she was with a man she had just met like her mother; however, she knew his name and he made her feel beautiful. She kissed him back. She made Danny's job easy. She hungered for him.

"It's nice being an escort for such a sexy man." She eased her hand down his chest. "Cocoa skin," she marveled.

She pulled the spandex dress over her head and dropped it on the floor. She began to do what she heard other girls did for tourists to get big pay.

Danny stood and let her have her way with him. He had found himself a diamond. He had to get her back to Georgia to work her skills on potential clients.

In the morning, she found her way home. Tessa and her mother fiercely awaited her. She walked in the door now dressed in her own clothes. Danny kept the dress he had given her, to keep her from having to explain where it came from. Aniyah forgot the bathing suit behind the trashcan.

"Where were you?" her mother scolded her.

"It's almost daybreak," Tessa exclaimed.

"I fell asleep at the poolside."

"No one saw you at the pool. Don't lie," Tessa said.

"I went with new friends to another hotel."

Tessa noticed Aniyah was a little off-balance. "What else do you wish to tell us?" she asked.

"It seems like you have a hangover."

Aniyah became angry. "I haven't been drinking. I don't know which one of you is my mother at times. Aunt Tessa, you always act like you're the mother. Mama, make her stop treating me this way!" she cried.

"Don't hurt your Aunt Tessa's feelings. She loves you like you're her own daughter. She lost her baby daughter a year after you were born. Give her respect!" her mother yelled.

Aniyah broke down. "Sorry."

"Go to your room. Stay away from trouble. It's tourist time. Men prey on young girls," her mother warned.

Aniyah went to her room and slouched on the bed. She pulled out the money she had stuffed in her bra and counted it. She tucked the two hundred dollars under the mattress.

In the following days, she found ways to be with Danny. The last week of his two-week vacation, they lay in bed in his hotel room. They sipped on rum. Aniyah made sure she limited herself to one drink.

"My plane leaves tomorrow," he said as he kissed her on the neck.

Aniyah sat up in the bed. "No, don't leave." She wanted him to stay. The pay was good. Being his escort built her bankroll to six hundred dollars.

"I have to leave. Duty calls."

Aniyah pouted. She bent over to rest her head on her knees.

Danny massaged her back. "Hey, baby, come back to Georgia with me. You can make double the money living with me."

"Wow, that's plenty of money for my family."

"Oh yeah, baby, it is," Danny said as he pulled her back down on the pillow to saturate her lips with his.

Aniyah counted the money in her head. Her mother and her aunt wouldn't go for her leaving with a stranger, but she was tired of always hearing them speak of how hard things were around their house. Most girls had lots of clothes, but she had a few pieces her family brought home that their employers no longer wanted to be seen in.

"I'll go," she said. "But I have no plane ticket."

"What about your family? I don't want any police coming after me."

"I won't tell them. I'll run away," she said. "I'll make money, and then I'll come back with lots of it. My family won't be mad when they see all the money I've made."

Danny smiled. "They'll be so proud of you. But there's one problem: I'm short on cash until I get back. Use the money you already made from me to buy your plane ticket. I'm good for it when we get to Georgia," he said as he kissed her on the neck.

Aniyah was absorbed in the attention from Danny and didn't think twice. She used the money to buy her air fare. She packed the few clothes she had and left a goodbye note to her family.

She wrote, "Going on a trip to do great things for the family. I'll return when I have a big surprise for the family so we don't have to suffer."

She left in the middle of the night with a fake passport.

Aniyah reached Georgia. Danny got her settled into his home. The first week he wined and dined her. Then, the next week he gave her a story about how he had been laid off his job and didn't have enough money to pay her the money back he owed her, much less pay her for escort services. He slowly began to introduce her to his so-called friends, but in reality, they were clients for her.

Aniyah's first job was to entertain a bald-headed Chinese man. She was his escort for a dinner party. She did everything Danny told her to do to keep the client happy but inside the car, the client touched her on her breasts. Aniyah pushed his hand away. "I'm just your escort. Danny is my man."

The client laughed. "Danny is your man? Danny is strictly about business. I'm one of his biggest meal tickets. He'll be mad if I tell him you're not being nice."

Aniyah didn't believe him. "Take me home!" she shouted.

The client picked up his cell phone and made a call. Aniyah heard him say, "This one is a lemon." He drove her to Danny's house. "Get out," he said as he pushed her.

"Pay me my money," Aniyah demanded.

Danny came running up to the car. Aniyah was happy to see him. She was convinced that he would straighten out the man, but instead, Danny snatched her out of the car by the arm. He threw her up against the car. He grabbed her by the neck. Aniyah trembled.

"Look, I hope you don't think you came here to Georgia to live on me. We need the money. Get back in the car and give the man whatever he wants so we can get paid."

Danny reached under her skirt and pulled her panties down, making her step out of them. He dragged her by the arm and pushed her back into the car. He stood outside the car and looked in. He watched as his client popped every button on her blouse. The client forced his face between her breasts. From there he thrust his way inside her.

Aniyah thought of her family. *Home wasn't so bad.* Once the client was finished having his way with her, Danny opened the car door and pulled her out. The client handed Danny her pay. After that day, she never saw one dime of the money that she made.

She wanted to go home, but was too ashamed because she made no money to take back with her.

Aniyah lived the escort life for years until Danny got tired of her and brought in a new girl he found while vacationing in the Caribbean. He tossed Aniyah out onto the streets of Georgia with the clothes on her back. He vowed to kill her if she ever said a word about his business. The only thing she knew to do was to start her own business.

Aniyah went to nightclubs to look for men. She made money, but it had its price—bruises, black eyes, and two abortions.

Finally, she struck it big. A club owner knew of her work. One of South Carolina's very important men needed an escort.

Aniyah was informed that the service was private because the man was well known and married, but he paid well. The man could be a major client for her if she played her piano keys in tune.

The club owner took her to an upscale hotel in the downtown area of Atlanta. He gave her a key to put in the elevator to get to the suites. Aniyah knocked on the door.

Rupert opened the door. "Hello, come inside."

Aniyah walked in. She saw an assortment of fruits on a tray. A bottle of wine chilled on ice. The man went over and poured them a drink.

"So your name is Aniyah?" he had said.

"Yes and yours?"

"That's not important," Rupert said.

Aniyah watched as Rupert poured two drinks. He handed her a glass. "To a wonderful night," he said as he raised his glass.

"I hope to fulfill whatever fantasy you have."

They sipped the wine. Rupert stroked her hair.

"You remind me of someone who used to work for me a long time ago. She had dark hair exactly like yours."

"How was she in bed?" Aniyah asked.

"Let's just say, I hope you can make up for what she lacked."

Rupert swallowed the rest of the wine and tossed his glass into a fireplace nearby.

He removed one strap at a time from her black dress, kissing her on the neck down to her shoulder. Aniyah stood and let him smell the scent of her body. He then took her glass from her, pouring the remainder of the wine between her breasts. He cleaned her up with his tongue. Rupert turned her on. Together they made their way onto the bed.

Aniyah undressed him. She saw the diamond ring on his finger. "Married," she whispered.

Rupert noticed he still had his wedding band on. "Not right now," he said as he slipped it off his finger. He pulled her close to him. Together they explored the juices of each other's bodies.

Aniyah woke up the next day cuddled in Rupert's arms. He snored as she removed his arms from her and got up.

Aniyah took a piece of fruit from the tray and chewed it. She opened the room door to get the morning newspaper. Flipping through the newspaper, she saw a photo of her date. The headline read, "Rupert Houston of Houston Commercial Construction Company to build a Houston Tower in Atlanta, Georgia."

Aniyah's eyes lit up. This was the man her aunt was pregnant by and the man who had shipped her back to Cancun, Mexico, to live with her family. She was quite aware that her aunt never told him she had a miscarriage because her aunt had received a small check from him for several years now for a baby that didn't exist. All her aunt's problems, Aniyah had learned from snooping in her aunt's journal.

Aniyah felt no remorse. She had struck it rich and would finally get the money she needed to take back home. The Sanchez family would never know where she got it. But they would be free of being slaves to others.

Before Houston woke up, she put the newspaper back outside the door for him to find.

"Where are you?" he wondered.

Aniyah grabbed two slices of an orange. She dived back under the bed covers. Rupert watched as she squeezed the juices from the orange onto her ample breasts. He sucked the juices from her.

She was paid well. Rupert ordered her to stay with him for the week that he was there. Her funds in her bank account began to add up. Rupert came to Georgia regularly on business with her as one of his main objectives.

The day came when he asked her to move to Lake Murray. He had purchased a home on the lake that she could occupy. She didn't have to worry about driving because he had limo service to carry her around. She went along with his program as long as he was good to her.

Aniyah lived there until he became tired of her, as other men had. The day came when he sent Clark, his driver, to tell her that she had to move out. She was handed two thousand dollars.

"Wow, tell Rupert, I mean Mr. Houston, that I said thanks," she said as happy as ever.

"Mr. Houston said you have to leave immediately. You can stay at an apartment he has for no longer than two weeks," Clark said sternly.

Aniyah's happiness turned into outrage. "Damn it, just like that he's kicking me out?"

"I guess so. I'll wait for you outside."

The driver drove her to a small apartment. "I feel sorry for you girls who think Mr. Houston is going to keep you forever. He has a wife and a family he loves."

That was all he said and left. Aniyah furiously vowed to get even with Rupert. She put her plans into motion. Now was the time for her to use what she knew about him to her advantage.

How would he feel if he thought he had slept with his own daughter?

Aniyah could not wait to see his face. She also aimed to find any dirt on his family to use against him.

Aniyah discovered Noelle's attraction to Baron. She had spotted them at a local café having coffee. They exited the café and Noelle reached up to put her arms around his neck. She kissed him. There was no obvious attraction on Baron's part. Aniyah could tell by the way he kept his hands by his sides. Noelle placed his arms around her.

Aniyah snapped a photo and had someone alter the photo—to strip them of their clothes. The alteration made them seem as though they were having passionate sex. The word was out that Rupert never wanted his daughters to have contact with his workers or helpers.

Aniyah vowed to be a part of his empire. He owed it to her for what he had done to the Sanchez family.

After several weeks, she contacted Houston. She demanded that he come to see her. She threatened to cause trouble for him.

"You're crazy," Rupert said as he entered her apartment.

"You dumped me like I was trash."

"You are trash!" he yelled. "Look at what kind of work you do."

"I'm going to move up in the world," she said as if she had a top-tier corporate position. She was only living off the money she had saved. With Rupert's help, she would give up the escort business. This was the man that had destroyed her family, so her goals had shifted.

Rupert laughed.

"Don't laugh too fast. I have info on one of your daughters," Aniyah said.

"You know nothing about my girls."

Aniyah laughed as he got serious. "The half-Mexican one."

Rupert rushed at her. He squeezed her shoulders to shake her. "How did you find out about her?" he wondered.

"Let go of me!" Aniyah fought back, having no fear of him. Danny had trained her well for physical abuse. "I want money."

Rupert shoved her. "I'm not giving you a damn cent. You better keep your mouth shut."

"Let me move back to the Houston Villa. I'll keep very quiet," she begged.

"Hell no! I'm finished with you."

Aniyah saw that revealing what she knew about his daughter wasn't working so she began to dance.

Rupert watched as she danced erotically. "You're a crazy bitch, but you're sexy."

Aniyah said nothing. She kept moving her body as she slipped out of her dress. Playing in her hair, she hummed an unrecognizable song.

Aniyah flagged for him to come to her. Rupert realized that he was playing with a hot candle. But he was going to take his chance and put the flame out. He moved closer to her.

Aniyah ducked under his arm and continued to dance. He discarded his suit jacket and pulled her into his arms. She unzipped his pants and released his manhood. She let him take her.

Rupert was exhausted. "You still are not getting a cent from me."

"Yes, I will, Papa."

Rupert almost choked on his words. "What the hell?" He jumped up.

"I'm your daughter." She laughed.

He rapidly put on his clothes. He wiped the sweat off of his face. He thought of how many times he had been to bed with Aniyah. He could not believe that he had fallen into a trap. He adjusted his tie. "How do I know you're not lying?"

"I'm Tessa Sanchez's daughter."

Aniyah explained his situation with her aunt in detail. Rupert had no choice but to believe that she was telling the truth because she looked so much like Tessa.

Aniyah blackmailed him. She was determined that he owed her dearly and insisted that she be listed in his will as the owner of the Houston Estate upon his death. Rupert told her that he would leave her the Houston Villa.

"You put me out of the villa. So I want the estate," she demanded. "Leave that place to your other daughters."

At that time, she didn't tell him of the photo she had altered of Noelle and Baron. She kept that secret to seal the deal with his lawyer—making sure Baron didn't mess her up with getting what the Sanchez family was owed.

Aniyah got her wish. She met with Rupert at Chavis Law Firm. She witnessed as he handed his new will over to Baron. Rupert gave her enough money to live comfortably. She took the money and stayed in the apartment for the time being, until she thought of the life that she wanted to live. Her next thought was to figure out who she would hire to get rid of him, but his heart attack had saved her the dirty work.

Aniyah fell off to sleep. Sex with Baron and Pete had worn her out.

Chapter 16

Tessa sat in darkness for two days before she decided to let any sunlight shine into her hotel room. She squinted as she opened the blinds to protect her eyes from the sunrays.

In a few days, she would have to check out of the extended stay hotel. She didn't know whether to pay more money for another week or head back to Mexico without seeing Baron.

She plugged in an iron that rested on an ironing board. Before she turned the iron on, she poured water into the spout for steam.

The room was silent—no sound from any radio or television. Tessa avoided listening to or watching the news. The reporters were fascinated with the Houstons' family saga as if they were the Kennedys.

Tessa carried on and pressed her blouse. Too quiet, she decided to turn on the television. She hoped that the media had found a new story to harp over.

The newswoman reported the weather before a newsman announced the top headline story.

The man reported: "The Houston Estate has been turned over to the illegitimate daughter of Rupert Houston. It's believed that the daughter is the child of one of his former Mexican housekeepers. We are in the midst of trying to gather more information. At this time, we do know that Mr. Houston's three other daughters, by his wife, Alana, were forced to move out of the estate—the home that they were raised in. It is believed that they are now living in one of his other properties, The Houston Villa."

Tessa clicked the television remote off and hurried to get her purse. She scrambled for Elsa's number. "Here it is." Tessa took out the slip of paper and called her.

"Good morning," Elsa answered.

"Elsa, it's me, Tessa. You didn't tell me Mr. Houston had another baby by a Mexican."

"Gracious Lord, you should know. It's your daughter."

Tessa confessed as she slipped her blouse on. "I have no daughter anymore. I lost my baby not long after I got back to Mexico."

"Well, rumor is, it's your daughter."

"No way; my daughter is long dead."

"But you made me think that she was all grown up."

Tessa calmed down. "I said that because all these years Mr. Houston sent me money to keep me quiet. He never knew I had no baby. I lied. I made him think my baby was alive. I sent him a picture of my niece."

Elsa grinned. "Good for the bastard. I didn't think this hot thing living in here could be yours. She's a mess."

"Stupid, like her father."

"A whore like him." Elsa laughed.

"Oh, she's *that* bad?"

"Girl, it's gossip city up in this place," Elsa said as she thought of Baron. "By the way, did you call Mr. Chavis?"

"I've been trying to think over whether I should call him or not."

"I'm glad you didn't follow my advice and call him. I was dead wrong for that. Don't bother to call him; he's messing with Aniyah. That's Mr. Houston's new daughter's name."

Tessa sat down in shock. Her deceased daughter's name rang in her ears. "You say her name is Aniyah. What does she look like?" Tessa wondered.

"I hate to say it, but she sure looks like you. They say we black folks all look alike, but I guess it goes for Mexicans, too. She's got the long dark hair and features like you—those pretty dark brown eyes."

"Oh, Elsa, what has my niece done?"

"Your niece?"

"Yes. Her first name is Rosie. Aniyah is her middle name, the same name I named my baby girl."

"Hush your mouth," Elsa said.

"Yes, Rosie ran away at sixteen. My family hasn't heard from her. Her mother almost died from a broken heart. She had a heart attack a few years back."

"Well, now that I know it might be your niece, I didn't mean to talk about her the way I did. But I saw her and Mr. Chavis with my own eyes." Elsa was eager to tell the story. "He showed Aniyah, Rosie, whatever her name is, to her bedroom. I tried to be nice and welcomed her with a glass of sweet iced tea. I got to the room door and it was slightly opened. I peeped in and there they were, sloping all over each other."

Tessa was hurt from the news. "My niece made love to Mr. Chavis?"

"Honey, I'm sorry to say, but yes. I don't think it's love on her part because there's more to the story."

"What else?" Tessa called as she took an aspirin out of her purse. She had a headache just that fast.

"Lord as my witness, as fast as Mr. Chavis left, I went back up to the room to check on her. Lord, God, strike me if I'm wrong. The girl had Pete, the new young helper, under her covers. I rest my case."

Tessa was upset with how her niece had turned out, but surprised at Baron's actions.

"I must come and see her for myself. In my heart I know this is my Rosie. I must stop her before she winds up in jail. Mr. Chavis— I never expected *him* to be this way."

"I didn't either but, you know the strange thing is," Elsa recalled, "he asked me to escort her to the room. She demanded that he take her. Now that I think about it, she might be holding something over his head. Lord, Tessa, I don't know. Folks is nuts these days."

Tessa cried, "Please, Elsa, I beg you not to say anything about my Rosie not being Mr. Houston's daughter. I'll get her out of there. I'll make her give back the house to the girls. Nothing good ever comes to those who steal from other's fortune. I'll call Mr. Chavis. I hope he won't lie to me. Tell me the truth. You know, I thought his heart was with me. I guess too many years have gone by and his heart faded away from mine."

"Maybe it didn't. He may see you in your niece. That might be the attraction."

"See you soon, Elsa. Thanks for telling me all this. I don't want Rosie to be put in jail. Please keep quiet."

"Girl, don't you worry. Just like I know how to spread gossip, I sure know how to hold on to it, too." Elsa laughed.

Tessa found the number to the Chavis Law Firm. Sara, the receptionist, answered, "Baron Chavis' office, may I help you?"

"Yes, my name is Tessa Sanchez. May I speak to Mr. Chavis?"

The receptionist assumed by her name that she was Aniyah Sanchez's mother. "Hold on for a minute."

Sara came back in a second. "I'll connect you."

"Baron Chavis," he said.

Her legs weakened as she said, "Hello, Mr. Chavis. This is Tessa Sanchez."

"It's so sweet to hear your voice. You sound the same as the day I first met you."

"I wish, at times, I looked the same."

"I saw you at the funeral," he said. "You're as pretty as ever."

She smiled from the compliment he gave her.

"I didn't see you. I guess I was so busy talking to the Houstons."

"You disappeared the same way you did years ago—just broke a man's heart." He flirted with her.

She couldn't believe he would flirt with her after being intimate with her niece.

"I need desperately to talk with you alone. Could you come see me at my hotel room?"

This is the invitation I've wanted for years—to be alone with you, not held hostage by your daughter, he thought.

"I can stop what I'm doing now and come."

"Thank you so much," she said.

"Tell me where you're staying?"

She explained to him her whereabouts. Baron never mentioned Aniyah to her. He wanted to keep her name out of their conversation for now. After all, he probably had lost any chance of having a relationship with Tessa, but his hopes were to keep her close to him as a friend.

Baron sped down I-20 to get to her. His phone rang off the hook. Between Aniyah and Noelle, he felt like he was in a tug of war. Noelle was no problem, but Aniyah might show up on his doorstep.

He knocked on the door. Tessa appeared at the door dressed in a mid-length floral skirt to match her yellow blouse.

"Good to see you, Mr. Chavis. Come in."

"Please call me Baron," he said as he made his way into the room.

She smiled. "Baron, it is. Have a seat."

"I'll stay standing. I've been sitting at my desk most of the day." He admired her. "Tessa, you haven't changed in looks either."

"A few gray strands."

"Join the family," he said as he patted his head.

Baron took his chances and gave her a kiss on the cheek. She blushed, but kept looking down at the floor.

"Hold your head up. Let the world see your beauty," he said as he lifted her face up.

"You always knew how to make a lady feel great."

"Tell me what's on your mind."

"Aniyah!"

Baron knew this conversation had to surface. "What about your daughter? You want to move in with her?"

Tessa dropped her head and shook it from side to side. "If this girl is the girl I truly think she is, she's not my daughter. She's my niece. Her real name is Rosie. Aniyah is her middle name and the name of my baby girl I had by Mr. Houston. But my Aniyah, born two months premature, only lived for a week after birth."

Baron couldn't believe what he had heard. All the time he thought he was sleeping with her daughter.

Tears flowed down Tessa's face. Baron took her in his arms for a few seconds, then he let go of her. He grabbed a chair and sat down.

"Mr. Houston changed his will for your niece. Everyone thinks she's his and your daughter. She looks just like you."

"Everyone in Mexico always thought I was the mother of my niece instead of my sister, Julia. Rosie was a troubled girl."

"I have a picture of her at my office in Mr. Houston's file. I wish I had brought the picture with me."

"What am I thinking?" Tessa said as she ran over and searched her purse. She pulled out a photo of her niece at age sixteen. She held the photo in front of him.

He studied the photo. The girl in the photo had on a long, wide floral skirt. She dressed so innocently, but her face looked the same, just without lots of makeup.

"That's Aniyah," he said.

Tessa cried. "I must go and see her for myself. I'm going to try to make her give back what doesn't belong to her. I need your help. I don't want her to go to jail."

As an attorney, Baron knew that Aniyah could spend time in jail for fraud. But he had his own reasons as to why he could not go after her.

"I'll have to see how I can handle this," he said, puzzled.

Tessa went over to him. She put her hand on his shoulder. "I've heard the news about you and Rosie."

He jumped up and blabbed off at the mouth. "It's not what you think. She came after me. She's crazy. She has this picture of Noelle and me making out. I mean, she fixed the picture to make it look like we were having a thing, but we never had sex. I promise you, just a peck on the lips—no sex. I only did that to get back at Houston for having what I really wanted, and that's you."

"Is that all there is to the story?"

Baron stared in her eyes. He couldn't lie to her. "Okay, your niece and I had sex, but it's because she has the picture. I don't want her to embarrass Noelle or send the picture to the press. I need to get it from her."

"You're a grown man, Baron. You owe me no explanation. I could see the fire in your eyes that night when you saw Mr. Houston and me. We hurt you."

The attorney stood up. He brushed her hair with his hands. "Houston did what he did to spite me. I could never hold that against you."

"All is forgiven," she said as tears flowed down her face again.

"Don't cry, my love." Baron pulled her into his arms and kissed her, allowing his hands to gently caress the small of her back. As the kiss intensified, his heart hammered as he wrapped his arms around her tighter, drawing her deeper into his chest. He circulated his tongue inside her mouth before letting up, giving her pecks of kisses on her lips.

When the kiss ended, an overwhelmed Tessa touched her bottom lip with the tips of her finger. He grabbed her from behind and nibbled on her neck, caressing her full, ripened breasts.

She leaned back against his chest, her head tilted over her shoulder as she locked lips with him in a passionate kiss. She turned to face him, staring into his lustful eyes. "It's time. I have fantasized about you for a long time."

"I've always wanted to feel your flesh against mine."

"We wait no more," she said, as she went over and closed the blinds to bring darkness to the room.

Tessa turned around and removed his clothing. In return, he dropped her clothes to the floor as she stepped out of her skirt.

Baron reached around her and unhooked her bra. Releasing her breasts, he took one for his pleasure. The bra fell to the floor as she removed her underwear.

He lifted her up and took her over to the bed.

Baron laid her down and explored every inch of her body. Together the rotation of their hips danced in harmony.

After a night of passion, Baron woke up to see the table in the room was set for two. The delicious aroma of bacon and eggs made him crave for food. Tessa was awake. She went out and brought breakfast back for them.

"Hungry?"

"For you," he said, yawning.

"I mean for a morning meal."

Baron got out of bed, went over to her, and pulled her close to his naked body. He held her tight. "Thanks for looking out for my stomach."

He let go of her and headed to the bathroom to freshen up for breakfast.

Returning to the room, he joined Tessa at the table. She noticed that he wore his underwear, covering up the muscle she loved most.

Baron took a bite from a strip of bacon, and then he took a swallow of the orange juice that she poured for him.

"Tessa, my love, what do we do now?"

"I have to go and straighten out my niece. My plane leaves in a few days to go back to Mexico."

"You can't go back," he said as he reached over and held her hand.

"I have no reason to stay here. I have work in Mexico."

"You have me; please don't leave."

"I have no home here. I'm using money I had saved to stay in this place," she said as she looked around the hotel room.

He noticed that her plate just sat in front of her. "You've eaten already?"

"Not hungry. I'm so nervous for Rosie."

"Trust me; she can handle herself in a lot of ways."

Tessa could tell by the statement he made that he found pleasure from being with Aniyah. "I'm just nervous for her."

"I have the perfect job for you."

"I dare not work at the Houston Estate."

"Come work in my home. It's not like the Houston Estate. It's a four-bedroom home. You can be the lady of the house. You'll sleep in the master bedroom with me or I'll sleep in the guest-room."

She tapped him. "I'll take the first offer. I want to be in bed with you."

"Be my wife—Mrs. Baron Chavis," he proposed.

Tessa couldn't believe that he wanted her to marry him. She thought he just wanted a servant and a woman to have in bed. "Me, your wife?"

"Yes. Say yes!" he rejoiced as he took his finger and rubbed it across her lips. She looked up into his eyes. She became mesmerized by the way he didn't bat an eye.

"Yes," she said with joy.

They forgot about the rest of the breakfast they left on their plates. Baron scooped her up into his arms. He messed in her hair as if he were shampooing it. She held him around his neck. They kissed passionately.

Shoving his hand up her dress, he removed her panties, then lifted her up and laid her on the bed. He released her favorite muscle for her to feast her eyes on.

Tessa hungered for him as she reached up and pulled him closer to her. She fastened her lips to his. He forced himself inside her with such power that it made her scream. He kept his eyes glued to hers as he caressed her breasts. All their worries vanished as they got lost in passion.

Tessa packed her bag and left with Baron. He dropped her off at his house and went on to the office.

Baron gave her full access to the Houston limo service, even though he rarely used it. He enjoyed driving his own vehicle.

Tessa admired his home. She was ready to finally be the woman of the house for the man she loved.

Chapter 17

Kenley's plans were to visit the estate as much as she could to keep an eye on the house. In reality, she wanted to make Aniyah so miserable that she would be forced to leave.

She put her key into the lock of the front door and entered. She sniffed a stale odor. Kenley covered her nose; it wasn't the pleasant smell of fresh-cut floral arrangements that were used as accent pieces throughout the home.

The house was silent until she looked up and saw Pete coming from the east wing. He froze at the top of the stairs. The dark hair on his head was fluffy. He wasn't looking fresh in his uniform of black pants and a crisp white shirt. Kenley came to the conclusion that he looked like he had just gotten out of bed.

"What's going on here?" she asked. "I know you're not getting relaxed in my parents' house."

Pete did not know how to respond to her. He hunched his shoulders and mumbled, "I no speak no English."

Aniyah heard voices. Strutting toward them, she wore a short red robe. The robe hung open and a red nylon baby doll gown was exposed under it. "Oh, hell no! Just what are you doing coming here to my house?" she shouted as she looked down over the banister rail.

Kenley held up her key. "In case you forgot, we share the house—that's what Father said in his will."

Aniyah tapped Pete's shoulder. "Wait for me in the bedroom."

Pete did as he was told and dashed to the east wing.

Aniyah made her way down the stairs. "Girl, I'm not no baby-sitter. You need to go back to your other two uppity sisters."

"I see what's going on here. You want to keep me out of here. You're playing around with the help."

"And? I'm grown. What's it to you? Go to school. Do something. Just disappear," Aniyah said with her hands on her hips.

"I'm not! I'm going upstairs to hang out in my room."

Face to face, Kenley tried to go around Aniyah but Aniyah blocked her. .

"Oh, no, you're not!" Aniyah shouted.

"You smell just like this nasty odor in this house," Kenley said as she turned up her nose.

"Incense smells way better in a house. Flowers should stay outside just like you should."

Aniyah lifted her left hand as if she was going to strike her.

"You touch me and the police will be all over this place. I'll have you arrested for abusing a minor."

Aniyah backed off. She didn't want the police anywhere near her. She thought about the years she would get for fraud, and she changed her tune. "Heifer, go ahead upstairs. But the next time you come here, the locks on the front door will be changed."

Aniyah stepped out of her way and Kenley ran past her up the stairs. "Miss Half whore." Kenley yelled back at her.

"You're jealous." Aniyah laughed. "I know, little sister, you've got the hots for Pete. I saw you looking at his cute butt. I'll share him with you when you're old enough."

"I'll eat dirt before I ever go behind a whore."

Kenley went into her room, happy the decor still looked the same. She ran downstairs to the kitchen. Elsa and another servant were busy cooking.

"What's that smell?" Kenley asked as she walked in. Again, she covered her nose.

Elsa turned to see her. "Is that one of the cutie Houston girls coming in here?"

"It's me." Kenley giggled as she ran over and gave Elsa a hug. "I've never been in this kitchen and it smelled so awful."

"I'm making chitterlings for your newfound sister. And would you believe, she wants red rice and black beans to go with it?"

"They smell like the way she acts—funky."

"Why didn't you tell me you were coming by? I would have fixed you a pan of baked lasagna."

"Elsa, with garlic bread?"

"Spread with butter." Elsa licked her lips.

"I'm getting hungry. Don't tease me."

"You're welcome to have some of this." Elsa pointed to the pot that the chitterlings were in.

"Disgusting!" Kenley turned up her nose.

Aniyah heard Kenley as she spoke to the help, but they all became silent when she entered.

"Do you have anything else better to do than to mess with the cook? I told you to disappear."

Aniyah waved her hand at Kenley. She looked at Elsa. "Where's the soda I asked for with plenty of ice?" she yelled.

"Sorry, I forgot." Elsa went on to find Aniyah the soft drink.

"No yelling goes on in my parents' house. Do you have any class?" Kenley asked.

Aniyah walked up to her. She pointed her finger in Kenley's face. "Girl, you're working my last nerve."

"Back off," Kenley said, and then yelled, "You're a whore and your mother is a bigger whore."

Aniyah pushed her. "You have a fresh mouth."

When Elsa approached them with the drink in her hand, Kenley snatched the glass of soda from her. She tossed it on Aniyah. Kenley ran out of the kitchen, leaving Aniyah's nightgown drenched in soda. She called back. "Talk to you later, Elsa."

Aniyah grabbed a dishtowel and wiped herself off. She called. "Fix me another damn drink."

Elsa and the other servants laughed amongst themselves after Aniyah left.

A few days later when the servants were off duty in their quarters, free to do what they want, Kenley decided to come back to the Houston Estate. She tried to enter using her key, but the lock did not work. She tried several times.

"I don't believe this."

The driver saw her struggling with the key. He tilted his hat. "Do you need my help, Miss Houston?"

"No." She sighed. "The locks have been changed."

Kenley thought for a second. She recalled the secret passage to the house. When she turned ten, her father had told her about the passage. "Wait here," she said, "I'm going down to another entrance."

The driver got out of the limo and watched her walk in the heat. He wiped sweat from around his neck. "It's some kind of hot out here, Miss Houston. Come back and let me drive you to the entrance."

Kenley stopped and yelled back, "I'm good. Go on and wait for me near the help's residences."

The driver watched for a moment as she took her time walking down the front of the house. After a few steps, Kenley looked back to see if he had followed her orders.

Just that fast, the driver had driven away to the servants' quarters. He reared his seat back to take a nap. He figured this was going to be a long evening.

Kenley dashed through a walking path attached to the house. She made her way behind a palmetto tree. Under a fake patch of grass hid a trap door. She twisted the lock and pulled the door open.

Making her way into the wine cellar, she reached out into the darkness for a string hanging from a light to turn it on.

She could see the rows of wine bottles labeled by dates on the wine shelves. It had been a long time since she had come down to the wine cellar. Her father had forbidden her from going in there. He told her it was not a place for a young girl to be.

Kenley walked down a narrow hallway to get to the stairs that led to the ground floor of the house. She stopped at a bookshelf that stood against the wall. It was filled with books.

Browsing the collection of romance books, she saw that there was a journal in the midst of the books. She took it out and opened the first page. Her mother's name, Alana Houston, was written in script on the page.

The young Houston realized that this was her mother's personal journal. Alana dated each page of her thoughts. Kenley read the first note in her mother's handwriting.

I know Rupert loves me but he can't be true to me. He has a love for other women. He doesn't think I know it, but I do. It hurts. But he's such a good man that I forgive him for his unfaithful ways. I know the baby Tessa is carrying is his. I'm appalled because I'm with child while his whore is, too. I could never tell Rupert I know the truth. Maybe he loves her and if I uttered a word to him he would disown me and put her in my place. I'll just keep it to myself. He's good to me, and I don't want to show I don't appreciate him. I will continue being the sweet and loving wife he married. Let him have his fun. I can live with it for the sake of my family.

Kenley was annoyed. "Mother, it's not all right. You knew, and yet you let Father run wild. I can't wait to tell Milandra and Noelle that you knew about Father's other women."

Kenley read many of her notes. But the note that touched her most was one of the most recent: *I know my heart is weak. Any little upsetting thing can shut it down. But what keeps my precious heart beating are my loving daughters. My girls and my home have been my strength to overlook the evildoing that I've allowed Rupert to get away with.*

Kenley wiped a tear from her eye. She was more determined to get Aniyah out of the house. *The estate had been nurtured by Mother's hand, not Father's mistresses.*

Kenley left the journal on a table. She left it in sight for her to take with her when she was ready to leave.

Tiptoeing quietly up the staircase, Kenley heard voices when she reached the top step. She opened the door and saw Aniyah and Baron in the midst of an argument. She realized that he must have driven up while she was in the wine cellar.

Aniyah was dressed in a white baby doll gown. Baron was still suited from work. Kenley listened to their conversation.

"I think you know, as well as I do, we're not a match. Your father has left you a nice home. You seem to like Pete, so move on," Baron said.

Aniyah yelled, pointing her finger at him, "I'm training that young thang. And don't tell me what I should or shouldn't do. It's not your call. I call the shots when it comes down to what I want.

You'll come whenever I call you because I have the picture of you and my sister."

Kenley watched as Aniyah stepped out of her lingerie and flung her arms around Baron's neck.

Aniyah smothered his lips.

Baron thought of Tessa being at his home. "I'm not having this," he said as he took her arms away.

Aniyah grabbed his crotch. "This is payback for the way you rich men treat us common women."

Baron held her tightly by her right wrist. "I said I'm not having this anymore."

He hurried out of the house to keep from revealing that he knew the truth about her. Instead, he would leave Tessa to handle her niece.

Aniyah slipped her clothes back on. She hollered out the door at him as he drove away. "We'll see about that."

Miss Half definitely has serious mental problems, Kenley thought as she watched and listened.

Aniyah came back into the house and made a call for a driver. She stood at the door until the driver appeared. "Come in here." She waved at him.

The driver removed his hat as he entered. Aniyah thought that he was gorgeous. The spice of silver mixed with black in his hair turned her on. She dropped her lingerie to the floor.

"How about it, driver, would you like to drive in my car?" She giggled.

The driver trembled; his eyes were glued to the curves of her body. His eyes popped opened when he saw the plumpness of her breasts. Over the years, his wife's breasts had found their way going in the same direction of the region he lived in—south.

"I can't, Miss Sanchez, I'm a married man. My wife also works for the estate," he said nervously as he dashed out of the door.

Aniyah ran outside bare bodied. "You and your damn old wife are both fired." She slammed the door.

"Pete," Aniyah screamed, "where are you, darling? I need your services. Mama is hot!"

Kenley stayed put until she watched Pete and Aniyah go down the hall in the direction of the staircase toward the mediation room on the lower level. She knew they would be busy taking care of Aniyah's sexual needs.

Kenley decided to snoop around. The photo on her father's computer of her sister and Baron had to come from Aniyah, and she intended to search for it. She thought that this had to make her father angry when he had received it, especially since he wanted to be the one to find the perfect man for his daughter.

She dashed upstairs to Aniyah's bedroom. She checked her computer for the image. She found it in her picture file and deleted it.

It did not take long before Kenley found a box in the closet with plenty of lingerie in it. She dug to the bottom of the box. There was a manila envelope. Inside the envelope was the photo Aniyah had altered. Kenley needed her email and password to log onto her Internet account. She scrambled through the box until she found a small, white envelope labeled *PERSONAL*. She looked inside the envelope and found a slip with Aniyah's email address and password. "Dummy," she said, running back to the computer and logged on to the Internet. She searched her email. There she found the email to her father. She deleted it.

Kenley made her way out of the room with the manila envelope in her hand.

About the time she got to the staircase that led downstairs, she heard Aniyah's voice. She ran to the west wing of the house to her room and peeked out.

Aniyah and Pete played lovebirds up the stairs all the way to the east wing. Once they vanished into the room, Kenley made her way to the wine cellar. She picked up the journal and left through the secret passage.

Running all the way to the servants' quarters, Kenley was out of breath. Her hair became drenched as it sweated from the heat. She tapped on the window of the limo and startled the driver as he was asleep. He jumped up and saw her face leaning against the window.

"Open up," Kenley called.

The driver unlocked the door, then got out to open the door for her, but Kenley had already gotten into the limo.

He looked into his rearview mirror at her in the back seat. He asked, "Miss Houston, is everything okay?"

"Get me to the Houston Villa as fast as you can," she said as she fumbled in a cooler to wet the dryness in her mouth with an ice-cold bottle of water.

Chapter 18

Kenley tiptoed into the villa but Milandra caught her. "Where have you been, young lady?"

"I went to the estate."

"It's appalling that you like being around that common trash."

"Actually, I hate her," Kenley said angrily.

Noelle came into the room with rollers in her hair and overheard her. "You can't go around hating people."

"You're going to hate her, too. I'm a great detective," Kenley said.

"What have you been investigating?" Milandra asked.

"See this?" She held out the journal. "This is Mother's diary. In her own words she said she loved us. That's what she says in it."

"Hand it here," Milandra, snatching it out of her hand.

"What's in the envelope?" Noelle inquired as she helped herself to it.

Kenley tried to take it back, but Noelle had already taken the photo out of the envelope.

Noelle stared at the photo of her kissing Baron in their birthday suits.

She leaned against the wall. "Where did you get this?"

"What is it?" Milandra said, forgetting that quickly about her mother's journal. She took the photo from Noelle. Her eyes lit up. She slapped Noelle with the photo. "You defied Father by sleeping with our lawyer."

"Of course not," Noelle yelled as she took back the photo. "This is some mistake. The truth is, I do like him, but I've never been to bed with him."

"You're a liar! The picture speaks for itself," Milandra yelled, jealous because her sister had had a man before her.

Kenley broke up their argument. "Milandra, she's telling the truth. Miss Half, our sister, did this. *She's* guilty."

"Why would she do this to me?" Noelle wondered.

"She likes Mr. Chavis. I know that much," Kenley declared.

"How do you know all these things?" Milandra asked.

Kenley explained how she discovered all the information. She told them about Baron and Aniyah's argument. Noelle was happy to know that he had pushed Aniyah away, but she was furious that the photo was created with her face on it.

Kenley gave them her last important discovery: "I also found the picture on Father's computer."

"No, please, tell me that's not true," Noelle cried

"I'm sorry, but it was on Father's computer," Kenley said.

Milandra put two and two together. "Father's heart attack. That's it! Aniyah must have given it to him."

"I'll strangle her! Father died thinking I had sex with his lawyer behind his back." Noelle screamed. She began to take the rollers out of her hair. She let them fall on the floor like bouncing balls. "I'm going over there and have it out with her."

"You'll do no such thing. Anyone that does something that despicable can do bodily harm to you. Just stay away from her. The important thing is that Kenley got the picture from her."

"Thanks, Kenley. I owe you," Noelle said as she gave her sister a hug.

"Just help me get around Miss Half, so I can still have my sweet sixteen pool party. I don't want to go to the yacht club. Mother is not here for the traditional one."

Noelle smiled. "You'll have the pool party there." She was ready to get even with Aniyah.

"We'll have to show the picture to Mr. Chavis," Kenley said.

"No, we're not going to show him a nude picture of him and Noelle," Milandra said.

Noelle knew this would be the time for her to go to see him. She fluffed her hair with her fingers. "I'm going over to his house tonight. I'll discuss this matter with him."

"Wait, before you go, there's something else," Kenley said.

"Oh God, please don't let it be about me." Noelle wondered what could possibly be next.

"Mother knew Father was having affairs with the help. It's all in her diary. I feel so bad for Mother. She really loved Father. She praised him. She thought it was her duty to take his crap," Kenley said.

"Watch your words," Milandra said. "We'll read for ourselves what Mother really felt."

"I'm going to see Mr. Chavis," Noelle said.

"Call him first," Milandra insisted.

"I will not," Noelle said because she wanted to see him. She ran to her room and slipped on a leisure suit.

"Go to bed, Kenley. Stay away from the estate," Milandra scolded her.

Kenley pouted. "I need to keep going there to keep an eye on Miss Half. The whore changed the locks on the doors."

"I guess she changed it for her safety," Milandra said.

"She doesn't want me coming over there—talking about how she's not a babysitter. She makes me ill."

Milandra became curious and asked, "How did you get into the house?"

"Father shared one of his secret ways of getting in the house."

Milandra laughed. "It's under a patch of grass."

"He told you, too."

"Yes, and Noelle also knows where it is."

"I thought I had my own secret passage."

"Run along. I'm going to sit and read Mother's words."

Chapter 19

Tessa rested in the arms of Baron in his family room. They watched a romantic movie that he had purchased on the way home. She lounged in her bra and panties. His chest was bare, but he wore pajama bottoms.

Baron kissed Tessa on the neck and tickled her nose with his tongue.

"You're supposed to concentrate on the movie," she said as she tried to feed him buttery popcorn.

Baron turned his head away. "The movie is making me hungry for you, not popcorn."

Tessa tossed the popcorn into her mouth. Baron noticed two actors in the scene were making out. He reenacted parts of the romantic scene.

He cupped his hand under her chin to turn her face toward him. He smothered her lips with his. He flicked the television off and got on top of her. Tessa grabbed the remote from him and flicked the television back on.

"Come on, let's make our own movie," he begged.

"I've been waiting to see this movie. I'll make it up to you when it's over." She smiled.

Baron saw that she was absorbed in the last part of the movie.

He sat up and pouted like a kid until the movie was over. He spoke, "When will you go speak to your niece?"

"I'll go see her tomorrow."

He admitted, "I saw her earlier. She's crazy."

"What happened?"

"She threatened me, insisting that if I don't become her man, she'll continue to blackmail me."

"You didn't tell her you knew she wasn't my daughter?"

"No, I wanted to make sure you spoke to her first. I'm trying to see how I'm going to get that picture from her."

"You will," Tessa said as she made her way into his arms.

Noelle made her way out of the house. As usual, when the Houstons called for a ride, the driver was prompt. She ordered him to take her to the home of Baron Chavis.

Peeping down into the envelope at the photo, Noelle wished she had shared a moment of passion with Baron and her father would have thought they were a compatible couple.

What was going through Father's mind the day he saw the picture?

One thing she realized—it took him to his grave. As much as Noelle cared for Baron, she could no longer defy her father—even in his death.

She shed a few tears. The driver looked through his rearview mirror and witnessed her wiping her eyes.

"Everything okay, Miss Houston?" he asked.

"I'm fine. Thanks for asking."

The driver stopped in front of Baron's home. Noelle got out and rang the bell. She saw a glow of dimmed lights in the house.

Inside, the bell startled Baron and Tessa. "Who could that be?"

he wondered. He peeped out of a side window. He prayed it wasn't Aniyah.

Noelle stood on the porch. He knew he had put her off more than she could stand, but to show up at his house, she must be desperate for him.

"It's Noelle Houston."

Tessa picked up the bowl of popcorn. She whispered, "I'll be ready for you when you come to bed."

Baron couldn't wait to get rid of Noelle. He ran and opened the door.

"Elle, what's wrong?"

She wept. "We have trouble."

"Explain!"

Noelle handed him the envelope. He pulled out the photo of them. He calmly said, "Where did you get this?"

Surprised that he showed no signs of excitement, she said, "You act as if you've seen this before."

"I have," Baron acknowledged. "I tried to keep it away from you. I was hoping I could get it and destroy it before you got a hold of it. Where did you get it?"

Noelle made her way to his sofa to have a seat. She saw two glasses on the table. "You have company?" she asked.

"Never mind that. Tell me where you got this."

Noelle explained how her sister was at the estate. Baron was thankful that he had not fallen weak to Aniyah's advances because Kenley would have seen them.

"Now we can rest knowing that the picture is in our hands and not in Aniyah's. She's terrible. You must stay away from her."

"Did you know about Father's encounters with the help?"

"I was aware of it, but it wasn't my place to tell."

"Mother called Aniyah's mother a whore."

Baron wondered if Tessa was eavesdropping on the conversation. Truthfully, she was. She listened from the top of the stairs. She heard Noelle loud and clear.

"Believe me, Noelle, Tessa isn't a whore. I don't want to speak ill of your father. So let's leave it that way."

Noelle was upset. "What I hate more is how Father hurt Mother's heart. And as much as I hate to, I have to hurt your heart." She wept.

He let out a sigh of relief. "What are you saying, Noelle?"

"I can't defy Father. He died because he thought I defied him by being with you—someone he trusted around his family. As much as you have my heart, I can't be with you," she cried.

Baron held out his arms. "I respect that. I'll always be some part of your life because of the closeness I have with your family. Hey, I'll be your big brother." He smiled. "I do understand."

Noelle made her way into his arms. He patted her on the back. Tessa heard their voices become silent for a moment before he spoke.

"I'll get rid of this picture right now." Baron tore the photo up into tiny pieces. He let Noelle out of the front door so that he could go back upstairs to be with Tessa.

"I guess you heard everything," he said.

"Yes, they think of me as a whore, and that's fine. My heart still goes out to those girls," she said.

"In due time, they'll see the light about their father."

To Baron's surprise, Tessa didn't utter another word. He led her into the bedroom. Together they shared the warmth of each other's bodies underneath the covers.

Noelle got to the limo and broke down into tears. She knew from the two glasses that she saw on the table that Baron had company.

She looked up to the second floor of the house as the lights went out. Some woman was getting what she couldn't have.

The driver saw how distraught she was. He walked over to her. "Miss Houston, let me take you home."

He took her by the hand and helped her into the limo. She leaned against the window and looked out into the darkness of the night. The driver handed her a tissue.

"Thank you," she said.

The driver looked through his rearview mirror. "Miss Houston, the pain will get easier in due time. I think I know what you need."

Instead of driving her to the Houston Villa, he drove her to the Houston Estate. Noelle looked up to see that she was on the grounds of her once happy home. The driver drove her to the far end of the acreage of land. He got out of the limo and opened the door for her.

"Come on, I think you need to get in touch with the calmness of the lake."

He held his hand to her and helped her out of the limo. Noelle stepped out.

"Yes. My mother always loved coming to this end of the estate. This is where she came for peace."

Noelle walked closer to the lake. She looked out to see tiny flickering lights coming from the homes across the lake. Far away, a light glowed from atop a docked boat. She took a deep breath. "Oh, how tranquil the water looks. It makes you feel you can conquer all the worries of the world."

"Yes and when you stand still and be quiet, you can hear the water talking to you."

Noelle smiled. "Mother used to say the exact same thing."

"Your mother is the one who told me that." He smiled.

Shocked, she said, "How marvelous she shared her words with you."

They both stood in silence. Noelle closed her eyes as she listened to nature. She took plenty of deep breaths, and then she folded her arms because of the breeze coming off the water.

The driver took his suit jacket off. "Here, take my jacket and put it around you."

"Thanks, what is your name?"

"It's Sid."

"You have been working for my family a long time."

"Yes, I wouldn't trade this job in for anything. I enjoy watching elegant ladies."

"Thanks for your kind words. I'm feeling better already."

Noelle moved and the jacket fell from her shoulders onto the ground. She picked it up and brushed grass and dirt from it. "I apologize; I'll have your jacket cleaned."

"It's fine. No harm done."

He took the jacket from her and tossed it back around her shoulders. She turned to face him. His hazel eyes were like stars in the sky to her. That moment felt so romantic to her. Tears rolled down her cheeks from the thought of how much time she had missed from having companionship with a man.

"Don't start crying again, Miss Houston."

"Call me, Noelle."

"Noelle it is," he said as he tilted his hat.

She took his hand and rested it on her face. She kissed the palm of his hand. Sid, the driver, stood his ground. He had to be cautious at what moves he made. His job was on the line.

"What's this all about?" he asked.

"It's my way of saying thank you for being a gentleman. Just this simple thing you've done for me tonight makes me so grateful."

Noelle took it another step, making Sid feel uncomfortable. She reached up and hugged him. Sid kept his hands at his side.

"Don't be afraid to hold me," Noelle said. "I give you permission."

Sid held her in his arms. His jacket fell off her shoulders again and he warmed her up with his muscular chest.

Noelle rested her head on his shoulders. She began to sing an unfamiliar tune to him, moving gradually to her own beat. He saw that she wanted to dance so he rocked from side to side while she hummed.

She stopped and looked up at him. "Kiss me," she whispered.

Sid brushed his hands through her curls. "As much as I want to, I can't at this time. I didn't bring you out here to seduce you during your weakest moment. I don't want you to do anything tonight that you'll feel ashamed of in the morning."

"I will not have any regrets," she whispered. "Are you married?"

She realized that she had forgotten to ask him his marital status.

"I'm single."

"I'm free as a bird myself." She smiled.

"I would love to get to know you."

She patted him on the cheek. "A gentleman you are."

He took her by the hand. "Let's walk along the lake and talk."

They walked part of the lake before they removed their shoes and played in the water. They threw rocks into the water. Her night had turned into a date.

Sid told her how he worked long hours for the Houston Estate because he was single. He was not like the typical guy who hung out in clubs or bars. He wanted a woman of substance.

They made their way back to the limo. Sid drove her away from the estate and back to the Houston Villa. He opened the limo door and she stepped out.

"Thanks for a lovely time," she said graciously.

"I enjoyed your company as well. I don't have a lot of money, but I'd sure like to take you out for a bite to eat."

"It doesn't take money to have a nice date. Tonight was free. I had a marvelous time. You know, you were right. Tomorrow I probably would have felt terrible about making love with you just to soothe my pain."

"I'm not going to say I didn't want to make out with you. I sure did, but I want it to be when you're ready. I hope we get to that point someday," he said bravely.

Sid caressed her hand and said goodnight. Noelle went into the house. She watched out of the window as he drove off. She marveled over the fact that he had lots of communication with her mother. She felt her mother had given him tips on how to handle a woman. But Alana did not know that the tips would become helpful to use on her daughter.

Chapter 20

Tessa took Baron up on his offer and used one of the Houstons' drivers to escort her to the estate. She waited until the servants left before she went to see Aniyah. She was ready to confront her niece. She rang the bell several times before Aniyah made her way down the stairs.

Aniyah opened the door to see her aunt. She wished she had peeped out the door—she would not have answered it.

Tessa saw that Aniyah had grown up. No longer did her niece wear the long floral skirts she and her mother had made for her.

Aniyah was dressed in a turquoise spandex dress. She was masked with makeup and big, hoop earrings hung from her ears.

Aniyah was amazed at how her aunt had matured with age. She saw that she still wore the simple floral skirts that she hated wearing as a teenager.

"Tessa!" she hollered.

"Rosie, my troubled niece," Tessa said as she reached out and hugged her. Aniyah, in her own way, was happy to see family.

"What are you doing here, Tessa?"

"Stop calling me by my first name as if I'm your friend. I've always been your Aunt Tessa. Today is no different. But, I guess it's a different time to you because you have everyone here thinking you're my daughter. How can you run away from home and take the life of your dead cousin?"

"Come in, Tess…Aunt Tessa, I can explain. This is all for us—the Sanchez family."

Tessa entered the house. She recognized that the odor in the house was nothing like the Houston Estate used to smell.

"Let's go into the kitchen," Aniyah suggested.

Tessa followed behind her. She watched Aniyah's rear. The dress fell just below her bottom and it clung to her hips. "Rosie, how can you wear such clothing? It doesn't suit a young lady."

"Hush!" Aniyah yelled as she placed her right index finger over her lips. "Stop calling me, Rosie. It's Aniyah to everyone here."

"You must take back your own name."

"It is my name. It's my middle name."

"You know what I mean. Use your first name, Rosie. My Aniyah would have never dressed in such a way if she had lived."

"This is the style I like. I'm not an old lady like you."

Tessa sat at the kitchen table. She recalled making many meals for the Houstons. She placed her purse on her lap.

"Please explain." She waited to hear her niece's side of the story.

"Aunt Tessa, Mr. Houston was a cruel man. I read your diary. He raped you. He got you pregnant and did away with you like you had a disease. It's his fault you lost your baby. Can't you see I'm doing this for you and the family? The Sanchezes can now live good like the Houstons."

"Nonsense! The Sanchezes may not have lots of money, but we have respect for the people that we are. Never would we take from others to suit our own needs. You must give this all back."

Aniyah poured a glass of water. "You want something to drink?"

Aniyah knew they needed cooling down.

"Not at all."

"Aunt Tessa, no way I'll give all this back. Everyone thinks I'm his daughter and let's keep it that way. You have to go along with it. We can bring my mother here from Mexico. She doesn't have to work at all."

Tessa stood up and went over to Aniyah at the sink. She yanked her by the arm. "Are you not a Sanchez? I can't take from others. Your mother would be heartbroken if she knew this. I won't allow you to do this to those girls. For God's sake, Rosie, they lost their parents. I know what it is to lose someone close to you. I lost my baby."

"You got over it, and so will them uppity broads."

"Please, have a heart. Give back what's rightfully theirs."

Aniyah jerked away. "I'm not giving up any of this." She walked to the other side of the kitchen near the pantry. "Maybe I'm my father's child—the man whose name my mama doesn't even know," she said. "I can't even begin to look for him because she doesn't have any idea how he looks. He was a stray cat who was hungry for milk. The milk satisfied him, and then he left me to be born with no father. All I had was a mama and an aunt who only showed me how to kiss up and be a slave for others. I never could be around boys because you and Mama were so protective of me. I wasn't happy with my life, so I ran away."

"We didn't want you to have to go through the same things we went through," Tessa said tearfully.

"It's too late. The man I left Mexico with treated me like trash. He made me what I am today."

Aniyah pulled her dress off. She stood nude in front of her aunt. "This is how I made my living—letting men touch me in places I didn't want to at first. But this is my tool for survival."

Tessa picked up her dress. "Put it back on. You don't have to be this way. You're a pretty girl. You can find the right man, settle down, and have a happy family."

Aniyah laughed as she slipped her dress back on. "I'm not being a housewife who sits at home and makes babies while my man goes out to wine and dine others. That's how Rupert was."

Tessa wondered about something. "You call him by his first name as if you know him well. How do you know so much about Mr. Houston?"

"I was introduced to him. I was his escort when he came to Georgia."

Tessa began to learn about how her niece lived. "Oh, Rosie," she said as she sat back down in the chair and shook her head in disbelief.

"I didn't know who he was at first. I did my job as a woman. He paid me well."

"How could you degrade yourself?"

Aniyah yelled in her aunt's ear, "I had to survive. I had to find money so that I could bring back to Mexico for you and Mama."

Her aunt jumped up and shook her. "We had jobs, Rosie Aniyah. All we wanted was for you to be a happy girl."

"Watching you guys struggle is not a happy life." Aniyah pulled away from her.

"How do you go from sleeping with Mr. Houston to being his daughter?"

"Once I found out who he was, I decided to make him pay. He moved me here. I lived where his uppity daughters live now. The Houston Villa was our love nest. I fed him his nightly meals and I got paid dearly until he decided to replace me with someone else. That's when revenge came into my heart. I told him that I was his daughter while we were in the sack. I also showed him a made-up picture of his cutie lawyer and daughter making out. I guess the man's heart couldn't take it. It sent him to his grave."

"You were with him when this happened?"

"No, I wasn't. The stress got to the bastard."

Tessa decided to ask about Baron while she was telling all. "Why would you be cruel to his lawyer?"

"I needed something on him to make sure I was taken care of." Aniyah laughed. "Damn, the man is good in bed."

Tessa wanted to agree with her, but she said nothing about her relationship with Baron.

Aniyah smirked. "He has a crush on you. I took care of him for you."

"Rosie, I pray for you."

"Aunt Tessa, I don't need your help. I live well now and so can you. We can live in this house. We can have the world."

"I beg you to do what's right. You can go to jail."

"I won't, if you keep your mouth shut."

As she got up to walk out, Tessa said, "Sorry, but I can't do that."

Aniyah walked over to a drawer and took out a switchblade. She wasn't about to let her aunt spoil her new life.

"You win, Aunt Tessa," she wept. "I'll give back everything and go home to see Mama. I do miss her."

Tessa looked back at her niece. "I'm happy that you have come to your senses. It's for the best."

"Aunt Tessa, please help me pack," she begged. "I'll leave with you."

Tessa started to go and hug her niece. But Aniyah thought quickly "Please, don't come near me. It will only make me cry more."

"All right, let's get your things."

Tessa led the way upstairs. "What room have you called your own?"

"I'm in the guest bedroom. But I want to show you something in Mr. Houston's office that he kept on you."

Tessa was anxious to see what souvenir Rupert cherished about her. She made her way into the office.

Aniyah held tight to the blade. Once her aunt stepped into the office, she rushed and grabbed her from behind.

Holding Tessa's left arm from behind her back, Aniyah flicked the blade to release the knife. She held the knife to her aunt's throat.

"Don't say a thing or I'll cut you," Aniyah threatened.

Tessa trembled as she kept her mouth shut. She realized that the person who held her wasn't the girl in Mexico who she helped raise.

Aniyah pulled her to a chair. She pushed her down in the seat. "Don't move," she ordered.

Tessa watched as she rummaged through drawers, but she didn't seem to find what she was looking for.

Tessa saw that her niece was somewhat concentrating on finding something in the closet. She jumped out of the seat and tried to make a run for it, but Aniyah caught up to her.

She snatched her aunt by the hair until she fell on the floor. She dragged her back into the study near the entrance of the closet that she was previously looking in.

Tessa screamed from pain. Her head throbbed from the hair-pulling.

Aniyah spotted a roll of twine. "Sit up," she said, pointing the knife in her aunt's face. "Put your hands together in front of you."

"I'm your mother's sister. I beg you, please don't do this to family."

"How can you sit here and tell me about family when you want to destroy my future? You'd rather save your dead baby's daddy's family than your own. Forget you."

Aniyah tied her aunt's hands in a tight knot. "Put your damn feet close together," she demanded as she wrapped the twine around her aunt's ankles and knotted it.

"You have disgraced the family." Tessa cried.

"Remember, I have no family, so shut the hell up."

"Please, Rosie, don't do this."

Aniyah slapped her aunt across the face. "It's Aniyah to you."

"No, my beautiful Aniyah died a long time ago."

Her words didn't faze Aniyah. Her niece figured that no one would be looking for her aunt. Everyone would assume that she went back to Mexico.

Aniyah found some masking tape. Tessa gagged as she tried to cough while her mouth was being taped.

Aniyah opened another closet that had been emptied out by the Houstons. She put her arms under her aunt's underarms and dragged her across the room into the closet. Tessa shook her head as she mumbled, "No."

Then Aniyah went into the bedroom and cut open the seams of a pillowcase. She cut a long strip. Tessa watched her come back in the closet, praying that maybe she realized she made a mistake.

Aniyah tied the pillowcase strip around her aunt's mouth to add reinforcement. "There, that should do it."

Aniyah sat down in the office chair and closed the knife back into the blade. She wrote on a sheet of paper. "Do not enter this room or you'll be fired."

Aniyah looked over at her aunt sitting inside the closet. "See, all you had to do was enjoy all of this with me. We could be shopping and having fun, but no, you care more about the uppity broads than you do your own. You'll rot in that closet."

Aniyah got up and taped the note on the outside of the door.

Exhausted and in pain, Tessa prayed that Baron would not think that she decided to go back to Mexico.

Chapter 21

The sweat ran down Milandra's face as she played a tennis match with Nolan. He had persuaded her to play a game of tennis with him in exchange for paying for the services he rendered on the property. It was down to the last point. Milandra served the ball. Nolan hit it back across the net. She ran down the court and hit the ball back to him. The ball landed on the opposite side from where Nolan stood. He tried to run and catch up to the ball as it bounced on the court, but he missed it.

"I won!" she celebrated with excitement.

"You're a pretty good player. I want a rematch."

"Do I sense that you hate losing?" She smiled.

"It's okay as long as it's to a pretty lady. I can't complain. I do think your long legs distracted me."

"Excuses, I see."

They walked off the court over to a cooler with ice-cold water in it. They hurried to satisfy their thirst. They took long swallows from their water bottles.

"This is so refreshing," Milandra said.

"Hits the spot," he said.

"Let's go inside and have lunch. Elsa came over to prepare a fruit salad and sandwiches for us. She has probably already set the table."

Nolan rolled the cooler near the entrance of the house for her.

"Don't bother to bring it inside; the cooler can stay there. One of the help will take care of it."

Nolan followed her into the house. "I need to use the john."

"Who's John?" she questioned.

Nolan laughed. "I'm referring to the bathroom."

"Sorry, not up much on slang talk. You know where the bathroom is. You're welcome to use it."

Nolan went to handle his business while Milandra went to freshen up.

Nolan found his way out to the sunroom to see that the table had been set with a bowl of fruit salad, fresh squeezed lemonade, and all the trimmings to make a sandwich.

Upon Milandra's arrival into the sunroom, Nolan pulled the chair out for her. She sat down and he pushed her chair in. He opened her napkin and placed it on her lap. The cool, refreshing air from the central air unit cooled them off.

"This is a fantastic view of the lake," he said as he looked out of the picture window.

"I would agree. It's not as bad a view as I thought it would be. You should see the view from the estate. It's so breathtaking and it's so serene."

Nolan took a bite out of a slice of watermelon. "Maybe one day I'll get to see the view with you."

Milandra didn't answer him; she smiled as she wet her throat with lemonade.

"I'm surprised, no iced tea today?"

"We change up at times. Freshly squeezed lemonade is also one of our favorites."

Nolan took a sip of his lemonade. He grabbed two slices of wheat bread from the plate in front of him. Spreading mustard onto the bread, he layered it with pastrami, tomatoes, Swiss cheese, and romaine lettuce. He took a bite out of it while Milandra ate fruit.

"You're not up on sandwiches?" he asked.

"Oh yes," she said as she reached for the bread.

"Let me." Nolan took her plate and placed the bread on it. "Mustard?"

"Yes, a little."

Nolan pointed to each item. "Pastrami? Tomatoes?"

"No tomatoes—only cheese and lettuce."

Nolan finished and placed the plate back in front of her. Milandra cut the sandwich in half. He watched as she ate her sandwich with proper etiquette.

Milandra never leaned forward to go after her sandwich the way he did. She brought her food to her mouth. He loved her sophisticated manners.

"Do you have plans for the rest of the day?" he wondered.

"My day is clear."

"Great, how about you and I go for a swim?" he asked as his eyes fixated on the waterfall in the pool. "Today is hot enough for a swim."

Milandra thought about how she had never been seen in a bathing suit by a man, except for the pool repairman or the male servants. But a swim would surely cool her off from the heat that her body felt from the attraction she had to Nolan.

"I…" she said, her words trailed off.

"Would love to," he finished her sentence.

"Tell me, you don't have swimming trunks with you, do you?"

"I might be wearing them." He chuckled.

Milandra didn't remember seeing any signs of trunks showing through the white shorts he wore during their game of tennis.

"It wouldn't surprise me if you do. You seem to stay prepared."

Nolan laughed. "Girl, I'm playing with you. It'll take me thirty minutes to run and get my swimming trunks and a towel."

"No need to bring a towel. There are plenty in the pool's linen closet."

Nolan patted his stomach. "This will give our bellies time to settle down."

He ran off to get his swimwear. Milandra went to get her bathing suit. Going through the assortment of suits hanging in her closet, she decided on a black, one-piece bathing suit. She wrapped herself in a white cover-up. Milandra pulled her hair up and twisted it into a ball.

Nolan returned faster than expected with a Wal-Mart plastic bag in his hand. "I'm back," he said as he entered the house.

Milandra appeared in her bathing suit. Nolan admired the curves she hid behind her clothing.

She noticed his bag. "Walmart?"

"Oh yeah! I saw one on the way home. I thought, what the heck, Why go home when I can get one there?"

"I'll meet you at the pool."

Milandra made her way out of the house. Nolan hurried to change into his trunks.

Milandra looked up to see nothing but muscles popping out from his arms down to his legs as Nolan walked out into the pool area with his trunks on. Nolan watched as she feasted her eyes on him. He spun around. "You like my trunks?" he asked.

"Very vibrant!"

"I thought I would help brighten up your day."

Nolan made her laugh as he looked into her eyes and became blind by the sparkle in them.

"Stop teasing me." Milandra sat down on a lounging chair.

Nolan snuck a peek down her low-cut bathing suit before he sat down on one of the rows of loungers next to her. "Do you mind rubbing suntan lotion on my back? I don't want to burn," he said as he held a bottle in his hand.

Milandra's eyes lit up. She couldn't believe that he actually wanted her to rub it on him.

"Lost for words?" Nolan queried as he awaited her answer.

Milandra took the lotion out of his hand. "Turn around."

Nolan turned his back to her. She poured the suntan lotion into her hand and gently rubbed it into his muscles. She tried to show no signs of nervousness, but her hands trembled.

"Don't forget to apply some around my spine." He pointed to his back.

Milandra moved down to the top of his trunks. Nolan was tickled because he could tell that she was hesitant about coming in contact with him. She finished and handed him back the lotion.

Milandra lay back down on her lounger.

Nolan went on to apply the lotion on the front part of his body. He made conversation with her as he massaged the lotion on his chest. "Would you like some lotion?"

"Not at this time."

"Girl, it's hot out here. You know you need suntan lotion on you. You scared for me to put my hands on you?"

Nolan stood up and applied lotion to his legs. He massaged his inner thigh. Milandra began to have tingling feelings in her private parts. She would melt in the heat if he touched her the way he was applying the suntan lotion to himself. She didn't want him to notice that he was turning her on.

"Don't flatter yourself," she said.

"Girl, turn over on your back. I'll be real quick."

"You're so persistent."

Milandra saw a lot of her ways in him. Nolan sat on the edge of the lounger that she laid on and applied lotion to the back of her neck. He took both hands and massaged her neck and shoulders. He slid his hand under her bathing suit straps and applied the lotion.

She closed her eyes as her skin absorbed his strong hands. Her body ached for him. But that was forbidden.

Nolan poured more suntan lotion into his hands. He started at her feet and worked the lotion into her skin all the way up her legs, making sure that he did not accidentally slide his hands past her thighs. Milandra felt like he was her masseur.

Nolan patted her on the back of her leg. "I'm done."

Milandra was too weak from his touch to move. She whispered, "Thank you."

Nolan went back to his lounger. He looked over at her as he watched her take her time turning back over. He could tell that with a little more work she would release the roaring lioness that was hidden within her.

They lay back on the loungers and chatted for a while.

Nolan was ready for a dive. He got up. "I don't know about you, but I'm ready to take a swim."

Nolan ran toward the pool and dived in. Milandra watched as the water glistened like crystals on his body. He swam like a professional swimmer before he swam back over to the edge of the pool where she was. "What are you waiting for? Come join me," he said as he wiped the water that drenched his face.

Milandra got up and dived in. She swam around the pool.

"You're like a swan."

Nolan swam over to her. Together they swam all over the pool.

Milandra went over to the edge of the pool that was farthest away. She cleared her ears and eyes of water. Nolan joined her. He admired her breasts through the wet fabric.

"You're a great swimmer."

"Thanks," she said. "I've been swimming since I was born. My parents taught us girls to swim before they taught us to walk. How about you? You swim very well."

"My adoptive parents put me into swimming when I was seven years old."

"You say adoptive. You don't know your real parents?"

"No. My mother was on drugs. She left me with her best friend when I was born."

Milandra couldn't imagine not knowing her parents.

"It must be difficult, at times, to deal with not knowing who your parents are."

Nolan began to see the compassionate side of her. "Having *good* adoptive parents all my life, it never bothered me. They're the only parents I know."

"I can see they did a great job with you," Milandra said. She left him and started swimming.

Nolan followed and swam behind her. They completed two laps before they stopped again. Milandra stopped in a corner of the pool and Nolan blocked her in. He took his hands and wiped the water from her face. She felt more heat from him than from the sunrays.

He leaned forward and kissed her on the lips. Milandra froze. "I'm sorry if I'm out of bounds, but I'm so attracted to you that it's making me sick," he said as he kissed her again. "Don't tell me you're not sick for me, too."

"This is all new to me," she admitted.

"You have the best teacher. Let me help you through this journey."

Nolan took her into his arms and kissed her passionately. Milandra felt so weak from the kiss that she thought she was going to drown; Nolan held her up. He cupped his hands under her butt. Milandra panicked and swam to the steps of the pool and got out. She went over and sat in the Jacuzzi.

"I'm sorry if I was out of line," he called as he swam over to the steps of the pool and got out. He went over to the Jacuzzi. "Are you okay?"

"I'm fine. It's just that I'm not a loose woman."

Nolan eased into the Jacuzzi and sat on the opposite side of Milandra. "I'll talk to you from here. I know you're not a wild lady. I didn't mean to make you feel uncomfortable. Do you forgive me?" he asked as he reached out his hand to shake hers.

Milandra held her hand out and shook his.

"I apologize if I overreacted."

"No need to apologize. I'm attracted to you. I believe you're attracted to me but don't know how to handle it."

Milandra couldn't hold back her emotions. Her eyes became tearful. "Can we discuss something else?"

Nolan reached and turned the Jacuzzi on. Masses of bubbles began to form. He moved closer to her, held her hands, and stared into her eyes. "I'm yours whenever you decide you're ready for me," he said as he kissed her on the lips. Milandra kissed him back.

Nolan let go of her hand, got out of the Jacuzzi, and dove back into the pool. "What are you waiting for? Come join me," he said.

Milandra made her way to the pool.

Chapter 22

In the courtroom, Baron sat across from an employee trying to sue Houston Commercial Construction Company. Baron hoped the jury would be sympathetic because of the death of Rupert and render a verdict in favor of the company. The employee alleged that bricks had fallen on his cast-covered foot.

Baron argued that the employee had stolen bricks from the company and the incident had actually occurred at his home.

The jury returned from deliberation. The court officer called the court to order.

"Mr. Foreman, has the jury reached a verdict?" the judge inquired.

"Yes, Your Honor," the foreman responded.

"How does the jury find the defendant?" the judge asked.

"Not guilty."

"I have another win under my belt. Am I good or what?" Baron mumbled to himself.

The plaintiff's attorney looked over at him. As usual, his opponent was furious. Talk amongst the attorneys around the courthouse was that Rupert had the judges on his payroll, but there was no concrete evidence to prove it. In reality, they were wrong; Baron really was a good attorney.

Baron packed his briefcase and closed it. He walked over and shook the opposing attorney's hand as a symbol of professional courtesy, but he really wanted to smear another victory for Houston Commercial Construction Company in his face.

Hurrying out of the building, Baron made his way to his car. He tossed his briefcase in the backseat and got in. His stomach growled. Baron was hungry and he was sure that Tessa had cooked up a storm for him, but his first stop would be to pick up a dozen roses for his love.

At the florist's shop, he handpicked individual long-stemmed roses. He made sure that each rose was firm and unbloomed. The florist laid them down in a long white box that was wrapped with a gold ribbon.

He thanked the florist, left, and made one and more stop at a store that exclusively sold wine. He started to buy Tessa one of the finest wines in the store, instead he purchased one that he knew she loved—a bottle of plain old Sangria.

When he arrived at the house, he expected to open the door and get hit by the aroma from Tessa's fabulous cooking. Instead, the house smelled like peach air freshener.

"Tessa," he called as he went to the kitchen and placed the wine and roses on the table. The kitchen was spotless. The only pot on the stove was a teakettle.

Baron left the kitchen and he ran up the stairs. "Tessa," he called her again.

He looked into the backyard, calling her name, but there was no answer. *Tessa must be speaking to her niece.* He figured Tessa would come back and bring food for them.

After hours had gone by and night fell, Tessa never returned. Baron tried her cell phone several times, but all he got was her voicemail. He went on to make himself a sandwich from leftover chicken.

Tempted to call Aniyah, he grabbed his keys and left the house instead. He jumped into his car and drove over to the Houston Estate.

It was around midnight when he reached the estate. Baron rang the bell.

Aniyah came to the door dressed in a red bra and panty set. She was excited to see him. "Hey, sugar, you came to see me."

Baron didn't want to ask her about her aunt. "I was in the area and was checking things out before I went home."

Aniyah laughed. "Yeah right!" She pushed up her breasts with her hands. "You want this."

He decided to use his lawyer skills on her. "Do you have company?"

"Hell yeah, you now." She grabbed his tie and yanked it for him to come inside.

He followed her into the house, which would give him the opportunity to look around.

Aniyah put her arms around him and kissed him. He pushed her off.

"Stop it!" he said.

"You'll do what I say. Don't forget, I have the picture," she reminded him.

He laughed. "Not anymore, I've destroyed it."

She laughed back. "No, you didn't. You're bluffing."

Baron stepped closer up on her and looked directly into her eyes. "Do I look like I'm bluffing?"

Aniyah saw that he might be telling the truth. She hadn't checked her hiding place where the photo was supposed to be secure, so she left him and ran up the stairs.

Baron looked around as much as he could while on the first floor. He ran up the stairs and looked in the west wing. There were no signs that Tessa had been there. He headed to the east wing when Aniyah showed up furious.

She ran up to him, beating him on the chest. "You bastard, you found the picture. Give it back to me."

Baron shoved her off of him with force. Aniyah fell to the floor.

"I'm not giving you anything back. You had no right to twist things around for your own nasty reasons."

"Whoever's in the room, she's nothing but a slut!" he yelled, assuming she was entertaining a man.

In the office closet, Tessa tried to make noise. She could hear his voice. *Baron has come for me.* She prayed that her niece wouldn't harm him in anyway.

Aniyah got up. "Get out of here."

He yelled back, "I will! I can't believe you're nothing like your mother."

Baron thought that he would bring Tessa's name up, hoping Aniyah would give him a sign as to whether her aunt had been there or not.

Aniyah kept a straight face and said nothing about Tessa being there.

"That's why you don't want me. You love her! Well, she doesn't give a damn about you. She loved Rupert. She always said he was hot in bed," she lied.

He walked down the stairs to get out of the house. Tessa listened as the sound of the arguing faded away.

"I feel sorry for you."

"Go back to what you do best and be a yes-person for the Houstons. Just leave me the hell alone."

Baron slammed the door behind him. He still wondered where Tessa was. He went over to the servants' quarters and woke Elsa. She came to the door covered in a long robe with her hair tied up.

"Hello, Mr. Chavis. Something wrong?"

"Have you seen Tessa today?"

"No, I haven't."

"If she calls you, tell her to get in touch with me."

"Yes, Mr. Chavis."

"Elsa, don't tell anyone I was looking for her. Keep that between us."

"My lips are glued."

Baron called the limo service. He asked for the driver who had driven Tessa. The driver lied as he was instructed by Aniyah. "Miss Sanchez asked me to get her to the airport as fast as I could. I dropped her off and left."

Baron felt his stomach tighten up. His gut feeling was that something wasn't right. But he hurried home in hope that Tessa would be there.

He arrived home and there were no signs of Tessa. He glanced inside the closet. Her belongings were still intact, including her empty suitcase. But he used his connections as an attorney and learned that she did not take a flight back to Mexico. "Where are you, Tessa?" he whispered as he lay across the bed. He prayed that Aniyah wasn't holding something over Tessa's head that would cause her to run.

He realized that maybe the driver was lying and was following Aniyah's instructions. The Houston Estate was too enormous to check, but he had to find a way to search it for answers. He worried that Tessa was in trouble. The answers were with Aniyah. He tried to stay awake but could no longer keep his eyes open.

Aniyah ran back upstairs and into the office. She opened the door, went inside the closet, and slapped her aunt across the face. "No food for you tomorrow. You'll starve."

Tessa tried to talk but could not.

"Shut up! I don't see what Baron sees in you. He's hungry for you, but guess what? He had me and he liked all of this." Aniyah rubbed her hands over her body. "He took me for himself in his house. How do you like that?"

Aniyah knew that her aunt could not answer. She laughed at her and left the room, closing the door behind her.

Tessa tried to cry but she had already cried so much that her tears were frozen. She prayed that maybe tomorrow God would send an angel to save her.

Chapter 23

Sid picked Noelle up early that morning. She came out of the house wearing a simple baby-blue zip-up dress. He opened the door for her. "Good morning," he said.

"Morning, Sid, how are you?"

"Doing better now that I have such a lovely lady in my car."

Sid had become her permanent driver. He took Noelle to whatever destination she wanted. He thought that she was the sexiest woman he had ever seen. Today, she wanted to go shopping. He took her to a few shops, which included a party shop to purchase the necessary supplies for Kenley's sixteenth birthday. Lunchtime came soon after.

"Hungry?" Sid asked.

"Yes, I guess I've shopped up an appetite."

"I have a great lunch for us."

"Where did you get lunch from?"

"I had it packed just for you."

"Thanks, Sid."

Noelle thought that he was the perfect gentleman. He looked after her in every way while he was her chauffeur.

"So, let's see, where will we eat?"

"How about under a nice, big tree at the Houston Estate?"

"I don't think we should go back to the estate. It really belongs to Aniyah."

"The estate is so big, she would never know we were there. We'll go to the far end like we did before."

"I do love the grounds of the estate."

"See, it's perfect." He smiled.

First, Sid stopped to get some ice from the store and then drove Noelle to the estate. The security guard opened the gates for him.

Driving way out on the acreage to find a private spot, Sid parked the limo near a shaded tree to help block the hot sun. He turned on some soft music from the stereo in the limo. He took the lunch basket and carried it under the tree.

Noelle watched as he removed a large plaid blanket and spread it out on the grass. She eased down onto the blanket, pulling her dress down because she was too shy to expose her thighs to him.

The shade from underneath the tree cooled them off somewhat. Sid placed a sandwich on each one of their plates.

"You're always surprising me." Noelle smiled.

"I love your company."

"I enjoy yours, too."

Noelle looked forward to him picking her up every time she had to go somewhere. There was something about Sid that made her forget about Baron. She wondered if it was because he showed her so much attention.

Sid filled two crystal glasses with ice and poured tea into them. He added a small salad to their plates. He brought her favorite salad dressing—Italian. They also had potato chips to munch on.

"Lunch is delicious," she said as she took a sip of the tea. Her eyes sparkled as she glared into his eyes.

"My pleasure."

Sid watched as Noelle ate her food; she thought he looked cute in his work cap.

"Do you ever take that hat off?"

The limo driver realized that he still had his black work cap on. He took it off to show off his freshly cut hair. "I wear it so much I forget it's on my head."

Noelle smiled. "You look good without it."

Sid felt that she was flirting with him, so he flirted back. "Anyone ever told you that you have sweet-looking lips?"

Noelle touched her lips and blushed. She lowered her head as her cheeks turned rosy. "Never."

"I think you do."

"Well, all I can say is thanks."

When they finished eating, Sid gathered up the picnic items. Noelle tried to help.

"Stay seated. I'll clean this up." He hurried to gather everything while Noelle watched as he put the items into the limo.

Sid sat back down next to her. "It's so pretty on your family's land."

"Yes, I always loved the crystal blue waters. You can see it from everywhere," Noelle said, but became excited and stood up. "Look!" She pointed to a group of ducks flapping their wings in a small pond.

Sid jumped up to get a clear view of the ducks. But he became distracted when he spotted a group of sailboats. "I've got an idea," he said excitedly. "We can go for a ride out on the boat. I drove your father many times out on the lake in his boat when he just wanted to sit back and relax."

"Father must have really liked you. I never knew him to let anyone sail for him." Noelle smiled, feeling a connection with Sid through her father.

"How about it? I can take you for a spin out on the lake."

Noelle agreed. It had been a long time since she had taken a boat ride. "I don't know where Father's keys are."

Sid smiled. "It's a secret, but he gave me a key. He told me I could take it out; all I had to do was ask him beforehand, but I never did. I didn't want to take advantage of him. I enjoyed when we went out on the boat together. Mr. Houston took me fishing with him several times."

Noelle felt good hearing something positive about her father. She saw that Sid enjoyed her father's company.

"We'll go out on the boat later. I have a few runs to make for Mr. Chavis, then I'll be back."

They packed up and left.

Sid made his way back just as it got dark. He drove up in front of the Houston Villa. Noelle came out.

"Are you ready for the boat ride?"

"You want to go out *now?*" she asked.

"If you're scared to go out on the water at night, we can wait and go during the day."

"I'm not, but I thought maybe you'd be too tired from work. We can do it another time."

Sid wanted her company. "The water is what I need. Let's go," he said, knowing the soothing water was where he felt he could be at ease and open with her.

"Give me a minute to change," she said, still in her dress.

Noelle changed into a white shorts set; Sid sported a khaki shorts set. Her eyes wandered to the bulge in his pants and, immediately, she felt a warm, tingling sensation between her legs. Suddenly, Sid grabbed her by the hand, distracting her from the sexual tension that was mounting inside her.

They chatted as they drove to the boat. Once they arrived, he fired up the engine and sailed away as the stars twinkled in the sky. Noelle thought that it was so romantic, and she hoped that Sid felt the same way that she did.

"It's lovely out here at night."

"The deep orange moon among the stars is breathtaking," Noelle said as she looked up at the sky.

"Are you thirsty? There are drinks in the fridge."

Noelle went and got a bottle of water out of the refrigerator. She saw it was fully stocked with drinks, fruits, and cold cuts.

She went back to confront him. "I think this is what took you so long to come back. You were preparing the boat for our sail."

"Oh yeah?" He smiled. "We even have good old bologna sandwiches and chips."

"What am I going to do with you?" she asked as she felt loved and protected by Sid's caring ways.

"All I ask is for your company whenever you can spare time."

Sid drove over to a far end of the lake where there were no homes. He docked the boat and turned on some soft music. He reached out and asked, "Miss Houston, would you care to dance?"

Noelle, without hesitation, went to him. Sid put his arms around her and they danced until the music stopped. He looked into her eyes. Noelle looked back at him. She was attracted to him, and she wasn't going to be the way she was with Baron—sitting around waiting to see when he was going to make a move.

She put her arms around Sid. "Please, don't push me away again."

"Not this time. I feel we have gotten to know each other in our own way."

Noelle smiled as she locked lips with him. His lips felt soothing to her and she thrust her tongue into his mouth.

Sid took what she had to give him and in return, tongued her back.

Noelle stepped back. She pulled her top over her head, messing up her hair. She sported a white, laced bra.

Unhooking her bra from behind, she exposed a set of breasts the size of coconuts. He admired the abundance.

Noelle pulled down her shorts to expose her white, lace panties, then she reached up and removed his shirt.

He touched her breasts as she unclothed him.

Noelle ran her fingers down his chest, a chest rippled with muscles. She pulled him by the hand to follow her off the boat.

Sid drooled over her curvy hips as they made their way over to an oak tree.

They felt the warm night air against their bodies.

Noelle turned around, swung her arms around him, and kissed him again with all her might. "Love me," she whispered. "Show me what making love is all about."

"This is your first time?"

"I'm afraid so," she said embarrassed. "But I'm ready as ever to become a true woman."

She slipped her panties off; Sid followed, stepping out of his boxers. His erect, protruding manhood caught her attention. Noelle got down on the ground, resting her back on the green grass.

Sid got down on his knees and crawled on top of her, letting his groin rub against her.

Noelle longed to have a man touched her forbidden zone. Moisture built up between her legs and she reached for his manhood, nervous, yet, longing for him to enter her.

"Hold up, baby." Sid ran and got a condom out of the boat. He came back and put it on.

"I know you know what this is."

"Of course I do. Men use it to keep a girl from getting pregnant."

"Yeah, that's one reason."

Sid lay back on top of her and pushed his hardened groin inside her. He stroked her gently, letting her first time be of comfort.

Noelle let out a loud moaned that echoed into the midnight air.

He kissed her with passion and licked her like she was a lollipop.

She felt tingling sensations in her breasts. Sid pressed all the way down on her. He held her arms above her head.

Noelle kept her lips locked to his to keep from screaming. The pleasure of his body outweighed the pain.

Sid knew how to drive and she enjoyed the ride. Their body heat created pools of moisture from their intense passion. Noelle came for the first time. Her body felt rejuvenated. All her worries dissipated into the night air. He kissed her on the nipple and lay next to her.

"How was it for you?" he asked, hoping that she was floating like a boat on smooth flowing waters.

"I can't explain in words. But I do know I want you to take me again before we leave here."

"Only if you tell me I'm the only man you'll let have you."

She gazed lovingly, longingly into his eyes. Her heart palpitated. "You have my promise."

Sid let out a sigh of relief, happy that she felt a connection to him greater than a friend. He reached over, kissed her, and took a broken stick lying on the grass and gently tickled her. She was turned on again.

Noelle cried into the night as Sid tossed the stick away and gave her his own stick.

"I didn't know what I've been missing."

"That's okay; I'll help you catch up on lost time," he said willingly, in hopes that he would be good enough to be a longtime partner with the Houston girl. It was not her fortune that he was attracted to; her beauty, innocence, and sexual being turned him on.

Sid drove himself into her with all his power. Noelle screamed his name, "Sid!"

In return, he screamed her name, "Noelle!" They released their ecstasy and rested on the grass. "We can stay here as long as you want," he said as he held her.

"I wish we could stay here forever. It's so peaceful here."

"Who knows, maybe you and I will become one. Man and wife one day," he said wishfully.

Noelle smiled. "I believe our future is meant to be together."

They kissed and talked a little while. Sid drove the boat back to the Houston Estate. He took her home and again kissed her good-night. "See you tomorrow. I love you," he blurted.

"I love you, too," Noelle said joyfully, realizing since she couldn't have Baron, he was the type of man she had waited for all her life.

Noelle got out of the limo and watched him drive off. She ran into the house and took a shower. She cleansed her body, but hated she had to wash away the fresh smell of Sid's body odor from her flesh. Sadness came over her because she wondered, would her mother have been accepting of her newfound love? *Father would, no doubt, disown me.* Her mind wondered back to Sid and a smile quickly returned to her face. It was the passionate love that she had encountered that gave her a sense of peace.

Chapter 24

K enley made her way over to the Houston Estate for the
day. She hoped that Aniyah would let her in, but if Aniyah
didn't, she would go to Plan B—the secret passage.

The driver helped take her shopping bags, which were filled
with decorations, out of the limo. She was as ready as ever to get
things prepared for her sixteenth birthday celebration.

They carried the bags to the front door. She rang the bell several
times before Aniyah finally came and opened it.

"Oh hell no, not you again," Aniyah called as she blocked the
doorway.

"I need to get these things into the house."

Aniyah noticed the shopping bags in their hands. "Take your
stuff and get out of here."

"I'm planning my sweet sixteen pool party. I'm having it here.
It's traditional in my family. These are some of the things I need
for my party."

"Get real; you're not having a bunch of spoiled, rich brats up in
here."

"Before she died, my mother said that I could have a pool party.
What she says goes, even if she's not here anymore."

Kenley moved forward to go into the house. Aniyah swung the

door to close it, but Kenley pushed against it with the left side of her body.

"Please move out of my way. Some of these bags are heavy."

"I'm not!" Aniyah yelled. "Take your stuff and get the hell out of here."

"This is my house, too," Kenley said. "You're such a bitch."

"Watch your mouth," Aniyah said as she pushed Kenley out of the entranceway and slammed the door in her face.

The bags fell to the ground as Kenley stumbled. As the driver came to her rescue, he asked, "Miss Houston, are you okay?" He put the bags he carried on the ground and helped her up.

"I'm fine. Just gather up my things and put them back in the limo." Kenley brushed off her clothes.

The driver did as he was told. Kenley jumped into the backseat of the limo.

"Where would you like for me to drive you?"

"Straight down there," she said, pointing toward the walkway that led to the secret passage.

Kenley got out of the limo, and with the help of the driver, she grabbed all of her bags. They placed them on the ground.

"You can go. I'm going to stick around here for a while. Please keep your cell phone on. I'll call you when I'm ready to leave."

"Yes, Miss Houston. You sure you're going to be all right?"

"No one bosses me around and gets away with it. I'll be fine."

The driver tilted his hat and drove off.

Her eyes traveled around the area to make sure no one noticed her. The coast was clear and she opened the secret entrance.

Kenley tossed the bags of unbreakable things down the steps of the wine cellar. She carried the rest of them, storing them all in a closet.

Nearby where bottles of wine were stored, she opened a refrigerator filled with sodas. She took several swallows out of a Sprite soda to cool off. Once finished, she angrily squeezed the can and crushed it, thinking of Aniyah's head as she did it.

Kenley tossed the can into a trashcan before she climbed back up the steps and peeked outside. Again, the coast was clear. She eased out of the cellar. She went to walk toward the front of the house, but the servants were going home from a day's work. Her slender body disappeared behind a huge tree. As she waited, Aniyah came out of the house and got into a limo that had arrived to pick her up.

Yippee, the whore is leaving, Kenley thought, even though she didn't care where Aniyah was going. She watched as the limo disappeared down the path leading out of the estate.

Kenley ran back down into the cellar, leaving the bags in the closet. She hurried up to the main floor of the house. Since everything was quiet there, she went into the kitchen, grabbed an apple out of a crystal bowl filled with fruit, and she bit into it.

On the second level of the house, Kenley heard a radio playing in the east wing of the house, but she went to the west wing to check out her bedroom. She wanted to see if Aniyah kept her promise and changed her room, but the bedroom was the same way that her mother had the designer decorate it.

She peeked out of the wood blinds to the front of the house to make sure that Aniyah had not decided to return because she had forgotten something.

Kenley went down the hall to the guest bedroom where she knew Aniyah slept. As she got closer, the music became louder. She went into the room and searched around.

Aniyah had left a few dresses scattered on the bed. The closet had shoes thrown all over the floor. An empty glass and a bottle of rum were on the nightstand.

Kenley came out of the bedroom. She cautiously looked out of the window to be sure that Aniyah had not circled back. She was ready to use the basic skills she learned in martial arts on Aniyah.

Kenley decided to go into her father's old study. She saw the sign on the door. It declared "DO NOT GO INTO THIS ROOM." *I go where I please*, Kenley thought as she started to pull the sign down but then decided not to. She didn't want Aniyah to have a clue that anyone had been in the house. Instead, she just opened the door and went in. She looked at her father's empty desk— there weren't any photos of his family. His computer was in her possession.

Tessa was sound asleep but woke up when she heard Kenley in the room. She stayed quiet. Aniyah insisted that she would not get fed, but if she cooperated, maybe she would give her breakfast the next morning. She had to be sure of who was in the room.

Kenley went over to a drawer that held office supplies. She took out a letter opener with her father's name engraved on it. It was one of the things they had left behind while packing his things.

Tessa let out a sneeze. The sound frightened Kenley. She held the letter opener up for protection.

Pointing the letter opener toward the closet, the youngest Houston tiptoed over to the closet and opened the door fast. She screamed and Tessa made a mumbling sound.

Kenley saw that she was fragile, sweaty, and had a tear-stained face.

Tessa began to cry as her eyes pleaded for help. She was tied up and her mouth was bound with tape.

"I'll be right back," Kenley said frantically. She ran to search the drawers for scissors but couldn't find any. She ran down the hallway to the guest bedroom and found a pair of scissors in the nightstand.

"Who did this to you?" Kenley asked as she returned. She gently removed the cloth and tape from around Tessa's mouth.

"God bless you. You're my angel," Tessa cried. "Aniyah, as you know her name, did this to me."

"Who are you?" Kenley asked; she didn't recognize Tessa from the funeral.

"I'm Tessa Sanchez," she said as she gasped for breath.

"Aniyah's mother?" Kenley said, baffled.

"She's my niece. I'm not her mother."

"Really! And she did this to you?"

"Yes, my own family did this to me."

"She's going to jail."

Kenley finished freeing her. Tessa tried to stand up but fell back down; her body was stiff from sitting in the closet.

Kenley felt sorry for her. "Let me help you up. Hold on to me so we can hurry and get out of here before Aniyah comes back. Your niece is sick in the head."

"Not yet. We must leave things as they were. We don't want Rosie to notice I'm gone right away."

Kenley stopped for a second. "Her name is a lie, too?"

"Kind of, her middle name is Aniyah."

"She's a fraud."

"Let's hurry. I don't want anything to happen to you."

"I'm not scared. But I'll handle putting everything back in place. Hold on to the desk until I finish."

Kenley worked really fast, tossing the rope and tape into the closet. She closed all of the doors when she finished.

They hurried to the ground floor.

"We can't go out the front door. She may come back. Or some-one may see us," Kenley said.

Tessa gained strength and was able to walk and follow Kenley. "Where are we going?"

"Down to the wine cellar," Kenley said as they made their way to the cellar.

"I don't want to stay in the cellar. No telling what Rosie would do to us if she found us."

"Trust me. We're not staying down there. There's a way to get to the outside from the cellar. My driver is waiting on me to call for him to pick me up."

Closing the cellar door behind them, they hurried down the stairs, where Kenley called for the driver. She ordered that he pick her up as fast as he could in the same place where he dropped her off earlier. They were in luck. The driver was still on the property.

They came out of the secret passage and walked down the brick paved walkway. The driver drove up just a few seconds later. They quickly got into the limo.

"Get us out of here," Kenley ordered.

"Where do you want to be dropped off?" the driver asked.

"Just get us off the grounds of the estate," Kenley said.

"I have to make a call," Tessa said as she called Baron.

Baron answered the phone and was glad to hear from Tessa. "Where the hell are you? I've been worried sick about you."

Tessa said, "Rosie tied and taped me up in a closet."

The driver heard what she said. He looked through his rear-view mirror at her.

Kenley saw he was listening to the call. "Keep your mouth shut before you're to blame for someone getting seriously hurt."

"No problem, Miss Houston," the driver said.

Tessa told Baron about the whole event.

"Put Kenley on the phone," he said.

"Here, Mr. Chavis would like to speak to you." Tessa handed the phone to Kenley.

"Yes, Mr. Chavis."

"Do me a favor and take Tessa with you to the Houston Villa. I'll meet you there. Thanks, you saved a life. No telling what her niece might have done to her."

"You know Aniyah is a fake?" Kenley asked, startled.

"Yes, I found out a day ago. Tessa got in touch with me. I was in the midst of getting things worked out for your family."

"Hold on a second, Mr. Chavis." Kenley called to the driver, "Take us to the Houston Villa, please." She went back to her conversation with Baron. "I'm so happy she's not my sister. I can't believe she lied to take over our lives."

Tessa listened as Kenley rejoiced. She laid her head on the window.

Kenley said goodbye and hung up with Baron.

Tessa said, "I tried to talk to Rosie about how wrong she was to take your family fortune. She wouldn't listen to me. She became angry and threw me in the closet."

Kenley was concerned for the woman her mother had called a whore. "I'm sorry you were tortured trying to help me and my sisters. Did she feed you?"

"She got mad at me and told me I would starve."

"I know she's your niece, but the girl is schizophrenic."

Chapter 25

The Houston Villa was silent as Kenley entered with Tessa at her side. No noises coming from her sister's rooms assured Kenley that they weren't at home.

"Let's get you something to eat."

"I would love to take a bath, if that's okay, Miss Houston," Tessa said as she lifted up her right arm and sniffed her underarms. She turned her nose up. Her deodorant had worn off.

Kenley showed her to the bathroom. Inside a Jacuzzi tub, she turned the brass faucet on and ran Tessa's bath.

Tessa reached for one of many fresh 100 percent pima cotton plush towels that were stacked neatly on a nearby shelf.

"Watch the water," Kenley said. She left and returned with one of her white linen bathrobes and a brand new pair of panties. She handed the underwear to Tessa. "We keep extras around here."

"My angel, you are," Tessa said as she patted Kenley on the cheek.

"I'm glad to help." Kenley smiled and closed the door, leaving Tessa to her bath.

Tessa turned the faucet off. She undressed and eased her foot down in the water. "Just right," she mumbled as she sat down in the tub. She rested her head back, closed her eyes, and let the warm water soothe her body.

Downstairs, a servant was cooking dinner when Kenley entered the kitchen.

"Smells delicious in here. How long before the food will be done?"

"Are you hungry, Miss Houston?" the servant asked.

"I have a guest that hasn't eaten today."

"One plate of stewed chicken and rice coming up," the servant said.

"Thanks! I'll be back."

Kenley ran back upstairs. She spoke through the bathroom door, "Miss Sanchez, your meal will be ready when you come down to the kitchen."

"Thank you, Miss Houston," Tessa answered back.

It wasn't long before Tessa came downstairs dressed in the robe Kenley had given her. She ran into the arms of Baron as he entered the house.

"Tessa, I've never been worried about anyone the way I've been worried about you. Are you really okay?" he asked as he kissed her on her lips.

"Yes, physically I'm fine, but emotionally I'm so hurt about my Rosie."

Kenley watched the glow in their eyes as they embraced. She realized the true connection between Baron and Tessa. She interrupted them. "Miss Sanchez needs to eat. She hasn't had any food."

"I can't believe Aniyah didn't feed you," he said.

"Rosie became so mad after you left the estate," Tessa said.

"You were there all the time?" Baron asked, wishing he'd been able to search the entire house.

"I tried to make noise, but Rosie had her music playing so loud and my mouth was taped up."

"Where are Milandra and Noelle?" Baron asked as he turned his attention to Kenley.

"I have no idea," Kenley said as she held out her hands.

"Get your sisters on the phone. Tell them to come home quick. We have plenty to discuss and clear up," Baron said.

Kenley led the way to the kitchen as she got her sisters on the phone. She called each one of their cell phones and urged them to hurry home, not knowing she'd interrupted their dates. "They're on their way home," she reported to Baron.

In the kitchen, Tessa had taken a seat at the table; a plate of stewed chicken and rice was ready for her. She stuffed her mouth with a forkful of food, gobbling it down like she was a homeless person glad for a meal.

"I'll call the police," Baron said as he took a seat beside Tessa.

"No police." Tessa panicked. "I don't want my Rosie in jail."

"You're her auntie and look what happened to you," Kenley said as she poured Tessa a glass of tea and handed it to her.

"We have to put a stop to her or someone can get seriously hurt because of her. She might even try to come after you again. And the next time there is no telling what she'll try to do to you," Baron said.

Tessa knew what he said was true. She took a gulp of her drink and placed the glass on the table. "All right, call the authorities," she submitted.

The police arrived before the Houston sisters got home. Tessa explained to the police her ordeal and Aniyah's identity.

"Would you like to press charges?" the police asked.

Tessa bowed her head and tears flowed down her face. Kenley and Baron waited for her to answer. Finally, Tessa held her head up. "Oh, Julia, my sister, please forgive me. Yes."

Baron patted Tessa on the back, and then he left Kenley to stay with her while he walked the officers out.

By the time the rest of the Houston sisters arrived home, the officers had left. Noelle and Sid came first. Milandra came in behind her with Nolan.

With his eyes lit up and a smile across his face, Baron couldn't believe that Rupert's daughters were accompanied by men who were clearly not up to Rupert's standards. "You ladies have been holding out on me."

"Mr. Chavis, we don't have to discuss our private lives with you, only business." Milandra rolled her eyes at him. "What's the rush for us to come home?"

Milandra looked to see Tessa wrapped up in the bathrobe. She recalled who she was. "What is Father's whore doing here? Get out!" she yelled, pointing in the direction that would lead her out of the house.

"She's my guest," Kenley said as she kept Tessa company at the table.

"I'll leave," Tessa said and was about to stand up.

"No, you don't have to go anywhere. Milandra, you don't know what's going on. Before you pass judgment on Miss Sanchez, hear her out," Kenley said.

Nolan put his arm on Milandra's shoulder. "Give the lady a chance to speak."

Baron stepped in. "Let's all gather in the family room."

Baron led the way and everyone followed. They took seats around the room. Baron spoke first. "These past few weeks have been terrible for you all. But a brighter day is coming. Tessa has something to tell you."

"Aniyah, as you girls know her, is not my daughter. She's no daughter of your father. She's my niece, Rosie *Aniyah* Sanchez."

"What?" Milandra yelled. "We have been living here falsely? But the will stated father left the estate to her."

Tessa went on, "Mr. Houston thought she was truly his daughter. She made him believe that by telling him she was my daughter. You see, I did have a baby by your papa."

Milandra stood to her feet. "Get this whore out of here." She directed her attention to Baron.

"Have a seat and listen to her story," Baron said.

"Let her finish her words," Noelle said.

"Will everyone be quiet? This is like a story out of the movies. I want to hear it," Kenley said as she sat on the edge of her seat.

Milandra cut her eyes at Kenley. She sat back down in her seat with her arms crossed.

Tessa cried and took a deep breath. "Mr. Houston hated that my heart was with Mr. Chavis. He knew we liked each other. Mr. Houston decided to take me for himself. I'm sorry to speak of your papa this way, but he came after me as he did so many of the other female servants. I became pregnant the same time as your mother. Mr. Houston rushed me out in the night and sent me back to Mexico. I lost my precious baby girl. I named her Aniyah after my niece's middle name."

Kenley stood up and added her two cents. "The crazy girl locked her aunt up in a closet in Father's study."

"She did?" Sid asked. "Yeah, she's a crazy bitch."

"Your sister," Tessa said, pointing to Kenley, "she's an angel. She helped me out of the closet."

"Kenley, you went to the estate?" Milandra asked.

"Yes, I went shopping for my pool party. Aniyah wouldn't let me in. I waited until she left, and let's just say I found my way in. When I got upstairs, I found Miss Sanchez."

"You weren't supposed to be over there. You'll have your pool party here," Milandra said.

"It's good I did go to the estate. Miss Sanchez would still be locked up. Be thankful I was there. Hey, hopefully, fake Aniyah will be out and I can have my party at the estate." Kenley smiled.

"I am thankful," Tessa said as she took a tissue and wiped her tears.

"The girl must have mental problems to do the things she's done. But Father, how could he use women? And how could Mother sit there and let him do it? I don't understand it," Noelle said.

"Mother married Father unconditionally. She loved him. She let him have his way out of loyalty to her vows," Milandra explained.

"Your mother was such a sweet lady. I felt bad letting Mr. Houston touch me in ways he was only supposed to touch her. I stayed and took his abuse because I needed the money for my family. I guess I'm no better than Rosie."

"Please, don't put yourself in the same category as your niece. As my big sister would probably say, she's a lunatic," Kenley said.

Tessa bowed her head. "You girls...I'm willing to work for you for free. I owe a debt to your family. I, too, took money from your papa. I hated him. I made him think I still had our baby. I never told him I lost the baby. He paid me three hundred dollars a month just to keep anyone from knowing about our baby."

"You're a thief like your niece. Yes, you will work off every penny you owe my father," Milandra yelled as she ran over to Tessa, pointing her finger in her face.

Kenley hurried and stood in front of Milandra. She argued at her sister, "Are you kidding me? I say she owes nothing. I love Father with all my heart, but she did what she had to do to pay him back."

"You're out of line, Kenley. Stay in a child's place," Milandra ordered her.

"Sometimes you can be so heartless," Kenley said and marched back over to her seat.

Nolan wanted to jump in and agree with Kenley. But he wasn't about to jeopardize his hopeful relationship with Milandra. He would find a way later to make her have forgiveness in her heart.

"Stop bickering," Noelle said. "Milandra, I have to take sides with Kenley. I love Father, too, but he was wrong. Tessa, you were wrong too, but you did it because it was your way of getting some kind of payback from my father. That's all in the past. Let's move on. There's been enough hurt for all of us. Milandra, Father is gone."

"Come on. Lighten up, Milandra," Nolan said. He couldn't keep his mouth shut any longer. He patted her on the hand.

Milandra felt smothered from everyone ganging up on her. She threw her hands up in the air. "Fine! I won't punish you, Tessa. But your niece will pay dearly. She took our grieving time and turned it into a circus. I want her behind bars," she demanded.

"The police are on the case as we speak. They'll be arresting her soon," Baron said as he stood up. He helped Tessa out of her seat. "You ready to go?" he asked as he grabbed her by the hand.

Everyone in the room saw that there was a definite bond between them.

"I'll have to put my clothes back on," Tessa said.

"Keep on the robe. Think of it as a gift from your angel." Kenley smiled.

Tessa gave Kenley a hug. "I would love to be the help for your party. That's if you like, Miss Houston."

"Just be a guest chaperone." Kenley smiled and gave Tessa a hug.

Baron and Tessa made their way out of the house.

Chapter 26

A niyah sat at the bar sipping on rum as she waited for her latest client—or what she would call her latest victim. *What does this fool look like?* Aniyah thought. She hoped he wasn't too old that she had to be a home attendant instead of an escort.

Her goal was to turn the Houston Estate into quarters for male clients who needed escorts while they were in town. With Rupert's fortune, she'd hire girls to entertain them.

This client had come along before she could get her girls set up. Aniyah figured *she* would start out with the client, then pass him off to the first girl she hired.

Kenley, Aniyah thought. Kenley was turning the same age as she was when she started out. But to her, Kenley didn't have what it took to carry out the job. She crossed Kenley off the list as one of her potential girls.

The phone rang several times before Aniyah heard it among the noise in the bar. "Hello," she hollered.

"Change of plans," the caller said.

"Oh crap, he decided on someone else?"

"He's not a client who wants to appear in a public place. He wants you to meet him at a hotel in the downtown Columbia area," the caller said, and then he gave her the hotel name and location.

"Let him know I'll be there shortly," Aniyah said, but she didn't bother to leave right away. She figured she'd let the client hunger for her. The clients were always informed that she was the hottest escort any man could want.

Taking the last sip of her drink, Aniyah hopped down off the barstool and strutted out of the bar. A drunken man watched her from behind. His eyes traveled down the back of her red dress that hung right below her butt.

Clark, Rupert's former personal driver, had become her driver. He had driven her to the hotel.

Aniyah ordered the driver to turn the volume up on the radio while she snapped her fingers to a song by Mary J. Blige.

"That's my girl."

The driver looked in his mirror and laughed as he watched her dance in the seat.

The song went off and a slow jam came on. "You can turn that down, Clark." Aniyah wasn't up on the tune playing. She wondered if her aunt was asleep in the closet. This was another burden she had—thinking of what to do with her.

Aniyah dismissed thinking of Tessa when she arrived at a hotel with revolving glass doors. She made her way to the front desk.

Just as was told to her, her client had left a key for her to his suite.

Inside the elevator, before she reached the tenth floor, she took out a compact mirror and made sure her makeup and hair were intact.

Aniyah slid the key in the door and walked in to see that there was no one waiting for her. A dim light came from a lamp in the room. She tossed her purse on a desk and took a seat on the end of the unmade bed.

Aniyah made a call back to her contact. "What's going on? There's no one here."

"Be patient. He's on his way. This is a big deal. So don't mess this up. This could be the start of a booming business for you."

Aniyah giggled as she kicked off her red pumps. "I'll have that sucker's tongue hanging out of his mouth. He'll be begging me to be his forever."

She hung up and made her way over to a radio and flicked it on. She went into the bathroom and removed her dress, ready to greet her client in a red sheer bra and panty set.

The footsteps of someone entering the room alerted her that her client had arrived. Aniyah opened the door to see a man with a shaved head and a thick mustache on his face. His weight was that of a linebacker. Something about his face looked very familiar to her.

"You finally made it," she said, puzzled, but in hopes his eyes burned from looking at her curves.

Aniyah stared into his eyes. Right away she recalled the hazel eyes. "Danny!" she screamed as she reached for her purse on the desk, forgetting about her dress and shoes. She tried to rush past him to the door, but his huge framed blocked her.

"It's been a long time."

Danny snatched her belongings out of her hand, attempting to throw them back on the desk, but they landed on the floor instead.

Aniyah's eyes watered. "Please let me leave."

"When I say so."

Squeezing her in his arms, Danny landed a kissed on her lips. Aniyah tried to push him off but he was too strong. He pulled her by the arm and shoved her onto the bed. "You're here to give me services. Handle your business."

"I thought you were someone with some damn money."

Danny pulled a roll of bills out of his pocket. "Does this look like tissue paper to you?"

"Who did you con out of their money?" Aniyah asked as she tried to get up, but he still held her down. She struggled with him as he reached to pull her panties off.

Danny punched her in the face. Her left cheek stung from the blow.

"You still don't understand you're supposed to please the client," he said.

Aniyah begged, "Don't do this, Danny. You replaced me with another girl. Why are you bothering me?"

"I hired you for the night. Haven't you learned yet to never cancel a client in the middle of working with him?"

"I changed my mind."

"Too late." He laughed as he unfastened his belt buckle and removed his pants.

"I thought you meant good back then. You made me leave my home to go to Georgia with you just to use me."

"I didn't make you do a damn thing you didn't want to. You know you love you some Danny." He laughed louder.

He lay down on her. Aniyah punched him in the back numerous times. Danny had enough of her so he grabbed a handful of her hair and yanked it. She screamed, so he forced his tongue in her mouth to silence her.

Aniyah bit him on the lip. He felt the pain and he slugged her across the face again. She cried in pain.

Danny snatched off her bra and squeezed her breasts until she felt excruciating pain.

"It hurts!"

"Shut the hell up and I'll stop."

Aniyah quieted down as tears drowned her face. Danny released her breasts. He spread her legs apart and entered her.

"You used to love it," he whispered in her ear as he worked his muscle inside her.

Aniyah wondered how his six-pack had turned into a potbelly. Danny began to suck on her neck.

She wondered if the money in his pocket was meant to pay her for her deeds. Aniyah decided to play him for a sucker, please him, empty his money roll, and then pass him off to one of her new young girls when she hired them to work for her escort business.

Pressing her lips hard against his, she worked her body right along with his.

"I knew you wouldn't give this good loving up."

"You're right. You're the client. I aim to please," Aniyah said as she counted the dollars in her head that he would pay her.

As much as Aniyah tried to not enjoy it, she felt the passion she had for Danny all over again.

She rested on the pillow, sweat rolling down her neck as she watched Danny get out of bed. He picked up his underwear and put them on, followed by his pants.

"I'm out of here," Danny said as he tossed his shirt on.

Aniyah sat up on the bed. "Where's my money?"

"Money! Girl, you get nothing from me. I'm not paying for something that already belongs to me."

"You bastard, give me my money," she shouted as she ran over to him and beat on his chest.

Danny lifted her up as if she were a pencil. He slammed her against the wall. Aniyah trembled.

"I know you don't need money. I've read about the fortune you came into. You owe me commission on that money. I'll be in touch in a few days. Just get ready because I'll be moving into the big house with you. I have to clean up some unfinished business in Georgia. I'll be back as soon as I can. So make room for me."

Danny put her down. Aniyah stayed put as she stood against the wall like a statue. She wanted to get out of the room alive.

Danny smothered her lips with a kiss and disappeared out of the room.

Aniyah hurried and put on her clothes. She called her contact and yelled, "Thanks for that bullshit client." She hung up right away.

Back to another bar she went, drowning her sorrows with rum. She sniffed the smell of Danny's cologne coming from her neck so she took a napkin off the counter and wiped her neck off.

She carried on a conversation with a man sitting at the bar with her. He flashed a few hundred dollars in her face. After too many drinks, she took the strange man to the estate with her.

Chapter 27

Milandra and Noelle entertained their male friends with a game of Yahtzee while Kenley watched them play. In the middle of the game Milandra got out of her seat. "Let's go," she ordered.

"Where?" Noelle asked.

"To the estate," Milandra said.

"Let's just play the game," Noelle said.

"It's not a good idea for you and your sisters to go over there," Nolan said, putting his two cents in.

"We need to show this Rosie girl we're no pushover sisters," Milandra said as she sat back down to rejoin the game.

Kenley agreed. "I have a few words for her."

"Just because we carry ourselves as graceful ladies doesn't mean we're weak," Milandra acknowledged.

"The girl is crazy. You see what she did to her own aunt. She'll think nothing of bringing harm to us," Noelle said.

"She can't tackle the three of us," Kenley said.

"I agree with Nolan, let it go. Let the police handle it," Sid said.

Milandra backed down. Kenley, bored from their game playing, went upstairs to her room to watch television.

An hour later, her sisters escorted their male friends to the door. Nolan placed a peck on Milandra's cheek, but Noelle wasn't ashamed to give Sid a kiss on the lips in front of her sister. They waved goodbye to them and went back in the house.

"We've met some wonderful gentlemen," Noelle said.

"Yes, they are so attentive to us. They are such great friends," Milandra said.

"I don't know about you, but I'm in love with Sid. I think you love Nolan, but are too scared to show it. You don't want to admit we've found love from the common man."

"They are not men Father would approve of us marrying."

"Milandra, Father wasn't planning on accepting any man for us—rich or poor," Noelle said as she started to unbutton her blouse to get ready for bed.

"What are you doing?"

"Getting ready for bed."

"Call for a car; we're going to the estate."

"I thought we agreed we weren't going over there. She's probably already been picked up by the police."

"You recalled she wasn't home earlier. They might wait to pick her up tomorrow."

"I don't think they work that way. I'm sure the police are still waiting at the estate for her."

"Please, let's just go and see because if she's there, I want to confront her. I can't go to bed without venting my thoughts to her. Go on; call for a ride. I'll get Kenley," Milandra said.

Noelle made arrangements for a limo to come right away. Milandra went upstairs and brought Kenley back down with her. They locked the house and went to the estate.

No signs of a police car were on the property. Word was left at the security desk to call them when Aniyah arrived home. The house was dark with no sign of life in it. Milandra rang the bell several times but got no answer.

Kenley suggested she go through the secret passage. She hurried and made it into the main floor of the house to open the front door for her sisters. Aniyah hadn't come home yet. The women sat in the kitchen until they heard her come in. Kenley secretly took a knife out of the drawer and kept it by her side.

Aniyah walked into the house staggering. She and her male friend were all over each other. She steadily kissed him, not hearing the sisters walk into the foyer where they were.

Her male friend noticed them and jumped. "We have company," he said as he adjusted his pants.

Aniyah turned to them. "What the hell are you broads doing in my house?"

The sisters smelled the odor of liquor.

"Correction, whore," Kenley said, "this is the home of a Houston, which you're not."

"Go upstairs and wait for me," Aniyah ordered her guest.

Kenley stepped in front of the staircase. "Go home!"

"I suggest you do, Sir," Milandra said. "No need for you to get in any trouble for a slut."

"All you tramps get out of my house!" Aniyah yelled.

The stranger saw this was about to escalate into a catfight that might involve the intervention of law enforcement. He was on parole and wanted no part of that.

"Call me—" He patted Aniyah on the behind. "—when things cool down." He dashed out the door.

"Is this about me not letting you in here earlier? So you go running to get your sisters to back you up?" Aniyah asked as she focused on Kenley. "They don't scare me. So get out," she yelled as she held open the door.

Milandra walked up closer to Aniyah. She yelled, "You're despicable. To let my father believe that you were his child and make him do the honorable thing by leaving you in his will is pretty low, I must say."

"How many times do I have to repeat myself—I'm his daughter!" Aniyah shouted.

"The hell you are," Noelle said.

Kenley laughed. "Tessa! Does that name mean anything to you?"

Aniyah tried to make her way up the stairs but Kenley blocked her by stretching her arms out.

"Girl, you want to get your little ass whipped? Get out of my way," Aniyah said as she put her finger in Kenley's face.

Kenley held up the knife. "No, Rosie. Isn't that your real name? Explain to us why you're running around here using your dead cousin's name?"

Noelle saw that her sister held up a knife. "Kenley, put that away. We're only here to talk."

"Kenley, do as Noelle told you," Milandra called.

Noelle went over to the stairs and snatched the knife out of her sister's hand. "I'll take it back to the kitchen," she said as she left the foyer.

Aniyah laughed as she tried not to show any emotion about Kenley discovering her birth name. "The little bitch can keep the knife. I'm not scared of her ass."

"Leave our house right now, or I'll get another knife and cut you up!" Kenley yelled.

"Hell no. How many times do I have to say it, or do you all have a hearing problem? My name *is* Aniyah."

"Call the police for Rosie Aniyah," Kenley said as she winked her eye at Milandra.

Milandra took her cell phone out of her pants pocket and started to call 9-1-1. Aniyah ran over and knocked it out of her hand.

Kenley came to her sister's rescue. She pushed Aniyah to the floor and ran to pick up the phone. Aniyah staggered to stand up to get to the phone. Milandra tripped her with her foot. This gave Kenley the chance to get to the phone.

Noelle came back to see Aniyah on the floor and Kenley on the phone.

Instead of calling the police, Kenley called their lawyer while she kept an eye on Aniyah, still on the floor with her hair out of place and her dress rose up, exposing her thighs.

"I called Mr. Chavis. You speak to him," Kenley said as she passed the phone to Milandra.

Milandra held the cell phone to her ear until he answered.

He tried to scold her. "What are you doing over there?"

"I'm handling my family business and you have no right to question a Houston," Milandra relentlessly said.

"I apologize but the police will handle Tessa's niece. I'm on my way there," Baron said.

Aniyah tried to stand up but Kenley grabbed her by her hair. She pulled her to the stairs. "Let me go!" Aniyah yelled.

"What kind of woman are you?" Milandra asked Aniyah as she watched Kenley drag her.

"Stupid—that's what she is," Noelle said.

"You tied up your own aunt and put her in a closet. How crazy are you? Your own family!" Kenley yelled as she yanked Aniyah's hair.

"Ouch!" Aniyah said, coming into the realization that her aunt Tessa was no longer upstairs. She wondered where she was.

"She deserved it," Aniyah screamed. "Just like your papa deserved it."

Kenley slapped her on the face. "Respect my dead father."

Aniyah laughed. "I had plenty of pleasure from your papa. He was a male whore. He took me as his woman. The house you live in is where we made our love nest. I had him where I wanted him—right by the balls. That's when I told him I was his daughter. You should have seen the look on his face. That's what sent him straight to his grave."

"Shut up!" Milandra said hysterically. "Respect my father."

"He never gave my family respect!" Aniyah screamed.

Milandra lost control. "Move out of my way, Kenley."

Kenley stepped away from Aniyah. Milandra ran over and kicked Aniyah with so much force that it bruised her right leg.

Noelle pulled her sister away. "Control yourself, Milandra. She's not worth it. The law will take care of her."

Milandra fell to the floor and cried. It hurt her to have heard nothing but negative things against her father. She couldn't believe there was a cruel side of him that made him abusive to women when he had daughters of his own.

Baron and Tessa entered the house. Tessa saw her niece at the foot of the stairs. She ran over and whacked her across the face and she cried to Aniyah, "I will never tell your mama I found you. She almost lost her life worrying about you, Rosie. A heart attack almost took her life. I'd rather her think you're still lost. She would be so hurt to discover that her daughter was being so manipulative and cruel to others."

Aniyah sobbed, "Stop lying on my mama. Aunt Tessa, you're a traitor and I hate you!"

"Everyone be quiet," Baron said.

"Boss those heifers over there, not me," Aniyah yelled to him.

"I'm not here to boss anyone. I'm saying let's all calm down. Aniyah or Rosie, whatever your name is, you need help to deal with whatever pain you're going through," Baron advised her, trying to give her the benefit of the doubt since she was Tessa's niece.

"What are you now—a damn shrink? You need help on how to screw a woman. You're crappy in bed." Aniyah laughed. "You're a sucker, just like Rupert."

Noelle couldn't believe Baron had slept with Aniyah.

"Stop lying," he said, even though it was the truth. Tessa also knew she was telling the truth, but she protected him in front of the Houstons.

"Rosie, no more lies," Tessa said.

Aniyah sat on the steps and yelled, "I don't care whether you believe me or not. He screwed me."

Noelle comforted Milandra. Kenley ran up the stairs. She grabbed some of Aniyah's belongings and tossed them in a pillowcase that was on the bed. She brought the stuffed pillowcase to the staircase.

"Here are your things. Take them and leave me and my sisters alone," Kenley yelled. Everyone looked up and moved out of the way as the pillowcase tumbled down the stairs.

Kenley came down the stairs. Aniyah tried to attack her but Baron stopped her.

"I'm sick of you for real, little creep. Enough is enough. You're a pest," Aniyah said.

Upset with Aniyah for going after her sister, Milandra ran over and pulled her by the hair.

"You high-class bitch, let go of my hair," Aniyah argued.

Baron dared not to stop Milandra; he watched her as she dragged Aniyah out the door.

"Please, Rosie has done wrong, but she's my niece. Don't hurt her," Tessa begged.

Noelle could see by the look in Tessa's eyes that she was in as much pain as they were, but in her own way. She called to her sister. "Milandra, let's not get in trouble with the law."

Milandra listened to her sister and let go of Aniyah.

Aniyah sat on the outside of the door and tried to pat her hair neatly in place.

Two officers, who were notified by security that Aniyah had arrived home, pulled up to the front door.

Aniyah stood up and still tried to put on until the end. "Officers, please make them leave my house," she yelled.

"Are you Rosie Sanchez?" the officer asked Aniyah as they got out of the police car.

"I'm Aniyah Sanchez."

"Liar!" Kenley shouted. "She's a fake."

The officer noticed Tessa from speaking to her at the villa. "Can you identify your niece for us?" the head officer asked.

Tessa pointed at Aniyah and cried, "She's my niece. Her name is Rosie Aniyah Sanchez. She's using her middle name and my dead daughter's name, Aniyah, for her own."

One of the officers went over to Aniyah, grabbed her hands, and put them behind her. He handcuffed her and read her Miranda Rights.

"You traitor. Aunt Tessa, how could you do this to me?"

Kenley took one of the officers upstairs and showed him the rope and tape Aniyah had used on her aunt. The officer took the items for evidence.

"I want to make sure you have the story of what happened," Milandra said. "She got this home because my father left it to her in the will under the assumption that she was his child. She isn't."

"I was told this earlier by Mr. Chavis," the head officer said. "Is this true?" he asked as he turned his attention to Aniyah.

She laughed. "She's jealous because I'm our papa's favorite daughter."

Tessa begged, "For God's sake, Rosie, stop lying. You know you're not Mr. Houston's daughter. His real fourth daughter is dead."

"Is this true?" the officer asked Aniyah a second time.

"I'm not answering any more damn questions. I plead the fifth. Speak to my lawyer right there." Aniyah pointed to Baron.

"You're her lawyer?" the officer wondered.

"No. I'm the Houstons' attorney," Baron said.

"He's my lover and he's my lawyer." Aniyah blurted to the officer.

Tessa yelled, "Rosie, stop making a fool of yourself."

Aniyah turned and looked at her. "Rot in hell, bitch."

Those words made Tessa feel like her niece had taken a knife and stuck it in her heart.

The officer took Aniyah out and put her in the police car.

Baron ordered them all to go home. The girls locked up the house until they could get all the paperwork straightened out.

Chapter 28

Baron and Tessa arrived at Baron's home. Tessa was distraught. "Thank you so much for making the Houstons listen to my side of the story."

"They should know what really went on; even if it's not anything they wanted to hear."

"I guess it's hard for them to hear that their papa was cruel in his own way."

Tessa took off her blouse. Baron came up behind her and put his arms around her. He caressed her breasts as he kissed her on the neck.

Turning Tessa around, he put his lips to hers. They kissed passionately. He unhooked her bra to release her breasts. He cupped one as he took it for his pleasure.

Tessa moaned from the delight of his teeth biting on her. She helped remove his shirt, and then placed kisses on his chest and all the way up to his neck and lips.

Baron eased up as he thought of the roses and bottle of Sangria he bought for her. "I'll be right back."

"I'll make you a warm bath."

"I'll do that for you when I get back," Baron said as he went downstairs and took a bowl of strawberries and a chilled bottle of wine out of the refrigerator. He placed the bottle under his right arm and grabbed two glasses. He left the bouquet of roses on the kitchen counter and he went back to join her. When he entered the bathroom, Tessa already had the water running in the Jacuzzi tub. "You don't listen. I told you I would do that for you."

"It's okay." She noticed the treats he held. "What do we have here?"

"A few goodies, but I do have one more thing to get from downstairs." He set the bowl of strawberries, wine, and glasses on the edge of the tub and then ran back down to the kitchen to get the roses.

After the tub was filled with water, Tessa turned the jets on.

"Roses for a beautiful lady," Baron said as he walked into the bathroom.

Tessa relieved him of the bouquet of roses. She took one of the roses, plucked the petals off it, and tossed them in the water to let them float. She removed her panties, stepped into the Jacuzzi tub, and reached for his hand.

"One more thing," Baron said. He left and came back with a few candles. He placed three candles on the tub and lit them. The rose petals glowed as they floated in the water. He poured two glasses of wine. He removed his shorts and eased into the tub so his body would adjust to the water temperature.

"You're so romantic," Tessa said.

Baron gave her a peck on the lips before he leaned over and took a strawberry out of the bowl, putting it between his teeth and brushing it across her lips before she gripped it with her teeth. She chewed on the other end of the strawberry until their lips met.

Tessa reached for a strawberry and rubbed it on his chest to lick the juices off him.

Baron picked up the glass of wine. He poured some in her mouth, letting some trickle down her left breast. He sucked the wine off her. She playfully poured the wine on top of his head, and then she licked it off every place it appeared on him.

Tessa stood up in front of him, took one of the long-stemmed roses and began to dance with it. She rubbed the rose across her body as she danced. He admired her moves. Her hips swayed from side to side. Her breasts jiggled as she danced. She sat back down in the water and slid the rose down his chest to his manhood. He moaned.

Baron took another rose and worked her body with it. She moaned from the tingling sensation she felt.

Tessa whispered in his ear, "I thought we'd never see each other again."

"I would have come to Mexico to find you."

"You would have brought all this chocolate to Mexico for me?"

"Yes, just to dip you right in it." He giggled.

"Dip me in chocolate now."

Baron took her in his arms and held her tightly as he kissed her with force. The water splashed as they became one. "I love you, Baron," Tessa screamed.

"Love you forever," he said, forcing himself inside her harder. She scratched his back as she held on to him. She tickled his neck with her tongue. Together, they rocked to their own beat until they reached their climax.

Chapter 29

B ack at the Houston Villa, the girls went straight to the kitchen. Noelle opened the refrigerator. She searched for something to eat while her sisters took a seat at the table.

Milandra couldn't believe her sister had an appetite. "How can you think of food? All I want to do is move back to the estate."

"I'm just happy I get to have my pool party there," Kenley said, smiling as she thought of her birthday.

"Kenley, is that all you think about?" Noelle asked as she took out a glass casserole dish of lasagna.

"You had your day; I'm looking forward to mine." Kenley pouted.

"How do you work this microwave?" Noelle asked as she played around with the buttons.

Kenley got up and went over to help her sister. "Move out of the way." Kenley pressed on the buttons as if it was a calculator.

"And when did you learn how to work a microwave?" Noelle wondered.

"Elsa taught me how to use it," Kenley bragged.

The aroma of the tomato sauce perfumed the kitchen as it heated up. Noelle, with a dish towel in her hand, took the glass dish out of the microwave. She and Kenley made plates for themselves.

"Well, Milandra, are you going to join us?" Noelle asked as she went on to taste some of the lasagna on her plate.

"Yes." She pouted as she sniffed the aroma of cheese as well. She grabbed a plate out of the cabinet and joined her sisters.

They sat together and ate the lasagna. Kenley's thoughts went to boys as she chewed her food. "I can't wait to have a boyfriend," Kenley said.

"You have plenty of time," Milandra replied as she took her napkin and wiped sauce from her lowered lip.

"I won't wait as long as you and Noelle," Kenley said.

"Please don't wait as long as us." Noelle laughed.

"Father kept you away from men while he had fun with lots of women," Kenley said.

"I wish I could confront Father. I would ask him to explain in his own words all his best-kept secrets," Milandra said as she ate.

"It's no secret. Father probably thought men would treat us the way he treated women—terribly," Noelle said.

"Not Mother. He treated her with respect," Milandra said, defending him.

"You call it respect. He ran from her bed to others," Kenley said as she got up and poured iced tea for all of them.

"But Mother had everything a woman could want," Milandra said as she continued to defend their father.

"I guess we'll never know why Father was harsh to women," Noelle said.

"He *was* good to us. We have to forget about it and move on," Kenley said.

"We will as soon as we move back to the estate. I cannot wait to get out of this place. To think, Father entertained Aniyah here. It's dreadful! Just get me back to my bed at the estate," Milandra said.

"I hope I'm not sleeping in the room here, the room where Father had sex with her," Noelle said.

"The thought of her and Father in bed together is making me lose my appetite. I can't eat any more," Milandra said, dropping her fork on the plate.

"I think it's gross." Kenley frowned.

They left the dishes on the table for the servants to clean up the next day. They went on to sleep in the beds; they had no other choice.

Morning came soon enough. Kenley was excited about meeting with friends to talk all about her party plans. Her sisters cleared the morning schedule to have breakfast with their male friends. Today, they vowed to forget all about their problems and let Baron take care of their legal issues.

"Nolan said they'll be here at ten o'clock to pick us up," Milandra called from her bedroom to Noelle. She busily applied dark-brown mascara to her eyelashes.

"I'm doing my hair," Noelle said as she stroked her hair with a brush. "Has Kenley left the house yet?"

Kenley heard her sister's question. "I won't meet with my friends until this afternoon," she called from her bedroom; the rooms were adjacent to one another.

Downstairs in the kitchen, Pete, the servant, cleaned up their mess from the night before and prepared bacon, eggs, and grits for Kenley. He had been sent over by Elsa to work for the Houstons.

"Miss Houston, your breakfast is ready," Pete said.

Kenley came to the top of the stairs to see him. "I remember you. I thought you didn't speak any English."

Pete grinned. "I do a little."

"You're one of Aniyah's lovers."

"No, not me. She made me do things with her. I need to keep work so I did what she wanted," he admitted.

"Bring my breakfast up to my room."

Back in the kitchen, Pete prepared a tray of food for Kenley.

Not long after, he walked cautiously toward her room, careful not to spill the glass of freshly squeezed orange juice.

"Where would you like me to place it?" he asked as he smiled.

"Sit it on the bed and you better not come anywhere near me," Kenley said as she glanced at his cute dimples.

"Miss Houston, I no touch you."

Pete set the tray down. She knew he was the youngest of all the servants.

"How old are you?"

"Eighteen."

"I forgot your name. What is it again?" Kenley asked as she tried to recall what Aniyah had called him the day she had seen them together. She took a bite of the bacon as she listened to his answer.

"Pete," he replied.

Kenley saw him as one of her peers. "That crazy woman took advantage of you."

"Ad-van-tage?" he muttered.

Kenley realized he didn't understand her. "You know she took you for her fun," she explained.

"Yes, she wild." Pete giggled.

To make up for his encounter with Aniyah, Kenley asked, "You want to come to a party? It's my sweet sixteen birthday."

Pete smiled. "I would like to, but don't own any party clothes."

"Tell Elsa to give you a pair of black pants and a white shirt. They're available for the help when we have formal parties. You do have swimming trunks for the pool?"

"Yes, I do." Pete grinned.

"There'll be lots of pretty girls your age coming to the party."

"I will come for sure," Pete said.

"You can have fun, but no getting together with them. You know what I'm saying?" Kenley teased.

"I know. They're rich girls. They no want a poor guy like me."

"Yes, my snobby friends won't want you, so just have fun. After dinner, go by Elsa's and pick up the clothes."

"I will. Thanks for inviting me," he said, dismissing himself.

Milandra heard Pete out in the hallway. She called "Please unlock the front door. I have guests coming over. They'll let themselves in."

Milandra had already instructed Nolan that he and Sid could come right on in the house and make themselves at home. At times, it took her and her sisters extra time to get ready.

Pete followed her orders and unlocked the door. He looked out to see there were no visible signs of the guests. He pushed the door, but it didn't close all the way.

He went on to tidy up the kitchen.

Kenley left her food and peeped out the window to see that the lake was full of sailors on their pontoon boats. She could tell by the beaming sun that the temperature was near a hundred degrees. She was happy to be cooled by the central air throughout the house, but she would have to endure the sun soon enough.

Milandra is going to scold me for inviting the help as a guest to the party. I don't care because Aniyah did Pete wrong and he's cute.

Kenley grabbed her iPod and placed the ear buds in her ears. She listened to music as she ate the rest of her breakfast.

Baron found Tessa sitting at the kitchen table with her head down on it. He came up behind her and rested his hands on her shoulder.

"Is there something wrong?"

She sobbed. "I can't do it, Baron; not to my niece."

"Tessa, you must."

"I can't believe I pressed charges against my own family. Rosie is my only niece."

"I know it's difficult, but it had to be done. Your niece has to be punished for her terrible actions."

Tessa banged on the table. "She's family! The Houstons are loyal to theirs. I must be loyal to my family."

"You have this whole day to think about it. Whatever you decide, I'll still love you. But you'll be making a great mistake if you let her go, after what she did to you."

Tessa sat up and wiped her face. Her eyes were red from hours of crying. "I know they'll hold her for acting as if she was their father's daughter. That can be enough punishment for Rosie. I don't want her to feel like I betrayed her."

"You're too nice. Your niece betrayed you. She thought nothing of shoving you in a closet. Think about it. Give it lots of thought today. Be loyal to yourself first." Baron placed his chin on the top of her head. "That's one of the things I love about you. You always think of others."

Tessa patted him on the hand. "I'll make a decision before the day is over."

He went into his home office and made a few calls.

Tessa got dressed and headed over to the villa. Her decision was already embedded in her head. She wanted to be the one to tell the Houstons her decision. She didn't want Baron in the middle of it.

Chapter 30

The front page of the newspaper announced Aniyah's arrest. The headlines read: "No Fourth Houston." Danny read on and learned Aniyah's true identity. He spoke out as he read. "How stupid could that dumb broad be? Damn! I should have gotten to her sooner. I would've been loaded with cash. Those freakin' crazy Houston women jacked up my plans and the Sanchezes aren't any better. The dumb-ass aunt helped turned over her own niece to the Feds."

Danny read about how Tessa valued her family's name. "Value the money, broad," he yelled. He read on about where the Houstons resided at this time.

Danny grabbed a phone book and looked up the number for the Houston Estate. He called the estate and got one of the servants on the line. Pretending to be a magazine writer, Danny inquired about how to get in touch with the Houstons. He struck luck because he promised the servant a few dollars to give up their whereabouts.

He slipped on his clothes. He also took the knife he had used for his steak dinner, wrapped it in a cloth napkin, and left his hotel room.

Danny parked his compact car a little way back from the Houston

Villa, hiding it behind a bunch of trees. He constantly wiped the sweat that drenched his face as he walked up to the house. No signs of people, he hurried up to the front door and noticed the door was ajar. As he slowly stepped inside the house, Danny listened for movement. Right away he heard footsteps coming from the right side of the house. He assumed it was probably the servants in the kitchen because the aroma of the morning breakfast still filled that side of the house.

Coming from upstairs, Danny heard Milandra's voice.

She called to her sister, "Noelle, are you ready?"

"Not yet," Noelle replied.

Danny took off his shoes and carried them in one hand up the stairs. In the other hand, he held the knife. He went into the room he heard the first voice coming from. Milandra was not in the bedroom; instead, she was in her private bathroom.

Danny gently sat his shoes down on the floor. He tiptoed into the bathroom. Milandra stood in the mirror brushing her hair, fully dressed in a cream-colored, two-piece linen suit. She looked in the mirror to see Danny behind her.

Milandra went to scream, but he covered her mouth with his left hand while he held the knife to her throat with his other hand.

"Shh," he said. "Make a sound and you'll be scarred for life."

Tears ran down her cheeks. Danny kept his ears and eyes open.

"Point to where the closet is," he whispered.

Milandra pointed to a huge closet inside the bathroom. Danny was about to open the closet when Milandra bit him on the hand. He nipped her on the neck with the knife. As quickly as she tried to scream, he placed his hand back over her mouth. This time, though, he applied lots of pressure. "I see I'll have to slice you and your sisters into pieces."

Danny shoved her into the closet and she fell on the floor. He shut the door and locked it.

Milandra placed her finger on her neck to feel for blood. She cried, "God, why is so much pain coming to my family?" She took a dark-blue scarf off a dress and placed it around her neck to absorb the blood.

Danny left the bedroom. He kept a close watch on his surroundings as he made his way to Noelle's bedroom next. She hadn't gotten dressed yet. He walked in on her and saw she was dressed only in a white-laced bra and matching panties.

Noelle noticed him and tried to run. She screamed, but Kenley couldn't hear her because of the ear buds in her ears. Danny ran after Noelle and tackled her to the floor. He lay on top of her, then kissed the back of her neck, absorbing the perfume she wore. He eased the knife down the side of her face. Touching her just enough not to cut her. Noelle felt his erection against her leg.

"Please, don't hurt me," she begged.

"Do what I say and maybe I won't," Danny whispered.

As much as he wanted to have her, he had to stick to his plans. "Get up and keep quiet. Move and I'll slice one of those pretty tits of yours."

Danny eased the knife around her right breast, making a full circle. Noelle didn't say anything. She stood up. He grabbed her from behind, covered her mouth, and stuck the tip of the knife against her right cheekbone. He walked her through the hallway into Milandra's bedroom.

Danny unlocked the closet door and Noelle saw her sister on the floor. Before she could say a word, Danny pushed her with force. She fell on top of Milandra. They held on to each other. Then, he locked the door again.

Danny was happy that things were going smoothly. One more sister, he thought as he went into the last bedroom. Kenley sat on the bed, still listening to her music. She sang along with one of Beyoncé's songs. She wore a pair of pajama shorts and a sleeveless pajama T-shirt that resembled outerwear. He startled her when he snatched the iPod out of her hand. The ear buds fell out of her ears.

Kenley looked up, staring directly at the tip of the knife. She tried to crawl backward on the bed, knocking her breakfast tray on the floor. The remainder of the juice spilled on the carpet.

"Who are you?" she yelled.

"It doesn't matter. You move another inch and blood will be all over this bed."

Danny moved in on her and rubbed her face with his hand. Kenley stood still. Her eyes popped wide open as she placed her hands against her chest.

"You remind me of Aniyah, Rosie, whatever her name is, when I first met her—fresh meat for a man."

"What is she to you?" Kenley mumbled, but hoped he wasn't planning on hurting her.

"My escort and my money ticket, before you broads destroyed that."

Kenley thought quickly. "My family has plenty of money. How much do you need? My oldest sister is in the next room. She'll go to the bank and get all the money you want."

"Your sister isn't going anywhere at this time. She's safely locked up where you're going to join her."

Danny pulled Kenley by her T-shirt to join her sisters, still pointing the knife. He tossed her in the closet.

Kenley cried when she saw her sisters sitting on the floor. "I'm so happy to see you both."

"As long as you all cooperate, no one gets seriously hurt," Danny said and locked the door.

Inside the closet, the women listened until Danny disappeared.

"What are we going to do?" Noelle asked.

"Stay calm," Milandra said.

"Who is this man?" Noelle wondered.

"He knows Aniyah. He says we caused him to lose his money," Kenley informed them.

"No such thing," Milandra said as she fanned herself. "I think I'm going to faint."

Milandra removed the scarf from around her neck. Kenley noticed she had been bleeding.

"Oh, he cut you, Milandra. You may need to see a doctor right away."

"Lucky he didn't cut me deeper or I would be bleeding to death. I'm just getting overheated from being in this closet."

"Sid and Nolan will be here soon. I pray they don't get hurt." Noelle panicked.

"We need a way to call them," Kenley said.

"Your birthday gift," Milandra said as she pointed toward the package. "Noelle, hand me that bag."

Noelle reached under a blanket and pulled out a birthday gift bag with green tissue paper on top. "What's in it?"

"I don't want my present early," Kenley said.

"Sorry, but I have to open it. It's a cell phone," Milandra said. "Listen out for the man."

Kenley went near the door and put her ear close to it while she studied what kind of cell phone Milandra had purchased for her upcoming birthday.

Milandra opened the box. She took out a hot pink cell phone.

Kenley was excited. "You got me the hottest phone. Thanks, Milandra." She started to take it out of her hand.

"Listen out for the man. This is no time to celebrate," Milandra whispered.

"Call Mr. Chavis," Noelle suggested.

"No! He can't help us," Milandra said.

"He's a lawyer, Noelle," Kenley said.

"I'm calling Nolan. He and Sid are supposed to be on their way here. They'll handle this fat-bellied man," Milandra said.

"Yes, Sid does have muscles." Noelle smiled.

"Nolan is used to lifting things. He'll take him out," Milandra bragged.

"We should be calling the police," Kenley said as she kept her ear to the door.

Milandra called Nolan.

"Nolan," she cried. "I'm bleeding. A robber cut me. He has locked my sisters and me in the closet."

"What? You're joking."

"Hurry and come."

"Did you call the police?"

"No, not as of yet!"

"Tell me. Is the robber still there? What closet are you in?" Nolan asked.

"I don't know where he went. We're upstairs in my bathroom closet. My room is the closest to the stairs."

Kenley recalled that Pete, the servant, was downstairs in the kitchen. She yelled.

"The help is downstairs. He has no idea the man is up here. I hope he doesn't go downstairs and hurt Pete."

Milandra paid her no attention. She listened to Nolan.

"Sid is in the car with me. Stay calm. I'll call the police. Be there shortly. Remember, don't do anything to make him go off on you," Nolan said.

"I think he's coming," Kenley shouted as she moved away from the closet door. Milandra turned the cell phone off and pushed it back in the bag. Noelle tossed the bag back behind the blanket where it was. They huddled together.

"Let's pray," Noelle said as she bowed her head.

Danny had made his rounds in each of their bedrooms. He trashed their rooms, emptying out the drawers. He tossed mattresses off the beds and went through their purses. He was furious that all together, he tallied up less than two hundred dollars. Milandra had the most money in her purse.

Danny held the knife in front of him—ready to attack them if they charged at him. He opened the door to see the three of them jammed together.

"Three rich broads and all I came up with was a hundred and thirty dollars? Where's the money hidden in this house?"

"I told you my sister can go to the bank and get you much more money," Kenley offered.

"I guess you broads will be here 'til dark. I'll drive one of you to an ATM machine. No banks."

He pointed the knife at Kenley. "Come over here."

Kenley didn't move. Tears began to run down her face. "Why?"

"You don't get to ask questions. Do what I say," Danny said.

"No, I want to stay in here with my sisters," Kenley cried.

"I see you want a mark for life!" he shouted.

Danny took the knife and jammed it into the wall. He stabbed a hole into the sheet rock.

Noelle pleaded. "Please let my sister stay here."

Milandra kept her eyes closed; she didn't want to look at the man. She had seen enough of his disgusting face. The scars on Danny's face made her realize he had been in many fights.

With the knife aimed at her, Kenley crawled toward him. Danny jerked her up by the arm and pulled her out of the closet. He tossed her around like she was a Frisbee. He locked the closet door again.

"Please, don't hurt her. She's only fifteen," Milandra yelled.

Things became silent. The sisters couldn't hear what was going on. Danny took Kenley back into her bedroom. She saw that the room was in disarray.

Danny stood in front of her, steadily showing her the knife. "Take the top off."

Kenley wiped a tear from her eyes. She shook her head. "I don't want to."

Danny snatched her by the T-shirt and tried to remove it. Kenley fought back by giving him a karate kick, but he grabbed her leg and she fell down on the mattress that he had tossed on the floor. He slid the knife across her right arm to cut her. Blood gushed out.

Kenley screamed, "You cut me."

"Do as I say, or next time it'll be your damned face," he whispered.

Kenley settled down as she tried to wipe the blood. She didn't know how bad the cut was; all she saw was blood as red cherries.

Danny didn't give it one thought. He raised the T-shirt off her to expose her small breasts.

Kenley covered herself up with her hands while he loosened his pants. Not wanting to see his body, Kenley closed her eyes. She knew she had to think of something else or he was going to have his way with her before she bled to death.

Outside of the home, Tessa arrived. She saw that the door was ajar and walked in. "Hello, is anyone home?" she called as she waited for someone to appear. Pete, the servant, couldn't hear her. He had gone out back to throw away the trash.

Upstairs, Danny, so caught up in having his way with Kenley, didn't hear Tessa either as he removed his pants.

Holding the knife up in the air, Danny went to get on top of Kenley, but before he could lay on her, she jammed her right knee into his crotch with all of her strength. He let go of the knife and it fell on the mattress.

Danny grabbed his groin while Kenley picked up the knife and swung it at him. She cut him across his chest, slipped from underneath him, and ran out of the room screaming.

Tessa saw her make it to the stairs. Kenley held her hands over her breasts. They made eye contact.

Kenley screamed, "There's a man in my room."

"Come to me. Let's get out of here!" Tessa yelled.

Kenley rushed down the stairs. She cried, "My sisters are locked in the closet."

Tessa noticed the blood flowing down her arm. "You're bleeding. We must call for help," she said as she took a cell phone out of her purse.

She found some Kleenex in her purse and handed them to Kenley.

Nolan and Sid arrived, noticing no police had come as of yet. They parked at the back of the house near the kitchen. Nolan unscrewed two legs from a table that was on his moving truck for them to use as weapons.

Pete with a trashcan in his hand spotted Nolan and Sid with the table legs in their hands and became alarmed.

"It's okay. We didn't mean to frighten you," Nolan said when he recognized Pete's burgundy pants as the uniform of a servant.

"What I need you to do for me is call the police," Sid instructed. "Tell them to hurry up. A robber has the Houston sisters held hostage in a closet. You got that?"

"A robber?" Pete whispered.

"Yes, we got a call from one of them upstairs. We're going up to try to stop him."

All three of them entered the spotless kitchen. Pete picked up the cordless phone and made the call. He went on to place a garbage bag in the trashcan.

As Nolan and Sid made their way into the hallway, they encountered Kenley and Tessa.

"The robber is gone?" Nolan wondered.

"He's up in my room," Kenley said. "He may be hurt. I cut him with his knife."

"Stay put," Nolan advised.

"I've called for help," Tessa said as she glanced toward the top of the stairs.

Nolan listened for any noises coming from upstairs as he proceeded to go up. As he got closer, he heard Danny moaning from Kenley's bedroom.

Nolan rushed in the bedroom where Danny had taken the covers and wiped the blood off him. Nolan charged at him, whacking him in the knees.

Kenley had already pointed upstairs to show Sid where Milandra's bedroom was located. He ran up the stairs to rescue Milandra and Noelle. When he opened the closet door, Noelle ran into his arms. He kissed her with passion.

"I have to go, Baby. Nolan may need my help." Sid held the leg of the table in his hands. "Get some clothes on. The police are on their way."

Kenley, Tessa, and Pete watched from downstairs as Sid made his way into the next bedroom.

Sid saw Nolan had cracked the leg of the table on Danny. Of course, he got a few swings in for himself. Danny screamed in pain as he lay on the floor.

Milandra rushed to Nolan. He checked her neck. "You're lucky, baby, the knife didn't go any farther."

"Thanks for saving us," Milandra said as she gave him a hug.

Once the police arrived, Danny had to be carried out. Both of his legs were broken.

The police insisted Kenley be taken to the hospital, but she didn't want to go. Milandra had the Houstons' private doctor come to their home to tend to her wounds. Kenley had to have a few stitches in her arm.

Baron entered the house to see everyone gathered in the kitchen. Pete had cooked food for them. Noelle and Milandra had given their dates a rain check.

"What else can happen around here?" Baron asked. "Unbelievable. And you didn't tell me you were coming over here." He pointed at Tessa.

"I'm sorry; I came to speak to the girls," she said, but had yet to tell them her decision.

"It was scary," Noelle admitted.

"Where's Kenley?" Baron asked.

"She's taking a nap. Doc gave her a painkiller," Milandra said. "Have a seat."

Baron took a seat on a barstool near Tessa. "Nolan and Sid, I hear you're heroes."

"Man, we just did what we had to do," Sid said.

"Beat a man down." Nolan laughed.

"You got him pretty good." Sid chuckled.

Tessa was keeping quiet during the exchange, but finally she spoke up. "I have something to say."

Everyone saw the seriousness in her face. Baron wished she wouldn't upset them after what they had just been through.

"Rosie has done wrong, but no matter what, she's still my family. I know you are doing what you have to do to punish her for what she's done to you, but I'm sorry—I can't. I'm going to drop the kidnapping charges."

Milandra jumped out of her seat. "What? Are you as crazy as your niece?"

"Miss Houston, don't be so harsh," Baron said.

"I'm wondering about you, Mr. Chavis. What is it about her that makes you want to be with her?" Milandra asked.

"I love her unconditionally," Baron said.

Tessa cried, "Miss Houston, aren't you loyal to your family? You'll do anything to protect the Houston name. I must stay loyal to my family, too. I'm not saying Rosie is right for what she's done. I know it's wrong. I mean, she pretended to be my dead baby, but she's still my family."

Tessa got up and started to leave, but Baron stopped her. He held her in his arms. "Take it easy," he said.

"Milandra, as much as I wish she wouldn't drop the charges, she's right. The girl is her family. I know if it was you, I'd stick by you to the end, even if you were wrong. Her love for her family is no different than our love for ours," Noelle said.

Milandra took a swallow of cold water from a glass that sat in front of her on the table. "This day has been too much. Whatever you decide to do with your case against your niece is up to you."

Kenley came in the kitchen sporting a short set. Everyone turned to see her. "Hello, everyone."

"How are you feeling?" Milandra asked.

Kenley held her right arm close to her side. "I'm feeling a lot better."

"I'm sorry I couldn't rescue you the way you rescued me," Tessa said as she walked over and gave Kenley a hug.

"Your niece sure knows how to pick her men," Kenley said.

"Rosie?" Tessa questioned. "What does she have to do with this?"

"He knows her. He said something about me reminding him of her when he met her around my age."

"He must be the man I heard she ran away with," Tessa said.

"He said he was going to get the money out of us that he should've gotten out of her. He's blaming us for her going to jail," Kenley explained.

"The police will handle all that. I'll find out more about him," Baron said.

"Jackass, he is," Sid said.

"I bet he's in a lot of pain at the hospital." Nolan laughed. "I bashed them legs good."

Tessa listened to them. She was ready to leave. She wanted to run and see her niece. She wondered if Danny was really the man who had persuaded her niece to leave Mexico.

"I will go see Rosie," Tessa announced.

Baron looked at her. "I don't think so. Stay far away from your niece."

"I must find out who the man is—what part he played in her life," Tessa said.

"I never want to see your niece *or* him again," Kenley said.

"Your niece is in a terrible state of mind," Baron said.

"I don't fear my family. Please call a car to take me to the prison."

Baron saw that she was determined to go. "I'll drive you."

"No, I'll go alone. You stay here with the Houstons and help them," Tessa said.

"I guess you're going to tell her you're dropping the charges," Milandra said.

Tessa bowed her head. "She's family." On that note, she left.

Chapter 31

Tessa didn't part her lips to say a word as she turned over her purse for prison security to check for contraband. She went on and followed what she was told to do for the rest of the check-in procedures to obtain visitation.

Afterward, she was led into a room where all visitors were asked to be seated.

Lightly tapping her feet on the floor, Tessa waited for her niece to come out.

Aniyah, dressed in an orange uniform, strutted into the room. Her once high-fashion hairstyle was pulled back in a rubber band. Her face was as dull as an unsharpened knife from the lack of make-up. Right away she spotted her aunt. She had assumed her aunt was a public defender assigned to her case, in hopes of getting her released. "Aunt Tessa, I'm happy you came to your senses," she said. She wanted to give her aunt a big hug but the handcuffs held her hands hostage. "You've come to get me out of this mess you put me in."

Tessa no longer tapped her foot, nor was there a smile on her face. "How can you say it's my fault that you're behind bars?"

Aniyah yelled, "You didn't keep your damn mouth shut!"

"Lower your voice, Sanchez," a tall, medium-built female correctional officer said.

"Calm down," Tessa said.

"We could have had the world," Aniyah said as she lowered her voice.

"Rosie, none of it belonged to us."

Aniyah raised her voice again. "Damn, when something is so easily placed in your lap, Aunt Tessa, you take it."

"Sanchez, you're too loud," the female correctional officer bellowed.

Aniyah looked back at the officer and rolled her eyes. She stared back at her aunt. "Look, just leave. I've had enough of you." She stood up.

"Stay in your seat, Sanchez, that's your last warning," the female correctional officer bellowed.

Aniyah eased back down in the chair.

"You're so bitter. Is that why you want to cause harm to others?" Tessa asked, and then she went on to a touchy subject: "It's just like your man friend who, today, tried to hurt the Houston girls at their home."

Aniyah laughed, as she was quite aware of who her aunt meant. "Danny went after them snobby Houstons? He's good for something."

"I'm so ashamed of you. You think it's funny to celebrate other people's misery. Your friend is in the hospital with two broken legs."

Aniyah laughed hysterically. "Good for him, too. I hate all of them."

"I think you hate yourself more. You're not the little, sweet girl I used to know. It's going to hurt your mama if I ever decide to tell her."

Aniyah squinted. "Leave my mama out of this. Just keep your mouth closed on my business. You're just like Danny—so controlling."

Tessa listened as Aniyah revealed the name of the man in the hospital. "He's the one that got you to leave Mexico. Isn't he?"

"Yes. I left with him because I wanted to get away from the poor life."

"Your mama and I worked long hours to give you a good home."

"Long hours to still be poor. You blew our chance to have all the money in the world!" Aniyah yelled.

"It's not money for us to *take*. Why can't you understand that?"

"You blew it!" Aniyah yelled as she stood up and turned to the officer. "Take me back to my cell."

"Don't go, Rosie. I have more to say," Tessa pleaded.

"My name is Aniyah and you're nothing to me. You're nothing but a Houston whore. I hate you!" Aniyah yelled as the officer took her away.

Tessa laid her head down and cried. She wanted to share the news with Aniyah that she would drop the kidnapping charges but her niece had become someone else—someone that she no longer recognized. Tessa mumbled as she hurried out, "God, my niece's soul is with the devil."

Walking out onto the patio of the Houston Villa, Tessa saw the Houstons and Baron chatting around a black cast-iron table for eight.

Baron noticed the redness in her eyes as she entered. He could tell she had been crying and went to her. "How did it go?"

Tessa shook her head. "Not good at all. My niece is in her own body, but her soul is destroyed."

"With time, everything will come to a peaceful resolution," he said.

Tessa walked over to the table and grabbed Milandra by the hand. "Please forgive the Sanchez family. We are really good people. I didn't drop the charges on Rosie. I know now that she must take the punishment for her wrongdoings."

"I'm glad you came to your senses," Milandra said.

"Let's start thinking of Mother and how beautiful she was. Let's start rejoicing the good soul she had. She was a charitable woman," Noelle said as she smiled.

Milandra knew what her sister said was true. Her mother would give to a stranger on the street. Alana never walked by anyone without saying "Good day."

Milandra looked over at Nolan, who was staring at her. Just looking into his eyes, she saw the compassion she always saw in her mother's eyes.

Everyone watched as Milandra stood up and gave Tessa a hug. "Forgive me. Forgive my father. I know Father didn't show you the good and nurturing side of him, but believe me, it was within him." Milandra let go of Tessa and grabbed her hand. She reached and took Baron by the hand. She locked his hand with Tessa's. "Be happy. Catch up on the love you've always had for each other."

Baron gave Milandra a hug. "Thanks, Miss Houston," he said.

"It's a new day. You're welcome to call me and my sisters by our first names."

"Thanks, Milandra." He smiled.

Nolan rushed over to Milandra and hugged her. Sid ran over and hugged Noelle.

Kenley watched as they hugged each other. "What's this? Everyone has someone to hug, but me." Kenley laughed.

Pete came out of the kitchen to the patio to check on their needs. Kenley ran over and threw her left arm around his neck. He kept his hands up in the air. He yelled, "I didn't do anything."

"No, you didn't. I'm not going to use you like that fake Aniyah." Kenley laughed as she let go of him. Everyone on the patio was silent.

Milandra was curious. "Pete, how did she use you?"

"In her bed. I had to or I would lose my job at the estate. To protect me, Elsa sent me on many errands," Pete admitted.

Tessa went over to him. "I'm sorry for whatever my niece did to you. You're such a nice young man."

Kenley went back over to him. She gave him a hug all over again. "You definitely need lots of hugs."

"Thanks," Pete said, smiling, enjoying all the hugs from Kenley.

Everyone else went back to hugging their significant other.

Chapter 32

Aniyah was convicted of all the charges against her and so was Danny, who was wanted for other crimes throughout the state of Georgia.

It was packing time for the Houstons. Milandra hurried to pack her clothes in boxes with the help of a servant. Kenley packed with the aid of Pete. He became her private servant, even though Milandra insisted she have a female servant.

"Remember, he's just help. So don't get any ideas," Milandra warned her.

In her room, Noelle let her clothes stay put. She wondered how she would tell her sisters that she wanted to stay where she was.

Milandra came into her sister's bedroom. "I know you're the first to be packed," she said, but she was startled to see the bedroom was neat and tidy—not like her bedroom, which had clothes laying everywhere to be boxed. "You haven't even started to pack. Nolan will have his movers here early this afternoon."

"I'm not moving," Noelle softly said.

"You can't mean that," Milandra said in disbelief.

Noelle stared out of the opened window, viewing the calm waves of the lake. "I've fallen in love with the Houston Villa."

"How can you? This is where Father kept his lovers. This is where that man attacked us."

"Yes, but it's here that I feel so much peace. I guess you wouldn't understand. You're so much like Father."

"I don't know if I should take that as a compliment or not," Milandra said as she walked over to her sister. She looked out the window to admire the view, too.

"I didn't mean anything negative by it. I know you love the prestigious life more than Kenley and I, so the estate fits you in every way."

"And you don't love money?"

"I do, but I don't want it to control me. I want to be free to be me. Every time I do something, I don't want to have to remember that I have to live up to being a Houston."

"You can't escape that, Noelle. That's who you are."

"Yes, it's my name, but I want to live it in the way that I want to—not by any *Houston* rule book."

"You really mean what you say?" Milandra asked. "You want to let go of all the ways a Houston should be?"

Noelle walked past her sister. She sat in front of a vanity table and brushed her hair.

"I just want to be myself as a Houston."

Milandra could see her sister wasn't budging. "Okay, if you want to stay here, fine. Kenley and I are definitely leaving here ASAP."

Noelle couldn't believe Milandra wasn't going to give her a good verbal fight.

"Thank you, Milandra, for respecting my wishes."

"Can you do one thing for me?"

"What is it?"

"Can we Houston girls still go to lunch every Friday, as Mother always had us do?"

"Of course!"

Noelle laid the brush on the vanity and stood up. As she embraced her older sister, her baby sister entered the bedroom.

"Do you need me to call Sid to help you pack?" Kenley teased since she saw her sister hadn't begun to pack.

"No. I've decided to stay here—at least for now," Noelle said.

"Wow! Is Sid moving in with you?" Kenley asked.

Milandra echoed, astonished, "Sid is moving in here with you?"

"Of course not. Those were Kenley's words, not mine. Now *that* part of a Houston, I'll keep. No man will move in here until he makes me an honest woman."

"You scared me for a moment," Milandra said, relieved.

They laughed as they embraced in a group hug.

The day went as planned. Noelle helped them with their clothing. Nolan's movers packed their bags and boxes into the truck.

Noelle walked her sisters out to the limo. A tear rolled down her face. "I'll come to visit soon."

"Tomorrow," Milandra ordered.

They gave one another pecks on the cheeks. Noelle waved until she could no longer see the limo. The first item on the agenda in her new life would be to call Elsa to arrange for a servant for her. That part of a Houston's life she wouldn't give up. Pete had already left to go back to the estate, thanks to Kenley, who pouted until Milandra gave in and allowed him to continue working at the estate.

Before the end of the day, the doorbell chimed and Noelle made her way to the front door. When she opened it, her eyes lit up. Who better to be her first guest than Sid. She smiled. "Welcome to my home."

Sid gave her a peck on the cheek and entered. "I went to the estate. Kenley told me you decided to stay here. I'm surprised."

"I think it's time I stand on my own two feet. I always stood in the shoes of my family. I'm kind of nervous, but I think I can do it."

"I'll help you any way I can."

"Come in the kitchen; there's a freshly baked sweet potato pie ready to be eaten."

"Sounds delicious." Sid followed her into the kitchen.

Noelle handled the pie carefully as she carried it from the oven to the table. She directed Sid to find a knife in one of the drawers.

After slicing the pie in sections, Sid placed a slice on each of their plates. Noelle got ice cream out of the freezer and put two scoops on his plate and one scoop on her plate. Together, they began to feast on the dessert.

"Yummy…delicious," he said.

"I love vanilla ice cream and pie together. My mother always had the cook prepare this dessert at least once a week."

"Did you bake this pie?" Sid asked, knowing she didn't.

"No way! The help baked it. You would never want to see me again after eating a pie I baked. It would be a disaster."

"One day you and I will make one together," he promised.

Noelle's voice was as squeaky as a mouse when she asked him, "You can bake a pie?"

"Oh yeah. I wasn't blessed with a silver spoon. I've watched my mother bake up a storm. It rubbed off on me."

"I guess sometimes letting others do for you can make a person like me lose out on doing simple things that may just be fun. I look forward to making pies with you." She smiled.

Sid jumped up out of his seat. He took the remainder of the pie off the table and tossed it in the trashcan.

Noelle watched him with her mouth wide open. He took their plates and dumped them in the sink.

"I can't believe you threw the pie in the trash."

"Oh, yeah. We're going to bake our own pie."

"Right now."

Sid ran around the kitchen and took out all the ingredients to make a sweet potato pie. Noelle stood back and watched him move around the kitchen like a professional chef.

"Come over here. I'll give the instructions and you'll do as I say."

"I think you're going to regret throwing the other pie in the garbage."

"My recipe is better. And your touch is going to make it taste even better."

Noelle did as he said every step of the way. "This is fun," she admitted as she stirred the sweet potato mixture.

She finished his last instruction. She placed the pie in the oven.

"There, the pie is cooking. Wait until Milandra hears that I baked a pie. She's going to think I've truly gone against being a Houston."

"Baking a pie doesn't make you less of a Houston," Sid assured her as he took some of the leftover pie mix around the bowl and scooped it on his finger.

Holding his finger to her mouth, Noelle licked off the pie filling. "Superb!"

Noelle enjoyed the sweetness of the filling, and then she saw the sink was full of dirty bowls. "The kitchen is so untidy."

"More fun for us."

Sid removed the bowls and filled the sink with soapsuds and water. He washed the dishes. Noelle occasionally checked on the pie as it cooked. She kept the light on in the oven.

"Get away from there," Sid said as he handed her a dishtowel. "You can dry the dishes."

"We should have used the dishwasher. That would have been quicker."

"We're doing it the old-fashioned way—with our own hands."

Noelle wiped over the bowls, half-drying them. She didn't feel like a Houston in the way the world portrayed them. She wished the media could have captured her having fun in the kitchen.

Turning off the oven, Sid gave her orders that the pie was ready.

Noelle covered her hands with oven mitts to avoid burning herself on the hot pie pan. She held her head back from the heat that escaped from the oven. "It smells so good," she said as she placed the golden brown pie on top of the stove.

"We'll let it cool down."

"I'm ready for a bite."

"Set the table."

Noelle got out two small plates. She placed a fork next to each plate and filled two glasses with cold milk. She waited for Sid to give the okay to slice the pie.

He turned around and smiled at her. "Miss Houston, would you like the honor of cutting your first baked pie?"

Noelle curtsied. "I thought you would never ask."

Sid took the pie over to the table and she cut it into slices. She placed a slice on each plate. Sid went back and got the ice cream out of the freezer.

"One scoop of vanilla for me," Noelle said.

He put two scoops on his plate. They sat down and absorbed the taste of the pie with the ice cream.

"This is magnificent."

"You should be proud, Miss Houston."

"I am...to have you come into my life."

They ate the dessert until their stomachs felt like lead balloons.

"Talk about overeating. I've had my share of pie tonight."

"You made my first night in this house without my sisters one to be remembered."

Sid got up and started to clean the dishes. Noelle went over to him. "Leave it for tomorrow."

She took him by the hand and led him upstairs to her bedroom.

"As always I ask you, are you sure you want to do this?"

"I'm a grown woman; you don't ever have to ask me that question again."

Noelle eased her hands up his chest and around his neck. Sid loosened the pins in her hair to let it fall. They kissed passionately.

Noelle stepped back and removed her clothes. He stared as she shared her bare flesh with him again. The light from a pole outside glowed through the window to shine on her body.

"Aren't you going to join me?"

Sid removed his clothes. Noelle hungered for him. Once his last piece of clothing exposed his masculine parts, she raced into his arms. He lifted her up and laid her on the bed. He climbed on top of her. There he explored her body.

Noelle moaned from the force as he entered her. She locked her legs around him. He moved like the waves of the ocean and she paddled along with him. She screamed, knowing that her sisters wouldn't have any say-so in her life. This was her paradise—to live her life as she pleased.

Sid rested under the covers with her. He held her in his arms close to him. "I'm not the man you or your father would see as a suitable husband, but I can make you happy. Just give me the time to show you that I'm worthy of you."

Noelle touched his mustache. "My heart tells me you're perfect for me. We'll let things fall into place." She kissed his chest.

Sid looked at his watch. "It's late. I better get going."

Noelle placed her finger on his lips. "No such thing. My heart says you're wanted here for the night. Go to sleep."

They slept in each other's arms.

Chapter 33

B ack at the Houston Estate, Milandra saw to it that the guest bedroom was completely redesigned. The mahogany king-sized bedroom set was given away to the Salvation Army and replaced with a king-sized, cherrywood bedroom set. The bedding matched the newly painted green wall color.

Their parents' bedroom was also redecorated. Milandra decided to move into the master suite, leaving Kenley on the west wing of the house. Her goal was to turn her and Noelle's old bedrooms into more guest rooms.

She hurriedly unpacked as Nolan carried up the last box of clothing. He dropped the box on the floor. Taking a hand towel, he wiped the sweat that dripped down the back of his neck.

"I'm tired. Girl, you Houstons don't play when it comes down to clothes."

Milandra laughed. "We have to stay ladylike at all times."

"I don't know if I can keep up with royalty."

Milandra looked at him, noticing that his face showed no signs of humor.

"Nolan, I don't expect anything extra out of you other than the person you are."

"Thanks, because I can't give you what you want. I don't have the cash to do it."

Milandra knew this would come into play sooner or later. She went up to him. "I'm not looking for the world from you—just your friendship."

"Friendship! Is that it? Milandra, you only want me as a friend? I'm a man who wants a wife and kids one day, but I get the feeling you don't want what I want."

"We come from two different worlds. We could never be man and wife."

"I thought you really dug me. Damn, I've never been used by a woman."

"I'm doing no such thing. I mean we can be together and have fun, but it wouldn't be appropriate for me to marry someone of your status. You don't have wealth."

Nolan hit his fist against the wall. "You're no better than Aniyah and your father put together. I'm out of here. Take my company off your list for services. I won't be doing business with you anymore," he said as he stormed out.

"Nolan, why are you doing this? You know how things can *only* be for a Houston," Milandra called.

Kenley overheard them. She saw Nolan leaving, slamming the door behind him, and Milandra running after him, tearfully.

"What's going on between you two?" Kenley asked.

"I have lost Nolan. He couldn't understand that we can only be friends."

"And why can you two only be friends?"

"We're from two different worlds. I can't marry a mover."

"He owns his own company," Kenley said as she sat down on the top step.

"Nolan doesn't have wealth."

"He has love for you. That should be good enough. I hope you didn't tell him he didn't have wealth."

"I had to be honest with him."

"You lost a man who worships you, and you dared to tell him it's because he has less. You can marry a man with lots of money and be miserable."

"Oh, Kenley, Father wouldn't want his fortune going to the common man."

"Mother would want you to be happy. Doesn't she count too, sometimes?"

"Stop making things difficult for me," Milandra said as she left Kenley and went back into her bedroom.

Milandra slouched down on the bed and wept herself to sleep. In her heart, she missed Nolan already but the damage was done. Her outspoken behavior had caused her to lose him.

Kenley went into her sister's bedroom. She saw that Milandra was sound asleep.

Tiptoeing over to a nightstand, she picked up Milandra's cell phone and carried it out into the hallway. She scrolled to find Nolan's number programmed in the phone. She called him. Nolan didn't answer, so Kenley decided to call him from her line. He picked up.

"Hello, this is Kenley. Please don't hang up on me. I didn't do a thing to you."

"I'm not going to hang up on you. I hope you're not calling me for your sister."

"She doesn't know I'm calling. The calls you got from her number, I made them."

"Are you trying to get us back together? It won't work. Your sister made it clear about what she wants—and it's not broke me."

Kenley sat on the floor in the hallway. "You have to understand Milandra. Yes, she's stubborn and bossy. She's not used to anyone else taking the lead on things except my parents. You are a new world to her. It's frightening to her that she has actually fallen for someone that doesn't have lots of money. In her head, love and wealth go together."

"You and Noelle were born in wealth, but you girls are so different. You're more open to things."

"Don't get me wrong, I'm spoiled in my own way. But Noelle and I take people for who they are. Milandra is the one that took after Father all the way. He taught her to believe that love and wealth are one and the same, but she's finding out through you that it isn't true. She's fighting against herself. Please give her a chance. I know she loves you. I could see it when you ran out of here."

"I don't know." Nolan paused. "Maybe I should keep my distance."

"Do you think you're in love with my sister?"

"You're straightforward."

"You older people make love a big project. So do you love her?"

"I feel like I'm falling in love with her. I hoped she was feeling the same way, but 'just a friend'—now that's cold."

"Please, she feels more for you than just a friend. I should have videoed her after you left. All I can say is if you think you're falling in love with her, make her see that being with you, a man who has less, can be worth more than any other man with money."

Nolan said goodbye.

Milandra woke up the next day with a pounding headache. She decided to stay in bed.

Kenley came into her bedroom. "You're still in bed?"

"I don't feel good," she said with an ice pack on her head.

"You're in love."

"Nonsense!"

Noelle came over to the estate and made her way into the bedroom. She saw Milandra still in bed. "I heard you were sick. That was the talk of the day as I came in the house."

"I have a slight headache," Milandra said.

"She has a love ache. She ran Nolan away and now she hates that she did it," Kenley said.

"Hush your talk," Milandra said.

"You let Nolan go? Why?" Noelle asked as she took a seat on the side of the bed.

"He doesn't have wealth," Kenley answered.

"Sid doesn't have wealth, but he's a good man. I would never throw him away. Milandra, how could you do such thing?" Noelle asked.

"You would marry Sid?" Milandra asked amazed.

"Yes, we've talked about it," Noelle said.

"My head is pounding more," Milandra said.

"You can get well really fast by just calling Nolan back over," Kenley said.

"He doesn't want to be a friend, so we're finished," Milandra said.

"Let's forget about wealth. Let's talk about him," Noelle said, taking the role of a psychologist.

"There's nothing to speak of," Milandra said as she pulled the covers over her head.

"Oh, yes there is. I know you've kissed him, but what about sex?" Noelle asked.

Kenley ran up to Milandra and pulled the covers off her face. "You had sex with Nolan? Tell us how it was?"

"Kenley, get out of this room. I'm not discussing sex with my sister who is barely sixteen," Milandra said.

"I can learn it from you or I can learn it on my own. Which would you rather I do?" Kenley giggled.

"Start talking, Milandra," Noelle said.

Milandra said, "I'm waiting to have sex until I'm married. And I hope, Noelle, you'll wait until marriage also."

"Too late. Sid and I have made great love," Noelle bragged.

"Good for you, Noelle. When I'm old enough I'm going to be just like you. I'm not letting a man out of my sight who gives me great sex," Kenley said.

Milandra sat up in the bed. "What have you become, Noelle? There's more to a relationship than sex."

"Well, Sid treats me the best in and out of bed. Nolan treats you wonderfully, from what I see," Noelle said.

"Yes, he's a gentleman, I will admit," Milandra said. "But no wealth."

"Oh you're driving me bananas. Forget about the wealth. Love him for who he is. Have hot sex, or I'll be pushing you around as an old lady in a wheelchair. You'll have to live with me. I'll feed you peanuts and crackers," Kenley teased.

Noelle giggled. "You better find a way to get Nolan back as soon as possible."

"I've messed up. I don't know what to do. He might never forgive me," Milandra said.

Kenley smiled as Nolan appeared in the room.

"Ladies, will you excuse Milandra and me?" he asked.

Noelle and Kenley left the room. Nolan closed the door behind them. He walked over to Milandra and took the ice pack out of her hand, placing it on the nightstand. He held her in his arms and looked directly into her eyes.

"You listen here. I'll be your friend for now or whatever you want to call it, but I'm going to work hard to build wealth because you'll be my wife one day. I love you, and I know you love me. We'll have to learn each other's lifestyles. Now get out of this bed and get dressed. We're going on a picnic."

Nolan walked over to the door and opened it. Instead of leaving, he turned and went back to her. He took her into his arms, kissing her passionately. "No man can love you the way I love you." He walked away, but he made one last comment before he left the room: "I'll wait for you downstairs."

Her face puddled in tears, Milandra decided to get out of bed and join her man.

Chapter 34

K enley's sweet sixteen birthday party was one of the things that kept her from thinking of her parents' death. She gave out all twenty-five invitations—including one to Pete. She had convinced her sisters to have her entire party at their home instead of the yacht club. Her concern was who would be her date. She went to Milandra.

"My party is not going to be so good," she whined.

"You have all the trimmings for it," Milandra said as she went over the party list.

"I have no date to walk me in." Kenley wept.

"Let's see if one of Father's colleagues' sons would like to escort you."

"A stranger. I don't want anyone to feel pity for me," Kenley wept.

"Well, do you have an idea?"

Kenley thought and whispered, "Pete."

"Who?" Milandra stopped writing and turned around to look at her.

"Pete."

"The help? I better pick out your date."

"I like Pete. He's fun and quite handsome. Please! He knows me."

"He better not know you too well."

"I'm just talking to him. I'm not mushy with him like you and Noelle are with your male friends."

"Hush your mouth!"

Although she wanted to say no to Kenley, Milandra didn't dare upset her sister. "Okay, it's your sweet sixteenth birthday. I'll grant it."

"Yippee," Kenley yelled and twirled around like a ballerina and ran to find her date.

Inside the kitchen, Pete was polishing a silver bowl. Kenley came up to him and tapped him on the shoulder.

He jumped. "You scared me."

"Sorry, I didn't mean to. But you must stop what you're doing."

"I have to finish polishing this bowl before Elsa comes back from shopping."

"I need to talk to you."

Kenley watched as he set the bowl down on the table. Pete turned and gave her his full attention.

"What you want to talk about?"

"I need you to come with me and buy a tuxedo."

"That's a funny name. What is it?"

Kenley laughed. "It's a fancy suit. You're going to be my escort for my party."

"Escort?" Pete said as he wondered what an escort does.

"You'll walk me into my party."

"Oh, I see, like a papa walks his daughter in for marriage."

"Yes, like that." Kenley giggled.

"How about your boyfriend?"

Kenley said sadly. "I have no boyfriend. Please escort me. If you don't, I won't have anyone."

Pete grinned. "For you, señorita, I do it. What about the pants and shirt I got from Elsa to wear to party?"

"Give them back to her," Kenley said. She abruptly kissed him on the cheek. "Thanks for being my escort."

The touch of her lips turned his groin into a frozen Popsicle. Without any thought, he in return placed a peck on her cheek.

Her heart fluttered as she wished he had kissed her on the lips. "Let's go get you a tuxedo." Kenley smiled as she took him by the hand.

The afternoon was filled with shopping and grooming Pete for the party.

The servants decorated the estate with an arrangement of assorted flowers and balloons. A garland of pink roses adorned the staircase banister. Pete proudly stood in his tuxedo, not daring to sit down and mess it up. With the help of Elsa, his hair was slicked back, and the shirt he wore was white and crisp. The black cummerbund lay flat around his waist. His shoes dazzled like polished silver.

Pete kept looking up the stairs as he waited for Kenley to make her entrance; it wasn't long before she stood at the top of the stairs. She was dressed in a simple, pale-pink, low-cut, backless dress with sequins. Her hair was pulled back into a curly ponytail, and it showed off her mother's diamond stud earrings that sparkled in her ears. She strolled down the stairs on pink diamond stud high heels to match her dress. Her cheeks were rosy from pink blush and her lips glittered with pink lip gloss.

Pete held his head up high to show off the black bow tie as Kenley stepped down the last step to stand in front of him.

"Wow! You're the most beautiful black girl I've ever seen."

She smiled. "You're the best looking Mexican boy in a tuxedo."

"Black-Mexican," he corrected her. "But thanks." He smiled.

"Pictures," Noelle and Milandra called. They had already snapped several shots as Kenley came down the stairs, as if the occasion was a photo shoot.

Kenley and Pete posed for photos. Kenley knew her friends would think Pete was her boyfriend. She didn't care because he was fine.

They made their way out into the entrance of the yard. Many young teens sat around the pool under tents decorated in pink and white roses. The tables were covered in white linen.

In the center of the tables were bouquets of pink and white roses. A white runner was put down on the walkway, which extended to a hand-built arch filled with pink and white roses.

Kenley and Pete made it to the entrance. She put her arm under his. Pete reached over and kissed her on the cheek. "Happy Birthday, Miss Houston."

"It's Kenley to you."

Milandra stood outside and held a microphone. She announced, "May I have your attention, everyone?" The guests became silent. "Everyone, please stand." The audience stood up. "On behalf of my sister, Noelle and I, we would like to thank everyone for attending Kenley's Sweet Sixteen Birthday Party. At this time we graciously introduce to you, our sister, Sweet Sixteen Miss Kenley Houston escorted by Mr. Pete Gomez."

Kenley walked down the aisle on Pete's arm. Cameras flashed in their faces. They showed teeth until they made it under the arch. There, Pete stepped back and cameras continued to flash. Some of the local media were allowed in to take photos. Under the arch was a table set up for Kenley. There, she sat and prepared to dine on her favorite dish—lobster.

Pete sat at a nearby table with Milandra, Noelle, Nolan, Sid, Tessa, and Baron. Even Elsa was able to sit at the table at Kenley's request.

Later on, a toast was made in her honor. Then it was time for the guests to change from their dainty clothes into their swimwear. The girl invitees changed in the pool house. The boys changed in an outdoor bathroom. Kenley changed into a two-piece swimsuit.

Milandra saw her make her way back out to the poolside. "That's not the bathing suit Kenley is supposed to be wearing. It's a one-piece. I must go and talk to her."

Nolan grabbed Milandra by the arm. He was about to comment but Noelle handled it. "Leave her alone, Milandra. It's her birthday. Please let her be happy for this day. She deserves some happiness after all the hardship we've been through."

Milandra stayed put.

Pete changed into his swimming trunks. He dove into the pool for fun—not to help clean it as he sometimes did. Kenley splashed into the pool. She and her guests played volleyball.

"We adults should go inside and let the young people have fun," Noelle said as she got out of her seat.

"We're not leaving a bunch of teenagers alone. The boys might get out of hand," Milandra said and she stayed put.

Nolan grabbed Milandra by the arm again, this time to help her up out of her seat. "We can watch from inside. They're not babies."

The adults went into the house. Milandra stayed close enough to see as much as she could at the pool area.

Kenley enjoyed her party. The end had come too soon. She saw all her guests to the door. Pete was the last one to go home. She walked him halfway to the servants' quarters.

"Thanks, Pete. I'll always remember that you're the one who made my sixteenth birthday the coolest."

"I had fun. It was like a fiesta," he said as he handed her the tuxedo.

"My sister will see that it gets back to the renters, but I better get back to the house. Milandra will be looking for me."

Pete reached over to kiss her on the cheek. Kenley turned her face enough for their lips to connect. He put his arms around her and pressed his lips hard against hers. Kenley could tell Aniyah had taught him more than he should know.

Pete tried to touch her breasts, but Kenley pushed his hand away.

"I'm not ready for that. A kiss is fine for now. I like kissing." She blushed.

"The other stuff—that's for my sisters. They're old enough. I just want to have fun being a teen."

"I understand. I like kissing you, too. I just thought…"

"I know you have experienced more. That crazy fake Aniyah."

"Yeah, she's a hot tamale." He giggled.

"I'm in no way like her."

"You're a princess," Pete said as he bowed his head to her.

"Thanks! I'm ready for bed. It's been too much fun," Kenley yawned.

"Kiss, one more time," Pete said as he pointed to his lips.

Kenley reached out and they pecked each other on the lips.

"You be my girlfriend?"

Kenley called out to him as she ran to go home, "Yes, but let it be our secret."

"Okay, goodnight," Pete said and ran off toward the servants' quarters.

Chapter 35

The fall season had arrived. The waves wobbled in the lake and gave off a cool breeze. Kenley hurried down to the lake to meet Pete. They had been boyfriend and girlfriend for two years. Her father's boat was their private spot away from everyone.

Kenley stepped inside the boat that was tied to end of the dock. She walked to the bottom level of it. Pete sat there drinking a soda.

"I thought you weren't coming today."

"It's Friday. My sisters and I have lunch together, something my mother used to have us do. It's the time we talk about our daily lives."

"You talk about us?"

"My lips are sealed," Kenley said as she took the soda out of his hand and took a sip. "Ah…that hit the spot."

"No kiss for me?"

"I forgot."

Kenley pecked him on the lips. "Turn on the television. Let's watch a movie."

"Not yet! More kisses," he said as he squeezed her close to him, pressing his lips to hers.

Pete touched her blossomed breasts. She didn't push him away. He caressed her breasts as he kept kissing her. Kenley let her hand travel to his crotch. She touched his muscle and felt it become stronger.

Pete nudged her to get on the floor of the boat. Kenley pulled him right along with her until he was on top of her.

"You're ready."

"Yes, I'm a woman now. I've been waiting for you to take me since I turned eighteen."

"Why didn't you say something?" He wanted to know.

"I'm a lady. I wanted you to approach me first."

Pete said no more. He reached under her skirt and went to pull her panties off, but felt nothing but her flesh.

"I told you I was ready for you," she whispered. She wiggled her hips and removed her skirt.

Kenley spread her legs apart. She gave him a clear view of her garden. "Put this on," she said as she handed him a condom.

He slipped it on and eased inside of her. A sharp pain hit her between the legs, but as he stroked her, the pain turned to pleasure.

As Kenley moved her body to his mambo, she was unaware that her sisters had made their way to the boat with their male partners.

Milandra led the way on to the boat. She went down the stairs and saw Pete on top of her sister. She ran over and slapped him on the back of his head. Nolan ran after her, pulling her off him.

Kenley lay nude. She hid her breasts with one hand and with the other she covered her garden.

"What the hell are you doing to my sister?" Milandra yelled.

"Kenley," Noelle called, in shock at the position Kenley and Pete were in.

"We're having sex!" Kenley yelled. "How dare you come and interrupt us? We are boyfriend and girlfriend. We have been for a long time."

"Kenley Houston, you've been having sex?" Milandra scolded her. Nolan and Sid turned their backs to them.

"Today is my first time and all of you ruined it for me!" Kenley yelled, pointing at her siblings and their gentlemen callers. She snatched her clothes and ran into a bathroom to get dressed. Pete grabbed his clothes and ran out.

Kenley returned fully dressed and saw that he was gone. "Where's Pete?" she yelled.

"I don't know where he went, but he's fired," Milandra said.

"Then I'll go with him. I love Pete just like you guys love each other. I love him," Kenley cried. "You ruined my first time!" she screamed and left the boat.

Milandra took the nearest seat as Nolan consoled her.

"Don't let this get to you. Your sister is young," Nolan said.

"Getting that first piece is a major thing." Sid smiled.

"I don't think this is something to joke about," Milandra said as she looked over at Sid.

"Sorry, I know this is a serious matter for your family." Sid saw that she didn't take kindly to his words.

"Stop running," Noelle called as she left the others behind in the boat to run after her baby sister.

Kenley fell down on the ground. She cried, "Please don't let her fire Pete. He's my boyfriend. I do love him, Noelle, with all my heart."

"Kenley, those are strong words."

"You love Sid."

"Yes, but we're much older. Loving a man is something you must be sure of. And you must find out if Pete really feels the same way."

Kenley got up. "I'll go find out. Just leave me alone to find out."

"All right." Noelle gave in.

Kenley ran barefooted through the grass to the servants' quarters. She ran inside the open door to Pete's room and saw he was packing his suitcase. She shut the door behind her.

"Pete, don't pack yet. We must talk."

"I must leave. Miss Houston fired me."

Kenley sat on top of his suitcase to block him from packing. "Well, this Miss Houston says you're not. I love you. Tell me the truth, do you love me?"

"My heart is for you. I waited until you were ready to be with me. I could have been with any other girl, but I chose not."

Kenley tossed her arms around his neck. She kissed him passionately.

"Forget my sister. I'm yours whether you work here or not. I'll see to it that you get work somewhere to take care of us." She continued to kiss him.

Pushing the suitcase aside, Kenley pulled him down on her.

Pete nervously pushed her skirt up. He pulled a condom out of his pocket and slipped it on.

Kenley laughed. "You secretly had a condom for us, too."

"Yes," he said as he entered her.

They made their own heat that caused them to soak in each other's sweat.

Out at the boat Noelle made her way back to her older sister.

"What did Kenley say?" Milandra asked.

"She says she loves him. She went to find out if he loves her."

"Nonsense. She knows nothing of love."

"Milandra, everything has changed. I believe we're going to lose our sister if Pete doesn't stay. Don't fire him."

"Let the young man keep his job. At least you can keep tabs on them," Sid said.

"He's right, Milandra," Nolan said. "Baby, they're going to find a way to be together. I know I would go to far lengths to be with you."

"This is a time I miss Father dearly." Milandra wept.

Noelle put her arms around her sister and held her. "We will be okay."

A storm was imminent; lightning lit up the darkness of the clouds. The sound of thunder echoed throughout the boat.

"I think we better get back to the house," Noelle said. She was frightened of storms.

They made their way off the boat, but they were not able to reach shelter before a downpour of rain came down. Their male partners tried to shield them from the rain, but their bodies were soaked as if they had gone for a swim.

Chapter 36

Elsa scrambled plenty of eggs for a morning breakfast for the Houstons and their guests. She flipped pancakes on a hot griddle, and in another large frying pan, sausage and bacon sizzled in hot grease. The back burner on the stove held a pot of hot grits.

Kenley made her way into the kitchen. She went over to the stove to steal a piece of bacon.

"Oh, no you don't, young lady," Elsa said, moving Kenley affectionately out of the way. "No one eats my breakfast until it's spread out on the table."

"It smells so good."

"It's gonna make you do a hallelujah dance when you taste it. I put extra love into breakfast this morning."

"Elsa, you're teasing me."

"Go on, find your place at the table."

Kenley went over to her seat at the table, which was covered in a white linen cloth. She poured herself a glass of orange juice from one of the crystal pitchers that were filled with orange and apple juice, already placed on the table.

Elsa brought serving dishes of food over to the table.

Noelle and Sid entered the kitchen. Sid absorbed the aroma. "Whew, I'm ready to eat," he said.

"It smells delicious," Noelle said.

"Go on and take a seat at the table. Don't do like your baby sister here and go touching things on this table," Elsa preached as she directed her attention at Kenley, who was sipping on juice. "Y'all know how Milandra is about every Houston being present at the table."

"Did I hear my name called?" Milandra said as she made her entrance in the kitchen with Nolan at her side.

"Thank God you're here. Your sisters are mighty hungry," Elsa said as she placed two plates of biscuits on each end of the table.

Two seats were empty. "Call Mr. Chavis and Tessa and tell them to hurry. We're not eating cold biscuits," Noelle said because she had invited them.

"Piping hot, they'll melt in your mouth," Sid said as he waited to snatch one up.

"All Houstons are here, that's good enough," Milandra said.

"Don't be mean, Milandra." Noelle snapped at her sister.

"Bow your heads," Milandra said and went on and blessed the food. She passed the food around the table.

"Where I come from, we just start grabbing food." Sid chuckled.

Milandra glanced over at him. "Manners must be used at all times," she commented.

"That's not necessary, Milandra." Noelle became annoyed.

"Okay, let's eat in peace," Nolan insisted, biting into a biscuit.

Pete entered the kitchen.

"You're still here," Milandra addressed him.

"Yes, he is. He's my boyfriend. Pull up a seat, Pete. Join us for breakfast," Kenley said.

Pete looked over at Milandra. She rolled her eyes at him, but said, "Sit down. You can keep your job, but I'll be keeping a close watch on you and my sister."

"Nolan, please keep Milandra busy, so she can stay out of my business," Kenley begged him.

Baron and Tessa entered the kitchen. "I hope there's still plenty of food left for us," he said.

"Mr. Chavis, I've cooked more than enough," Elsa said.

Tessa made her way to Elsa. She gave her a hug. "Elsa, it's always good to see you."

"I'm glad to see you, too, Sugar." Elsa smiled.

Tessa whispered in Elsa's ear. She held out her hand to show off her wedding ring. "I'm married."

"Well, I'll be. You tied the knot." Elsa grinned.

Milandra looked at Baron, who sat at the table and began eating.

"You married her?" Milandra asked.

"Oh yeah, we flew to Vegas. Got back yesterday."

"Milandra, let's respect Mr. Chavis' choice of wife," Noelle said.

"Everyone hold your juice glass in the air," Kenley said excitedly. "Cheers to the newlyweds," she shouted.

They tapped their glasses against one another's and chanted "cheers."

Tessa went over and sat next to Baron. She kissed him on the cheek. "Pass me the biscuits, hubby." She grinned.

"How cute." Kenley absorbed in their happiness. "We wish you both many happy years."

"I guess this is the moment," Nolan said, nodding his head at Sid. They took their partners by the hands. They each pulled out a small box. Kenley dashed out of her seat and got closer to witness what they were about to do.

Sid went first. He got down on one knee in front of Noelle. "You know how much I love you."

Milandra was ready to speak, but Nolan silenced her and got down on one knee in front of his hopeful future wife.

"Milandra, you know how much I love you," Nolan said, staring into her eyes.

Both men said together to their partners, "Will you marry me?"

Noelle flung her arms around Sid. She placed pecks of kisses on his forehead. "Yes!" she shouted.

Sid slid a diamond ring on her finger. "It's beautiful," Noelle gushed.

Nolan waited for an answer from Milandra. He knew it would be harder for him to get a positive answer from her.

"What are you waiting on, Milandra? Answer the man." Kenley nudged her.

"Think about it," Nolan said sadly as he got up off his knees. He pushed the box back in his pocket. Milandra saw the hurt in his eyes. A tear rolled down his face.

What am I doing? Follow your heart. She heard her mother's voice echo in her ears. *The man's hard working hands will bring him an abundance of wealth, but his love for you will bring you a lifetime of happiness.*

The room was silent. Milandra's face filled with tears as she jumped up and shouted, "Yes, I'll marry you."

Nolan took her into his arms. They kissed for what seemed like a long time. He eased the diamond ring onto her finger. He placed his hands on each side of her face. "One day, my love, I'll buy a bigger diamond—the one that you truly deserve."

"I accept this one to be your wife and no other one. I accept you for the man that you are. Your warm heart and soul are my riches from you," Milandra said.

"Thank God." Kenley sighed as she went over and placed her arms around Pete's neck.

"A double wedding," Noelle said.

"As soon as a wedding planner can organize it for us," Milandra agreed.

"The end of next year, I bet there'll be babies here around the estate," Kenley predicted.

Everyone looked at her.

"Please, not me. Pete and I cover up." She smiled. Pete grinned back at her.

"Kenley! Keep your personal things to yourself," Milandra suggested.

Everyone in the kitchen laughed.

Baron stood up and adjusted his tie. "Milandra, your father wanted me to be executor over the estate, but it's time I hand the power back over to you and your sisters."

"I'm willing to learn what I need to know about the business, but you must stay over it and run it. I'm getting married," Milandra said as she held Nolan's left hand.

"I would love to continue handling the business," Baron said as he sat back down.

Tessa whispered in Baron's right ear, "You're not going to tell them the full truth of what happened on the day their parents died?"

"No need," he whispered back. "Look at the glow in their faces. They're full of happiness. The way I felt about their father has nothing to do with how I feel about them. They're beautiful ladies who deserve wonderful lives."

"Baron Chavis, I've always loved you, and I love you even more at this moment," Tessa said, and then their lips connected in a long kiss.

On the other end of the table, Nolan and Milandra locked lips. Sid and Noelle kissed. Pete and Kenley made their way out to the patio area. There they snuck a French kiss.

Elsa looked around the kitchen at them. "Well, I'll be. I didn't know my cooking could stir up some heated bodies."

The couples let go. Nolan and Sid ran over to Elsa and kissed her on the side of her pudgy cheeks.

"Thanks for a great breakfast," Nolan said.

Chapter 37

The wedding bells chimed and the trumpet player tooted his horn as the Houstons became married women. After their guests left the wedding reception in the ballroom of the Houston Estate, Noelle and Sid went back to the Houston Villa to start their life as man and wife while Milandra and Nolan stayed. Kenley went to a friend's home to give them complete privacy.

Nolan carried Milandra outside to the backyard to the Jacuzzi. Candles lit the side of the Jacuzzi. A bucket of chilled wine sat on the edge. He removed her wedding veil. He unzipped her wedding gown to let it fall to the ground. Milandra stood in her white-lace undergarments.

She watched as Nolan stripped down to his boxers. They both stepped out of their shoes. Nolan picked her up and stepped inside the Jacuzzi. He sat her down on the bench inside and kissed her.

Unhooking her bra, Nolan released her breasts that got soaked from the water, as well as his tongue. She moaned from the tingling feeling running through her body.

They stood up in the Jacuzzi as Nolan pulled her closer to him, pressing her breasts against his chest.

Milandra began to find that she was doing things that were out of the ordinary. She rubbed him from his head down to his back, removing his boxers to release the biggest muscles of all. As she touched him a chill went through her body.

"I've been waiting on this moment for a long time," Nolan whispered in her ear as he felt her hand against his groin.

"I must admit I have wanted you to make love to me, but I knew I had to wait for marriage."

He smiled. "You're Mrs. Nolan Houston-Rice."

"Yes."

Nolan took her hand that held his muscle and moved it up and down. Milandra caught on quickly and began to handle the job on her own. He sucked on her nipples, making her crave for more of him.

Nolan must have known she was ready to move to the main course, because he moved her hand away and eased his muscle inside her. Milandra let out a cry of ecstasy.

He kissed her on the neck as he thrust back and forth inside her. She had never felt as powerless as she did at that moment—weakened from the force of his strength.

They exploded together. Milandra held him around the neck as she laid her head on his chest. His muscle was now as limp as her ponytail. Nolan kissed her on the cheek. "You and me, baby, forever," he whispered.

They stepped out of the Jacuzzi and picked up their belongings, making their way up to the bedroom.

Milandra pulled him to the bed. Nolan explored her body from head to toe. She screamed, "My husband."

Nolan thrust his muscle inside her and pumped her. He screamed. "My wife."

In jail, Aniyah picked up a newspaper while other inmates watched television. She read the headline: *Prominent Ladies Marry Ordinary Men*. She read the article to see that high-profile attorney Baron Chavis married Tessa Sanchez, ex-housekeeper of Rupert Houston and the aunt of the girl, Rosie Aniyah Sanchez, who was serving time for pretending to be Rupert Houston's daughter and kidnapping her aunt.

Youngest daughter, Kenley Houston, was allegedly dating one of the servants. The question was, if Rupert Houston was still alive, would he approve of his daughters' choices in men?

"Hell no! He's the only one that held the power to mingle under the covers with the maids." Aniyah shouted as she tore the paper into pieces. The guard heard her outburst, snatched her by the arm, and took her back to her cell.

Sitting far back on a cot, Aniyah thought, *I could have turned the Houston Estate into a place where lots of men would want to come and pick out his favorite escort.*

Aniyah took a nap and woke up to hear the announcement, "Lights out." In a flash, she was in darkness. One of the correctional officers walked past her cell and looked in.

"Wonderful dreams, pretty lady," the officer said.

Too excited, Aniyah ran over and held on to the cell bars. She watched the correctional officer check the next cell. She called, "Hey, do you need an escort?"

The tall, well-built officer came back to her cell. "And where are you going to escort me?"

Aniyah pulled the rubber band out of her hair. She opened the top button of the uniform to expose her ample breasts. The officer flicked the flashlight he had in his hands on her breasts. He then flashed the light on her face to see that she was blowing kisses at him.

"I can escort you anywhere you want to go. I can escort you to your wildest fantasy," Aniyah said as she batted her eyes. She shook her breasts, and then she moved her hips in a circular motion.

"I bet you can with boobs like them," he said, flashing the light back on her breasts.

"Come closer to me."

The officer cautiously came close to the bars of the cell. She puckered her lips and he kissed her between the bar rails.

"Sweet lips," the officer said.

"See, you pay me money and I'll escort you. We both win."

"Pay you? Lady, you're nuts. Go to sleep." He laughed.

Aniyah saw that he wasn't buying what she was offering. "I can show you more." She dropped her uniform to her knees.

The officer shined the flashlight on her body. "Hey, Kev," he called to another officer. "Take a look at this. We have a free peep show."

The officer's partner came over and took a look.

Aniyah was annoyed. She snatched up her uniform, slipping it back on because the officers laughed at her. She figured that the officers weren't worthy of her.

"Hey, pretty lady; give my partner a kiss, too. He may want some escort services." The officer laughed.

"No one makes a mockery of me!" she yelled, pointing her finger. "Forget it! You don't have enough money to take care of me."

The officer hit his club against the cell bars. "Shut up, and go to sleep. You're a fruitcake."

Aniyah spent the rest of the night fantasizing that she was the owner of the Houston Estate Escort Business and the Houston women were her workers.

Watch out, world, because when I get out of this hell hole, I'll have a new plan to score big money.

About the Author

Christine Young-Robinson was raised in Brooklyn and Queens, New York, but she now resides in her place of birth, Columbia, South Carolina. She is a wife, mother, and grandmother.

No stranger to the literary world, Christine has spent the last few years working with her children's books, *Isra the Butterfly Gets Caught for Show and Tell*, *Chicken Wing*, and young adult ebook, *Hip-Hop and Punk Rock*. Her short story, "Miss Amy's Last Ride," was featured in the anthology, *Proverbs for the People*, edited by Tracy Price-Thompson and TaRessa Stovall.

DO WHAT YOU GOTTA DO

by Christine Young-Robinson
Coming Soon from Strebor Books

Chapter 1

At last, Aniyah Sanchez would no longer be like a lion locked up in a cage. After spending four years in a South Carolina prison for fraud and kidnapping, she was being released.

As she stepped out of her cell, a male prison guard whispered in her ears, "Fruitcake, I'll see you when you get back."

Sniffing the odor of fish that escaped from his breath, Aniyah turned up her nose. Didn't he know after lunch to eat a peppermint?

"Good bye, Slut," an inmate yelled from another cell to her.

"You better get your last feel, Officer Mann," another inmate added.

The inmates laughed throughout the ward, including the guard who sported a broken front tooth. He cupped Aniyah's left breast with his right hand. Then he took the club he held in his other hand and placed it between her legs.

"I don't think so!" Aniyah snapped her head, brushing him away. "Your time has expired."

During her prison term, she had fulfilled the guard's sexual needs in exchange for protection from conflicts that she had endured with other female inmates.

Aniyah, almost jogging, hurried ahead until she came to a point where she met up with another guard, and other inmates that were being released.

Once the official documents were finalized, the guard let Aniyah out of the last door that gave her back her freedom. A chill ran through her body, but it quickly disappeared once the doors were slammed shut behind her.

Turning around, she took one last look at the place of residence she had called home. The fourth inmate in line, and in loafers donated by church volunteers, outside of the prison her feet made contact with the concrete ground.

Aniyah adjusted her eyes to the sunlight that blinded her. She pulled down on her red spandex dress that had risen up to her hips. It was the same dress she wore before she became a part of the prison system.

Her once slender hips stretched the dress to its limits, but Aniyah strutted as if the garment was brand-new. She faulted her excessive weight-gain from her no longer being able to shake her hips in the nightclubs because, in prison, most of the time she sat on her rear in her cell or in ongoing therapy sessions.

Under her armpit, she carried a plastic bag of her belongings and a pair of pumps. Her hands free, she twisted her flowing black hair up in a bun.

Other released inmates stopped to say farewell to each other, but Aniyah kept walking, too afraid that she might be called back by one of the guards.

Two female inmates ran past her, once they saw familiar faces of loved ones waiting to take them home. Aniyah was not looking for any family to come to her rescue. She would not know her father from any other black man on the streets. He was her mother's one-night stand with no name.

Julia, her mother, had died two months ago in Mexico, during the time dye eggs were given to inmates for holiday treats. Aniyah remembered the day the warden delivered the news to her. Guilt troubled her, since she had run away from home at the age of sixteen, leaving her mother behind to suffer a broken heart.

The only family she had left was her mother's sister, Tessa Sanchez-Chavis. And she was not counting on her self-righteous aunt to come to her rescue.

Where am I going? I have no idea.

As the heat beamed down on her forehead, sweat dripped down her neck. The spandex dress felt like rubber against her body.

"Rosie Aniyah Sanchez." She heard a name echoed in her ears.

Her eyes lit up, when she recognized the familiar voice. She locked eyes with her aunt. The solemn look on her face turned into a bright smile. "Aunt Tessa."

She studied her aunt, noticing how much she had aged. Streaks of gray highlighted Tessa's jet-black hair. Aniyah, elated, ran into her aunt's arms. "I can't believe you're here."

"You're family," her aunt said humbly, in her Spanish accent, giving her niece a kiss on the cheek.

Together, they strolled to a parked black Mercedes-Benz.

Admiring her aunt's ride, before prison life, without hesitation, if a man were driving the Benz, Aniyah would have easily flagged down the ride. She would have unraveled her bun to let her hair fall past her shoulder, propped one hand on a hip, and batted her dark-brown eyes. Then she would have worked her charm on the man behind the wheel, giving him her middle name instead of using her first name, Rosie. Simply played him for a sucker.

With all the counseling, her former lifestyle of being an escort and manipulating people, especially men, was supposed to be her past, but only time would tell.

Tessa unlocked the car door, and quickly Aniyah jumped in and took a seat on the butter-colored leather seats. It was not a man, but a free ride from her aunt would do.

"How did you know I was getting out?"

Tessa gave her niece another loving hug. Then she became emotional. "I've been keeping up with you. And although I can't forget what you did to the Houstons or me, you're still family. I have made peace with it."

"How about your lawyer-hubby, Baron?"

"He's Mr. Chavis to you for now on. And, he'll never forgive you for what you did to the Houston family, nor him," Tessa admitted with a hint of bitterness.

"It's not like it was his money." Reaching down between the seats, Aniyah picked up a bag of boiled peanuts. She cracked open the peanuts, tossing a few in her mouth. While chewing, she continued to speak. "The Houstons are garbage people. Mr. Houston was a male whore. How can you defend him?"

"Don't speak of the dead in a bad way," Tessa argued. She recalled working as a young woman in the home of Mr. Rupert Houston, owner of Houston Commercial Construction Company. He was a man who loved to have his way with his beautiful female workers.

Aniyah sucked her teeth. "Mr. Houston can rot in hell. And so can his spoiled-ass daughters." She slouched back in the seat.

In past years, Aniyah had crossed paths with her aunt's prior boss, Rupert. Her greed for money led her to become his mistress. He had promised her a false dream on Lake Murray, South Carolina, to later do away with her.

Aniyah vowed to get revenge on him. To keep her quiet, Rupert included her in his will.

Aniyah took a few more peanuts, folded the bag, and placed it back where she'd gotten it.

"I still say you were more loyal to his spoiled-ass daughters than you were to me," she said.

Staring at her aunt as she drove, Aniyah wanted to grab and shake her. Rupert's unexpected death left her a happy and wealthy young woman, instead of his three daughters until Tessa discovered her wrongdoings. Instead of living the life of royalty, Aniyah landed in prison.

Tessa sensed Aniyah was still bitter. "I believe in doing what's right. You had no right to do wrong."

"I didn't want to be a maid like you and Mama. I could have sent plenty of money to Mama." Aniyah lowered her voice. "Now she's dead."

Tessa was surprised. "I asked the warden to not tell you about Julia."

"You should have come and told me yourself."

"I didn't want you to be hurt. You couldn't go to Mexico to your mama's funeral."

"Did you go?" Aniyah asked sadly.

"I went to visit her in her sickbed a month before she went to her heavenly home. She wanted so much for you to come to her bedside. I simply couldn't tell her that I found you. You were in jail for doing bad things. It would have destroyed her. I stayed by her side to the end."

Tears flowed down Aniyah's face. "I'm glad you didn't tell her."

Tessa softly patted her niece on the hand. "Your mama loved you with all her heart."

"I know…I miss her." Aniyah wiped away her tears.

"Let's go shopping. You don't need to dress like you're a loose girl."
Tessa had witnessed her niece's dress code. The dress had risen up on
Aniyah. It resembled a tunic shirt.

"I'll go shopping. But I'm not throwing away this dress."

"It's too little."

Aniyah saw her aunt glancing at her. She tugged at her dress, trying
to cover her exposed thighs. "So I gained a few pounds. No big deal."

"After shopping, you'll trash it."

"This hot dress stays with me."

Tessa concluded that it was going to be a long day for her. The sooner
she took her niece shopping and got her settled, the sooner she would
be rid of her. She sighed. "Aniyah, you have always been difficult."

"I think for myself. No one tells me what to do."

After shopping, Tessa drove Aniyah to a two-story apartment complex
nearby the downtown city of Columbia.

Aniyah looked out at the buildings as Tessa parked. Startled, she said,
"This is where you and Baron live now. What happened to his house?"

"We still have our home. This is where you're going to rest."

Aniyah voice escalated. "Are you for real? Here?"

"I'm sorry, but there's no way Baron will let me bring you into our home."

"I'm your niece. He can now trust me."

"I'm afraid not."

Aniyah marveled. She heard the nervousness in her aunt's voice. She
was flattered that her aunt thought of her as a threat. In the past, she
had seduced her aunt's husband, prior to their marriage, in order to
manipulate him to get to his client's fortune.

They got out of the vehicle, carrying shopping bags by the handles.
Aniyah followed her aunt to the front door. Unlocking it, they entered
the one-bedroom apartment.

She proceeded to the middle of the living room, while Tessa, clenching
on to her handbag, stayed put near the door.

Aniyah felt her aunt's eyes pierced on her, well informed that she was
uncomfortable being alone with her, but her attention was focused on
her living arrangements. Next to a small wooden table, she tossed the

bags that she held on a futon. Then, she headed to see where she would sleep; leaving her aunt on edge to figure out if she would show any signs of psychotic symptoms.

Inside the bedroom, Aniyah spotted a four-drawer chest and twin-sized bed that was the bottom half of a bunk bed. Second-hand crap.

"I hope you like it." Tessa dropped the bags on the linoleum floor.

Aniyah mumbled under her breath, "No bigger than a jail cell."

Returning back into the living room, Aniyah decided not to complain. She was convinced without her aunt rescuing her, she might be sitting on a bench like a homeless person.

Aniyah grinned. "It's good."

"There's food in the refrigerator. I've stocked it with a few things, sodas and sandwich meats. In the cabinets, there're cans of corn, black beans and a five-pound bag of rice."

"Any steaks, lobster tails or shrimp?"

Tessa laughed. "There're frozen foods, and chicken for you to cook. Tonight you can heat a frozen chicken TV dinner."

Aniyah went directly into the kitchen adjacent to the living room. She looked in the freezer to see that few products loaded the freezer, including one iced tray. She slammed the freezer door shut. Then she opened the refrigerator section. Removing a can of orange soda, she snapped it open and took a swallow, quenching her thirst.

Tessa entered. As she watched her niece's every move, she noticed the spandex dress Aniyah wore had risen up her thighs. "I say you should change into something more appropriate."

Aniyah tussled with the dress. "Stop looking at my clothes. It'll fit fine once I lose a few pounds." Aniyah looked around the kitchen, noticing something was missing. "Hold up...no microwave?"

"You can use the stove to heat a TV dinner."

"Whatever." Aniyah rolled her eyes.

"Change your style of dressing. Start off fresh by getting yourself decent work. And, find a good man that you can start a family with," Tessa lectured with an air of sophistication.

Aniyah stared at her aunt as though she were a hated prison guard. She had not thought about a job. She twirled around. Cheerfully, she said, "I can use a money man."

"It's nothing like making your own money."

Aniyah walked past her aunt, stepping back into the living room. Tessa followed behind her while Aniyah searched for any sign of communication technology.

"No telephone in here?"

Tessa shook her index finger at her. "When you get work you can buy one."

"If you want me to get a job, at least get me a cell phone."

"For now, no phone. I'll be coming by to check on you."

Aniyah slouched down on the futon. She shoved her fist into the cushion, feeling the steel frame underneath.

"I hate being broke."

"In due time, you'll find work. Make your own money."

"I have no skills. No one will hire me."

"There has to be something you like to do or you can go to college."

"Aunt Tessa, getting out of jail is not the same as getting out of high school. I didn't just graduate. No college for me."

"You know how to clean."

Aniyah jumped to her feet. Her mind went to the days she was forced to clean the toilet in her jail cells. Enraged, she yelled, "Hell to the no. I'll die before I scrub another toilet."

"It's an honest living."

"Never!" Aniyah snapped as she sat back down. "I'll find something else to do."

"Start looking for some kind of work."

Aniyah banged her fist on the table. "I need money now."

Tessa eased her way near the door. Digging in her purse, she pulled out a few bills. "This should be enough to get you by."

Aniyah hurried over to her, snatching the money out of her aunt's hand. Before she shoved the bills down in her bra, she counted up to a hundred.

"The rent on this apartment is paid in full for three months. By then you should've found work."

"Give me a break. That's not enough time."

"You must have work by then. Baron won't allow me to give you any more money after that."

"He rules you."

"Nonsense. We agreed on that decision."

"Tell him what you want…you're his wife, Mrs. Tessa Sanchez-Chavis. Stop being too easy."

"I'm loyal to my husband. He's a good man. I won't let you ruin my marriage. Three months it is." Tessa peered at her through hooded eyes.

Aniyah heard the authority in her aunt's voice and said no more. She was not about to let three months turn into get-out-right-now.

"In the drawer, there's a nightgown for you to rest in." Tessa jingled her car keys as she made her way to the door. "I must go. I must prepare dinner for my husband."

"I need to eat, too."

"Heat your dinner. I pray you'll turn your life around. My sister would want that for you. I'll see you in a few days. And for God's sake, don't go anywhere near Milandra, Noelle or Kenley Houston. Baron and I have agreed not to disturb them about your release. They're in a good place in their lives."

Aniyah chuckled. "The fake sisters are history to me. I'm going to be in a much better place then, them uppity snobs."

"I have faith that you'll do fine, once you find work." Tessa noticed she still had the apartment key in her hand. "You'll need this." She tossed the key to Aniyah. "Don't lose it."

Following her aunt outside, Aniyah watched as she got into her vehicle. "Weak bitch," she hollered, once Tessa drove away.

Back into the apartment, Aniyah slammed the door behind her. She stood in the middle of the living room, sniffing the stale odor. She screamed, "I'm still in jail. The one time my aunt Tessa could do right by me and she put me in a hell hole."

Aniyah went into the bedroom. She bounced on the bed.

"Dead mattress," she fussed. "Aunt Tessa is going home to her fancy bed. I've got to sleep on a board for a mattress. Once again she shouted, "Weak bitch. Get a job, no way. My job will only be to find me a man with money. You and anyone else that gets in my way, will pay for treating me like I'm beneath you."